SELECTED STORIES

Rumjhum Nayak

Translated by

Ashok K. Mohanty

BLACK EAGLE BOOKS
Dublin, USA | Bhubaneswar, India

While strong humanism is the undertone of her stories, she is unique in her language and expression. As a lively and independent thinker, her composition is serious and deep. Stories are not only enjoyable but also educational.

- Padma Bhusan Dr. Pratibha Ray

Rumjhum's symbolic stories have been mesmerized by the discretion of the events and the deep expertise in the portrayal of characters, while the seriousness of the poetry in the style of the composition, the dramatisation of the drama creates an artistic dilemma.

- Mohapatra Nilamani Sahoo
Eminent Writer

Vitality, sensitivity, social awareness and the helplessness of the human mind are the remarkable revolutions of her story. The more she tries to cover this breadth and depth of literature, the more readers will be familiar with her new inventions.

- Professor Dr. Archana Nayak

Whether it is a story or a poem, the way in which the intensity of your consciousness, the seriousness of your thoughts, the passion of your description, the sigh of your heart and the tears of your eyes are expressed in each picture is truly incomparable. I found in the interlude of your story that the choice of right words under the emotion and feeling is an extraordinary combination. In my opinion, man lives and should live in this hope, to cherish such literature and derive pleasure by reading it in leisure.

- Dr. Harekrushna Satpathy
Former Vice-chancellor

Dedication

This collection of short stories is dedicated to Dr. Archana Nayak, my teacher and eminent writer. My pen has come alive because of her direct inspiration and blessings.

- Rumjhum

A Few Words

A creator is always sensitive about his creation. Everything that a man thinks does not come true. The creator decorates life with his or her thoughts with the help of his pen. Can one tell everything to everyone? There are many things that cannot be said in society. There are many sorrows that are hard to bear in life. It is not often possible to show how happy you are on certain occasions. There are a few memories which cannot be forgotten. I have tried to examine all this minutely and incorporate them into my stories. I have seen a few incidents with my own eyes. I have heard about certain things. I have experienced a few other things myself. I have built my world of stories by embellishing all this with my imagination. I have seen almost all the characters of my stories from very close quarters. I have tried to record these incidents and paint these characters before they moved away from me. I do not know if I have been successful in my efforts. However, my daydreaming mind has forced me to concentrate on literature when I have received a letter, a phone call, sms or what'sapp message from my dear readers. I have written more than one hundred stories till now. Pradipta Kumar Behura, the publisher and editor of *Lekhalekhi*, has selected twenty of them for this collection of short stories.

The love and affection of my relations, the blessings of the elderly people and above all the encouragement of my readers have provided me with the greatest gratification in my life as an author.

With gratitude

Rumjhum Nayak

Foreword

Rumjhum Nayak is now a very popular name in the field of Odia fiction. Her stories have great praise and passion. I must confess without hesitation that I enjoyed her latest collection of stories admired by my readers. There is a breath of fresh air in the narration (first person), in the pictures, imaged, snatches of conversation, half dramatized and crisp and also have the reflection of life around. Most of the characters are seen to be our next door neighbours or our own family members. These characters, not whole or rounded, are educated and are in the IT sector, have money and also a kind of egoistic profanity that is not warranted by the situational dynamics of the plots come. The first story – The Aroma of Kewda Flowers, is a result of a life almost lost and broken. The first love fails without any convincing reason. The lovers have never opened up to each other, rather they never tried, may be a chance factor plays an uncanny mischief, as a result Deepak and her infatuated girl friend drift apart. The woman, an IT professional maries a "shadow" for the "substance" never appears as except in a bitter grimace of memory in the narrator's monologue. The marriage fails, life flows as rocky beds but the aroma of Kewda's haunted her till the end.

The poverty and fate-freewill conflict of the traditional stories narrated the pair of hunger, torture and victimhood. In the shifting paradigms of life when poverty is <u>here</u>, freedom is palpable and the human will is free to make choices in life, we get the same conflict (interval) and failure. Life is lost without a search for meaning.

In the Lonely Bird (Eka Eka Pakhi Tie) almost the same failure of communication between winds, hearts and other civilized nuances. Desire for union is not dead but one takes the first step for reaching forward. The live confinements were limited, although today the internet is the connecting web. But the author by using the speech rhythms of modern people and by inter *sparring* the spoken Odia with English words is clearly reflected with our new reality. The cultural, moral and spiritual inheritance are all wasted in our bid to be of relevance on the digital civilization of present. The characters seem to be uprooted and never try to find or grow roots.

The two stories which have reassured me that humanity is not lost, the goodness is not lost and humans can make their own fate even without education if they are assessed with some love and passion. Those two are in search of Happiness and the last Bouquet.

Chemi and Sapana fight their imposed fate with their native talents. Chemi is in the rural area with inherited talents of making Ghee Pitha, "Chuda Muan" and Arisa etc. which every young girl learnt from their mothers or grandma's – It was a continuity of culture even in the midst of poverty and fatalism. Chemi and Sapana show us prove that by honest efforts, anyone can be self sufficient successful. Perhaps the tribe of good men are not dead.

Rumjhum Nayak's narrative style and choice of vocabulary are engaging. She has a sense of 'beginning and end'. No unnecessary lingering on emotional brooding. Her narrative structure is compact and focused.

About the translation, however, I have no comments to offer. However I wish easy flow of the monologues with ease and sharpness.

Rumjhum Nayak is a story teller of a great promise. I hope her space-time will embrace the uncanny complements of life and move towards the larger world of life's rhythmic variety.

I wish her all success.

Prafulla Kumar Mohanty
Chitrakabya
Sishu Bihar, Patia, Bhubaneswar-24

Contents

Fragrance of the *Kewda* Flower

You would remember that I had told you one day insistently that "I need a *kewda* flower." Good times never last long. You used to come to the gate of the college every day to see me off when the classes were over. You kept staring till my bus was out of your sight. I had been worried the other day when I did not find you outside my department when my classes were over. I found you talking to Sipra on my way to the canteen. I waited for you hoping that you would come to me after you were through with her. But you went forth instead of coming to me. I had started running after you. But Sipra stopped me in my tracks and said, "Do you know something, Sunayana? Deepak's father is serious. He is perhaps leaving for his village right now."

I was angry with you. But I was certain that you won't go away to your village without meeting me. It was almost a ritual for me from the following day to wait for you. I looked for you everywhere in the university. There were three other departments between your department and mine. I don't know how I covered the distance by myself every day. I went to the canteen after my classes. At times, my friends and I decided to have our snacks somewhere outside. You used to stand near the gate as I went outside.

Sipra said, "Your rustic boyfriend would be standing for you in this manner throughout his life. He would never have thought that you would fly away from him one of these days." I had never thought of being with you for all time to come. You always asked me what you would get for me from the village. My answer was, "Come back as quickly as possible." In fact, I wanted nothing more that day. I was eating *golgappas* near the gate one day as I was on my way home. You were holding the book that you had got for me from the library. You were watching how I was devouring the *golgappas*. My bus came after that. I forgot to collect the book from you and went away. You went away to your village the following day. The university was closed for holidays after that for three days. You came running to me and gave me my book when we met next and apologised for the delay. I had felt breathless while taking the book from your hand. What fragrance! I asked you if a bottle of perfume had overturned inside your bag. You said, "No! Father had sent some *kewda* flowers with me for Lord Mahadev yesterday. I had carried them in this bag." "Do *kewda* flowers have such fragrance?" You said, "Yes. There are *kewda* bushes throughout our village." I said, "The entire village must be fragrant in that case. Your house too!"

You laughed and said, "When would you come to my house?" I ignored your words and said, "Did you offer all the flowers to Lord Mahadev? Couldn't you keep one flower for me?" I had kept the book pressed to my nose. You said, "I will get you some the next time I go to the village." I had touched you for the first time and smelled your hand. You kept looking at me innocently like a small child looking at his mother. I reminded you about the *kewda* flowers every day after that. I asked you innocently when you were going to the village next. I had demanded *kewda* flowers from you one day obstinately. You had left for your village the following day as your father had fallen ill.

XXX

The compartments of Coromandal Express shook and the train came to a screeching halt. People were running inside the compartment. I sat up. I looked through the window. The train was standing at the end of a bridge. The river was nearby. A village could be seen in the distance. I asked a gentleman sitting in front of me about the name of the station. He said dejectedly, "There is no station here, madam. The train has gone off the rails. Who knows how long we are going to be stuck here?"

A sweet fragrance was suddenly in the air. I got up from my seat. A woman was selling some flowers in a basket. She had got up on the train after it had stopped. She was making entreaties, "Take these flowers. Offer them to Lord Mahadev. All your wishes will come true." I asked her, "What flowers are these?"

The woman said, "Ma! These are *kewda* flowers." The shivers of a twenty-one-year old ran through my forty-year-old body. I stood up and asked the price. The woman said that they were two rupees a piece. I asked her how many flowers she had with her. She counted and said that there were twenty-one flowers. I handed her forty-two rupees and returned to my seat pressing the flowers to my chest. My co-passengers were looking amazed. A gentleman sitting in front of me said, "Does anyone buy these flowers for money? These villages are full of *kewda* flowers." I kept the flowers carefully and looked at the woman. She was smiling at me while getting down from the train. I ran to her and asked, "Do you live in a nearby village?"

The train started to move. As the woman was getting

down hastily from the train, she said, "This village is famous for *kewda* flowers. The name of the village beyond the river is Amarsinghpur." The pent-up emotions of years had found their way into my eyes as the train started gathering speed. I had been looking behind me through the open door of the train.

You had left for your village Amarsinghpur after your father became ill. You did not perhaps find the time to inform me about it. The examinations were over. You would certainly have come back. You would have looked around for me in the university. You would have asked my friends about me. You might have even visited my house. My marriage was fixed within eight days of your departure. I went to the college after that. You had still not returned. My marriage was solemnised. I went to my in-laws' place. I went away to America with my husband a few days later. I looked for India in the map at times. Then I looked for Odisha. But I could never find your village from the map. It was difficult for me to adjust with this sudden change in circumstances. I was searching for the fragrance of the *kewda* flower in the well-lit streets of Manhattan in New York City. I was getting suffocated in that formal atmosphere. I had never thought that reality was so harsh. I missed my parents and brothers. I was not able to forget you. The time that I had spent with you had covered my insides like clouds. I thought about you a great deal more when I had difference of opinion with my husband.

You often said to me, "Sunayana, relationship gets spoiled when you argue with people. Why don't you learn to surrender?" I used to get angry with you at such times. Would you have surrendered to your wife? You are perhaps happier than me. I feel lonely with all the noise around me. I could not follow your advice and surrender myself. Time slipped away from my hands as I continued to make comparisons between you and me. I returned to my parents' place once again ten years after my marriage. I do not want to relive those sad days once again. I had been completely shattered before I got acquainted with sorrow. Father had found a suitable husband for me after I appeared for the M.A. examinations and before the results were out. He thought that he had discharged his responsibilities with regard to me. My conservatism did not help me in measuring up to the yardstick of competence. Father had passed away by the time I returned home as a pauper. I had been to the university to get my certificate after ten years. I was thinking a great deal about you as I moved around the different offices with the certificate pressed to my chest. I was having a breakdown as there was no one for me on whom I could fall back. A woman deserted by her husband is also not respected in her father's house. It was especially so when the father was not around. No one woke me up even if I fell asleep without taking any food. But you came in my dreams. You got down from the bus from your village and waited for me near the university gate. You carried a bunch of flowers in your hand the like of which I have never seen earlier. I felt breathless with the fragrance of those flowers. But there is only darkness before me now. I do not lose my way in the darkness. I meet my past in that darkness. You were waiting for me at one time. I had never had the occasion for waiting for you when we were studying.

These days I keep waiting for you all the time. I consider the time spent with you to be the most valuable time of my life and try to preserve them. There are no more any crossroads on my way. The road before me is unending. I believe that you must be looking for me as I keep looking for you. You say that people who cry are weak. Tears come to their eyes because they do not have the courage to face their situation. I had laughed at the time as I had not even heard the footsteps of sorrow till then. It was another matter that it was very near me at the time. You can see that the earth under my feet also does not belong to me. The sky is far above my head. I cannot even find a wall against which I can lean. How helpless can human beings be! There was a time when I lost my way with the chirping of numerous coloured birds on the branches of time. There is not even a leaf on those branches today. God had perhaps listened to my prayers before I had lost complete faith on life. A manager was needed in a private school in an *adivasi* village of Koraput. The qualification required was graduation. I had finished post-graduation. I got the job. I had not felt completely reassured. But I had found some of my self-confidence back. My brother rang me one evening a month after my joining and said, "A get-together of your batchmates is being arranged at the university. Reach Bhubaneswar within two days if you would like to attend it."

I had got on the bus from Koraput to Vizianagaram the day I had received the phone call. I had got on the train in Vizianagaram without any reservation. There was the same overwhelming desire in the eyes once again to meet the past. The train had gone off the rails near your village. The woman stood there with her basket of flowers. I felt you were sitting adjacent to me when I heard the name of your village from her lips. I recalled that the flower girl was saying that one's wish got fulfilled if *kewda* flowers were offered to Lord Mahadev. You too had said the same thing to me one day. Life is strange indeed. The sun had set in my life. But I was still searching for the first rays of the rising sun.

Someone seemed to be telling me deep inside me that you would certainly come to the get together. You too would have as much desire to see me as I have for you. It was the longest night of my life. I thought that the hills would crash over my head. I felt as if the sea was rushing towards me. I was afraid of thinking about you. I had kept awake throughout the night for fear that your memory will fly away to the sky like a dream. I had a bath early in the morning and offered all the *kewda* flowers to Lord Mahadev. I had not kept even one flower for me although I had preserved them in my memory for years.

I was wearing the pink-coloured sari that you always liked. But I was scared to go before you. I could see you clearly from where I was standing. But I was standing in such a place that you would not be able to see me. You were the same Deepak of seventeen years ago. You didn't seem to have aged in the least. Time seemed to have stood still for you. You seemed to be looking for someone in that large banquet hall. I knew that you were looking for me. You had not been able to recognise Sipra at first sight. She had put on a little bit of weight. You asked her something. She too was looking here and there with a grave countenance. There were sweat beads on your face. You took out the handkerchief from your pocket. You did not seem to be happy although you were meeting your old friends after such a long time. You looked so forlorn. I was feeling a shiver running down me as I found you looking sadder by the minute. I had no idea that love could be so profound. I was feeling small before the intensity of your love. Your face looked hazy before my tear-filled eyes. Your wife perhaps moved closer to you. You introduced her to Sipra. Your son looked almost exactly like you. He was as tall as your shoulders. I was not able to know whether you had surrendered yourself to your wife or not as I was standing some distance away from you. You were looking at your wristwatch repeatedly and glancing at the entrance to the hall.

The wound in my mind had automatically filled up after watching the freshness of my memory in your eyes. The rare fragrance of your love for me is my greatest asset at a time when my life is disintegrating. I returned to my place of work peacefully without meeting you after seeing a bunch of *kewda* flowers in your hand.

****

You, I and He

The boy had pressed the calling bell after Subrat left for office. It was as if he had been waiting for Subrat to leave for the office. My servant Manua asked him to sit down in the drawing room and came to call me. But I had arrived there beforehand. The boy stood up and wished me with folded hands and said that he had come from Subarnapur in Banki. I was surprised and asked him what I could do for him. I told him that my husband had already left for his office. "No, aunty! I have come to you." Aunty! "Do you know me?" The boy said, "No. There is a photograph of you and my aunt in our house." "How could it be so? I have never been to Subarnapur in Banki. I don't recall having seen you earlier too." I smiled and looked at the boy. He extended a letter towards me and fidgeted. Curiosity got the better of me and I came inside the house after taking the letter from him. I looked at the last line of the letter hoping that I would get the name of the sender there. But the letter had ended with the words, 'Yours truly'. No name had been mentioned. I glanced at the letter hoping to find the name of the sender somewhere. But the name was missing.

"Sunanda, I send you my love. I hope your family is fine by the grace of God. You will be surprised to get this letter from me after such a long gap. I have not been able to forget you even though a long time has passed in the meantime. I used to have affection for you earlier. I respect you now. Those two tiny eyes of yours look up at me from the pages when I read your writings. We had met at two opposite turns. We also got separated from each other in two different directions. You had said one day, 'No one will come forward to walk beside you. There would be no one with you to share the helpless moments of your life. Accept the man who has hidden your dreams inside his chest. The people for whom you do this penance will not value your time that is coming to an end.' But I had not paid any heed to these words. I had called you a very selfish girl and distanced myself from you.

"Your selfish comments were not the only reason why I hadn't listened to you. My fingers shake in shame when I am now trying to write you. You know it, Sunanda, that a prejudiced soot used to hang in some remote corner of my narrow mind those days. I could not bear to see your beautiful face, throaty laughter and carefree ways. I became intolerant when I heard the man I loved praising you. You were coming to the college in a car. I used to live in the hostel. We had different subjects. You used to wait for me for no reason when your classes were over. We went to the canteen together. You went home when your driver came and called you. I went back to the hostel. He used to stand on the way back to the hostel. We moved around the campus aimlessly. He talked about his career. He also made enquiries about you as we talked. I felt sad. I thought about you. You used to say, 'What is sorrow after all? Sorrow is only a river. You can reach the bank if you can swim. Otherwise, you will drown.' I found it difficult to pay my hostel fees. I borrowed books for my studies. Otherwise, I sat in the library for hours to make notes. You spent money like water. You bought books worth thousands of rupees from book fairs. You bought new clothes every week. You came to the hostel with new clothes for me on the occasions of Ganesh Puja and Saraswati Puja.

"I had no affection for you at the time. On the contrary, I was filled with loathing for you. Your mind was as colourful as the *Phalguna* sky. My mind was covered with the darkness of *Asadha*. As my love for you continued to decline and was about to be wiped away, you proposed one day, 'Susmita, let us go to your village some day.' Someone perhaps pressed her finger on the memory on which dust was gathering. You continued, 'Susmita, you say that your village is beautiful. You will introduce me to your parents, brother and sister. We will bathe in the river there. We will move around in the fields and catch butterflies.' I had stared at you in amazement. Can a twenty-one-year old girl doing her post-graduation look forward to catch butterflies? I had not obliged you. You too had never raised the matter of going to my village again. Your department's picnic was being organised at Nuanai. You asked me to come with you. Dipti, your friend from History Department, was also coming along with you. Cooking was being done in an islet inside Nuanai. The boys and girls were talking to each other in groups in the shade of trees. You were munching a cucumber that you had got from the cook. You were smiling like a mysterious heroine. The boys and girls wanted to go to Ramachandi. You did not agree. But you forced me to go with them. Dipti and I got ready to leave. But you stopped Dipti from accompanying me. I felt peeved. But there had been a change in my mood when I reached the Ramachandi Temple. It was a beautiful temple inside a coconut grove. The blue sea was behind the temple. The most amazing present of that day was that he too had come to the picnic that day. Other teachers of the Department of English had also come. I started mistrusting the man dearest to me from that day who stood very close to me and was smiling."

Her rose-coloured wrapper was flying on the silhouette of memory by the time I was halfway through the letter. Susmita .... She was somewhat dark-skinned. She had beautiful eyes, lips and nose. But the way she spoke was sickening. She wrinkled her nose at everything. It did not suit her age or background. I returned to the drawing room with the folded letter in hand. But the boy was no longer there. Manua informed me that he would come back in a while. I asked him if he had given him a glass of water or not. He said, "He was on the other side of the gate in a flash after handing over the letter. What could I do?" I asked him to inform me when the boy was back and went back to the letter.

"It was perhaps the month of December. A cuckoo was cooing on a solitary mango tree amidst rows of coconut trees. The boys and girls were busy chatting to each other. He called me to him very affectionately. He stood in the temple premises and was staring at the sea. He said to me, 'Susmita, tell your parents about our relationship after your examinations. You are just a student. But I am getting on with age. I am the eldest son of the family. I have already been working for five years. My mother breaks into a wail when she sees me. She is afraid I will remain unmarried all my life. Everyone is worried about me at home after my younger sister's marriage.' His eagerness had no effect on me. The feeling of jealousy in me had not allowed me to understand him.

"I had been blinded by mistrust and failed to see the bank of that silent mind overflowing. I had addressed him that day as Sir instead of the usual term of endearment I used for him. As such he was a lecturer in English in our university. I asked him, 'Sir, do you love me alone? Or do you propose to all my friends in this manner at different times?' He had never even thought in his dreams that I could behave that way. That too when I was fully conscious. He caressed his carefully groomed hair slowly and said, 'I do not like these kinds of jokes, Susmita. I love you alone.' I had been terribly angry. I said, 'Sir, please tell me one thing first. This is not the picnic of your department. Why did you come for this picnic? It goes without saying that your favourite student Sunanda has invited you to come to this picnic. Isn't it so? I cannot run after butterflies when I am twenty-one years old. The attraction of the sea, sky and the river cannot tie me down. I do not know the difference between the cawing of a crow and the cooing of a cuckoo. I do not receive T.S. Eliot's poetry books as presents. Nor can I buy clothes like the heroines of Shakespeare's love stories. I am a stable and level-headed person. I am not eloquent. I neither write poetry nor do I understand the psyche of a poet. Isn't that right? I am not Sunanda, Sir. I am Susmita. I am not planning to go on a honeymoon with my husband after my marriage. I have certain ambitions in life. I need money. I need a decent job. My family depends on me. I am not studying for the fun of it that I will become the eldest daughter-in-law of your family and light a lamp before your kitchen every evening.'

"Water ran over the huge tract of sand on the beach and returned to the sea once again. He too had returned. I have never seen him again since then. I had also not considered it right to tell you anything about it after returning from Ramachandi. The naughty smile on your lips forced me to keep myself away from you. I had been trying to avoid you from that day. But you were coming regularly to the hostel. I could not see your eyes when you returned without finding me at the hostel. But my friends in the hostel told me that you were weeping. You ran into me after a long time and said, 'Susmita! How you have changed! You are busy with your studies all the time. You don't have any time to think about me. Doesn't Sir come to you these days? I haven't seen him for a few days.' I had shot back, 'Do you meet him every day?' Without any preamble, you said, 'Almost every day. Except the Sundays.' I separated my wounded and bleeding mind forcefully from you with the solemn vow that I was not going to have any further relationship with you. The examination was in the offing. The results came out in due course. I had been posted as an ad hoc lecturer in Keonjhar Women's College after a year. I had received your marriage invitation there. Father had redirected it from home. I had not felt like opening the card out of anger and loathing. I was proud of the fact that I was a working lady. And you were only an unemployed woman.

"Your father may be a rich man. But what is your own standing in the society? Earlier you used to beg your father for it when you wanted to buy a new sari. You will now wear new saris with your husband's money. I have never tried to find out who you have married and how you have been getting on. Life gave me to understand gradually that living was not only a truth. It was the beginning of a greater misery. It is not just that I had kept no news of you. I had also lost him in the midst of the spider's nest of suspicion that had formed inside me. I mistrusted him because of you. I should have at least looked around for him after getting your marriage invitation. But how deep can be the roots of inferiority complex! I was convinced that he loved you. And I had put this poison as fertiliser at the roots of the tree of my love. Therefore, the tree died before it could grow. This too had given me a great deal of pleasure.

"Sunanda! I do not know how time flies. I am an adult lecturer who has lost her way in life. There is a long road ahead of me. But there is no tree with branches and leaves on that way where I could take rest for a while. I was arrogant enough to believe that I could spend the rest of my days by myself. But that firm pillar has become shaky now. Our family became more comfortable financially after I started working. I have a younger brother and a younger sister. Father looked around for a groom for my younger sister after their studies were over. My brother used to write me to send him money when he went to attend interviews for jobs. I never received a letter from him otherwise. My younger sister had passed B.A. from the college in our village. Father had retired from the village school. He had got my younger sister married with the money he had received at the time of his retirement. The groom belonged to the same village. Father had spoken to the secretary of the school and got him a job there. The younger brother got married to a girl of his choice. He has never been seen in the village after that.

"Sunanda, you must be amazed to receive this letter from me. You would be wondering why I am writing such a letter to you. I do not know whether you are a human being or a goddess. You had never got over your desire to visit my village. I came to know a long time later that you had come to my village with your husband. You had met my parents and made enquiries about me. You would have found it hard to believe that I never went home and I had no other relationship with my parents except to send them money every month. Why had you been to our house? My mother's eyes would have been filled with tears looking at the vermillion on your head. You had gone around the village. You had been to the bank of the river, the mango grove and the Shiva Temple along with your husband. I had been amazed when my younger sister informed me about it in a letter. What did you want to see? Did you want to see for yourself how pitiable my past was? I receive the U.G.C. scale of pay now. But you must have laughed at me looking at the barren land on the other side of me. This kind of perverted thinking had made me restless for a long time. My childhood was such a barren land that it was not even possible for a grass to grow there.

"We were three children in the family other than my parents. Father used to work as a schoolteacher with a paltry amount as salary. My ambitions were turning into grasslands only. I had never dreamt of a flower growing there. I had been obstinate about studying M.A. after graduating with first class and distinction. Father had made all kinds of sacrifices in order to fulfil my wish. I don't know how he was able to send me money every month. Being his daughter I have never tried to understand how he would have suffered. All girls are not fated to lead a family life. One cannot experience other people's happiness and sorrow if she does not have a family of her own. My arrogance and jealousy for you proved to be too much for my dreams. In the process, I was suffering the intense heat of the summer in the spring of my life. I always thought that he loved you on the sly. Therefore, I used to curse him all the time. I do not know when I became so indifferent towards life and so besotted with money in the process of wishing him ill and cursing him.

"Perhaps you do not remember what you said to me one day standing near the gate of the university and looking at the cloudy sky. You asked, 'Susmita, do you know the meaning of love?' I had said without looking at you, 'You might know.' You smiled and said, 'You won't perhaps be able to understand it the way I have. Love is not physical. It relates to the purity of the mind. A person who loves another selflessly only wishes him or her well. Susmita! I will be more miserable than you if you do not marry Sir.' I told you that it was all right. Before I could leave the place, you got inside your car and continued, 'Love finds fulfilment in sacrifices.' As your car sped away raising dust, I felt that you pricked my eyes with all the thorns available in the world. Were you telling me that you had sacrificed him for my sake? But it had happened before a long time ....

"I don't look at the full reflection of my body in the mirror these days. It's not as if I do not see it; I do not want to see it. I am a woman who is scared of her own shadow. But you had been able to understand this friend of yours who had not been able to understand herself. The person against whom I had held this grudge had never returned to me even once. I keep waiting for the postman every day hoping that he would miss me and write me some day. Sunanda ...!

"Love is like a beach according to you. Waves of happiness and sweet emotions come on that beach and return once again silently after reaching the shore. But I believed that love is like the sky. There are emotions like the moon and excitement like the sun there. I was looking for haughtiness in his silent eyes. He became restless at your capriciousness. I never tried to understand him. I was only getting angry with him. He said that he loved me a great deal. But he praised the way you smiled and the way you talked.

"He professed his admiration for you and said that

you were going to be a great writer in the future and you were going to have a happily married life. I moved away from him at such times and removed my hand from the grip of his perspiring hand. You and I had taken admission in the university the same year and got acquainted with him at the same time. You used to give us a lift in your car when we were in a tizzy after missing the students' special bus. I learnt that day that he was not a student but a teacher. It was natural for us to meet every day. We grew familiar with each other with the passage of time. He too belonged to a middle class family like me. Everyone came to know about our relationship during that period and the university walls were full with graffiti about us. I had been pleased that the most handsome lecturer of the campus loved an ordinary-looking girl like me. But you did something untoward one day. You paid money to the canteen boy and got the walls of the campus cleaned with a wet towel. Your strange act had not only surprised him. I thought he developed a great deal of affection for you because of it.

"It was unbearable for me when I found out that he was writing notes for you. His free access to your house was equally unbearable for me. He was acquainted with my intolerant nature. But he always tried to mould me in his ways. I had a lurking feeling that he was showing pity towards me as I was from a poor family. But I knew that I was going to get a salary some day that was as much as he was getting. I was certain that I was going to get a lecturer's job. I had a first class career and a burning ambition in me. I was certain about being successful in life. I have now gone much farther than where I wanted to be. The past has remained fragrant for me like incense sticks. It will perhaps keep me like that for some more days. Only smoke will be left after that. I do not know if I will be able to handle the suffocating smoke.

"Sunanda! My vanity is lying around like dry leaves before your magnanimity. How could you know about his mental derangement? Had you maintained a relationship with him after being separated from me? There was perhaps no intimacy in our love. I had an idea that I had come much further ahead disregarding the hand that had shown me the way before me. But it was only a delusion. I was only deceiving myself. I wanted him to come to me and beg forgiveness. I wanted him to explain to me that he had made no promises to you although he had a relationship with you. I wanted that he would tell me once again that he could not live without me.

"Sunanda! A person does not always do what he plans to do. He may not also get what he wants to get. I did not know that he had become completely alone after being separated from me although there were other people around him. You had provided support to the man who was my most intimate friend and who had lost his mental balance. I felt even more restless on getting the news that you were acting as a psychological prop for him than when I heard that he had become mentally ill. I hated you because of him. I tried to forget you after that. Just see what a selfish person I am! I have never thought of anyone except myself. But believe me. I had kept him hidden inside my mind. I could neither forget him nor could I bear his separation. The solitary moments spent with him were clinging to my mind. There were no flowers there. I did not want to take your help in looking for him even though the thorns kept on pricking me. I want to see him once before the memorial of my past turns into dust. I will beg your forgiveness and I need your permission to serve the man who had given me the first and last pledge in my life.

"Sunanda! The man against whom I hold all these grudges is far away from all dreams and realities. With whom can I get angry? What have I got from life? I have lost everything. And I have lost out to you, him and time. I have resigned from my job. There is no one beside me to see my vanity. My parents have left this world since long. I have moved far away from the families of my brother and sister. It's no wonder that the man who was bound by my love and who was so attached to you went mad when I disappointed him the way I did. You would have also wanted to go away from him when you learnt that I had deserted him because of you.

"I had been to the university a few years later and collected all the news. Your husband Subrat Mohanty is a psychiatrist. You are indeed a goddess, Sunu. That is the reason you could empathise with him under such circumstances. Although he is not completely fit, he is not a sick man anymore because of your support. Sunu dear! I had been to him without informing you in order to lose myself in his misery. I had thought that his hair would be unkempt, his clothes would be tattered and he would be having long nails on his fingers. I had thought that he would be standing inside a padded cell and he would ask me, 'Who are you? Where have you come?' But it was just the opposite. He was tidily dressed. He had his bifocals on his nose and he was sitting with a newspaper in hand. But the man was no longer there. He sat there like a tree that had been felled by an untimely thunderbolt. There were branches on that tree. But there were no leaves. My heart came to my mouth when I laid my eyes on him. Blood oozed out of my eyes. But he had been able to recognise me. He stared at my face and realised in a flash that my sparrow's nest had been destroyed. But he pretended as if he was not able to understand anything. The flash of lightning had been extinguished from his eyes as quickly as it had come. He was scared to return to me. He felt himself secured with your affection and sympathy. Age did not permit him to break that ring of safety and build a house of sand once again. Therefore, he had made out that he was a deranged man who was incapable of understanding anything. I had returned from him with the knowledge that he was all right. It is not so easy to forget him. My hope had been raised on seeing a few green grasses on the barren land. Flowers might not bloom there. But there might be a carpet of grass someday.

"Allow me to do it, Sunu. Forgive me for all my lapses. Just the way you used to save me one day from being censured by other people for my mistakes by saying that you were responsible for everything. I will also act like him. I hope his loneliness will provide support to me in my helpless life. Allow me to breathe peacefully for the rest of my life. The boy who is carrying this letter is the son of my younger sister. My sister died in childbirth when her second child was about to be born. Her husband married again. I have brought her son to me after that. I have lost many years of my life because of a lack of judgment and conceit. However, please consider my last wish as your own wish." Yours truly ....

Sunanda leaned back against the sofa with her eyes closed after reading the letter. The pages of memory were flying around her. She didn't know where they began and where they came to an end.

****

Ananda *Mastre*

For some reason I had the feeling that the gentleman was lost in the darkness of despair on seeing his face from a distance. His intermittent long sighs seemed to be filled with hot wind blowing in a desert. The peon informed me that the minister was asking for me before he could reach me. The entire state seems to have congregated on the corridors of the secretariat. People from all corners of the state gathered there. Someone was not getting his pension or salary. Someone was there to get the order of transfer cancelled. Someone was close to the minister. Someone else had arrived with a letter of recommendation. All the problems of the world seemed to begin and end there.

The day had passed somehow. I was busy throughout the day. I looked outside as I sat down in the car. The world outside looked hazy to me through the tinted glass. But I was able to see my old city, many new and old buildings that stood close together, the wide roads, tall trees and the light posts. Everything was running in the opposite direction. I was going ahead. I never had the time to look behind me. I had also never found any need for it. I checked the number of the incoming call before answering my mobile phone. I avoided calls from people who did not matter. I liked the way from the secretariat to my residence. I also liked that time. I used to live in the hostel when I was studying in B.J.B. College. When I sat on the scooter behind my friend Raju and passed this way, I had always thought that the people working in the secretariat were indeed fortunate. They had a direct connection with the people who decided the fate of the people of the state. I thought they were highly respectable. They constituted the government. I often went walking on that way later. I thought that the solitary bird perching on the top of the secretariat building was more fortunate than me. My thoughts came to an end with the sound of a car horn. The watchman had opened the gate and stood respectfully. As the car stopped in the portico, I looked at a bench on one side of the lawn. I felt dejected once again. There were problems at the office. It was the same at home too. As I entered the house hurriedly, something seemed to fly by my ears. I thought someone was calling, "Saura! Is that you, Saura?" I stopped in my tracks as if I had been chained.

I had lost that name in 1985 ever since I joined the civil service. Clay had been smeared on the name Saura and a shining, new glass nameplate bearing my name and designation had replaced it. Sourav Sundar Majhi, Chief Secretary, Odisha. It took me just a minute to get down the three steps and reach the lawn. I stared at the man who stood before me with perplexed and frightened eyes. The cloud that had covered my mind from the morning receded to a distance immediately. I was not unfamiliar with that grey beard, unkempt hair and sunken eyes. My driver and gardener had also followed me to the lawn. The gardener said, "Sir, we tried to dissuade him. But he didn't listen. He fell at my feet. He is an old man. Therefore, we have asked him to sit here." I felt bad. But my social status did not allow me to say anything there. I said to him, "Please come inside." I went inside my bungalow. I had been drenched in sweat. It was not because of the heat. It was because of fear, shame and regrets. Layers of dust had gathered on the past. But its existence had remained unimpaired. That thin and dark-skinned poor boy studying in class nine did not have the capacity to buy books at one time. This Ananda *Mastre* had given him books of Mathematics, Literature and Sanskrit and a hundred rupee note after the classes. I still worship him on the sly on Teachers Day on September 5 every year. *Mastre's* financial condition was not good in the least. He had not married. But he had to shoulder most of the responsibilities of a large joint family. He was a sincere teacher with a smile on his face all the time. He held the pleat of his dhoti in the left hand and carried two or three biographies of great men or novels in his right. He used to stop us on the way and gave us advices. He also gave us a book and advised us to return it after reading it. The children were forced to read the books. Ananda *Mastre* was certain to ask questions from those books the following day while teaching in the class.

I had asked the peon to make arrangements for his stay and food. But I was finding it difficult to go before him. Ananda *Mastre* had broken his piggy bank and passed on two hundred rupees to me that he had been saving for a long time when he heard from father that I insisted on studying at Bhubaneswar. He had said, "Go to the capital city. You will automatically find a roof over your head." Father was penniless. Ananda *Mastre* had given him new hope. His naked chest had seemed as dear to me as my father's wet *gamcha*. Father had held me tightly to his chest. Ananda *Mastre* had placed his hand on my head and blessed me. He said again, "Leave everything in the hands of God.

Never look back. Get on the bus and go on your way." I had never turned back from that day. I had never again set foot in the village. As a man looking for freedom flies in the sky, he loses his way and faces only darkness. He keeps track of only profits in his profit and loss account in the process of looking for happiness. I had almost stopped going to the village again. Of course, I was not enjoying myself in the capital city like other boys of my age. I had devoted all my time in preparing for the civil services examinations.

My shyness had got stuck somewhere like a bat. I had learnt to deliver long lectures about the country, the caste system and politics. That ideal student who had one day taken a solemn vow to eradicate injustice, atrocities and corruption dares to touch the sky above the capital city's skyscrapers today.

My mind went back to the village school, the dirty pond, the market where cows were sold, the uneven playground and the mango grove. The village came just after the grove. I recalled the wet eyelashes of Sumana, the only daughter of Ananda *Mastre's* younger brother. I had forgotten how rain used to play hide and seek on the quivering body of the unsought girl who had just turned into a young woman. I had now learned to heave a sigh of relief after moving miles away from all this. I have come to understand the meaning of joy of living only after reaching the capital city and finding the job to my liking. It is not as if my childhood memories had never agitated me. But that did not mean that I would have lived with those memories. I have built a beautiful present for me by colouring my discoloured, unnecessary memories anew. I have moved with the times. I.A.S. officer Sourav Ranjan deserves to be the son-in-law of a commissioner, politician, minister or industrialist. How did a village belle matter to me?

XXX

I had not gone before him till that time. I left for the club after making arrangements for Ananda *Mastre* to stay in the outhouse behind my quarters. After ordering for a peg of Scotch, I decided that I will enquire about Sir's problems the following morning. What was the matter? Was there a problem with his pension or did someone need a job in the village? A pitch road would already have been laid to the village under the *Pradhanmantri Gram Sadak Yojana*. In that case ...? Did he want a plot or a flat in the capital city? For whom did he want it? A girl was standing before me by the time I had taken the last sip of my peg of Scotch. Two plaits were hanging from her head. There was a bag in her hand and an umbrella over her head. As the two of us walked together under the umbrella, the girl took out a *pitha* or a fruit from her bag and pushed it inside Saura's mouth. Saura asked her if she had eaten. The girl nodded. He asked, "Did you bring this for me?" She laughed audibly. They had reached the pavilion of stone near *Gram Devati* (tutelary goddess of the village) by the time Saura had finished eating.

XXX

"Sir, shall I serve another peg?" I returned to my car without answering the waiter. I went back to my daydreaming days keeping pace with the speed of the car. Sumana – Ananda *Mastre's* niece. She was the only daughter of an educated Brahmin family. The people of the village did not take to it kindly that Ghania Majhi's son Saura Majhi should be so close to her. A meeting had been convened in the village to discuss the relationship between Saura and Sumana. Saura was studying in the final year B.A. at the time. Sumana was in class ten. Ananda *Mastre* had saved them from that predicament at that time.

Everyone in the village had been silenced. Ananda *Mastre* said, "I have asked Saura to guide Sumana in her studies. He comes to our house because of that." No one had the audacity to talk back to Ananda *Mastre*. Everyone knew that there was a temple inside him. The *Puranas, Bhagabata* and *Bhagavad Gita* were constantly recited before the deities in that temple. Sumana's face looked hazy to him from inside the fog of memory. That divine grace and divine words of Ananda *Mastre* – "Saura! Be careful about where you are going. What is your aim and future? The earth beneath your feet is still marshy. The sky above your head is still at an unreachable distance. You can reduce the distance between the earth and the sky if you want to do so. You have to equip yourself for the same." I had seen Sumana for the last time that evening. I had collected the drops of agitation shining in the corners of her beautiful eyes and returned to Bhubaneswar. I had gradually understood that dreams, love, frustration and thrills were only feelings. They turn into memories if you are capable of preserving them. But your life can change if you lose them. Memories do not help anyone to live. But one can keep himself young if he keeps his memories alive while compromising with the present. That can also be called life.

XXX

He stood up when he heard my car stopping in the portico. I recalled that the old man who was waiting for me at such a late hour in the night was one day my ideal. He used to walk ahead of me in order to ensure that my tottering feet would find their way on the uneven roads of life. He had numerous advices for his students. He used to say, "It's a great sin to tell lies. Never look at other people's wealth. Have faith on God. Do your duty. But do not expect anything in return." As I entered the room in an absent-minded way, I heard the words, "Saura! Saura, my boy!" I was losing myself on hearing his voice. I was getting drowned. I turned around and knelt down at his feet. He continued, "One cannot live with his ideals these days. You need a roof over your head, the ground beneath your feet, food for your stomach and to cover your body ...." He broke into tears as he said that. He stood with a great deal of difficulty leaning against my shoulder. I was scared to look at his face in the light. His eyes were sunken and covered with the protruding cheekbones. A bad odour came out of his body. "Sir?" said I. He said, "Who is Sir? One is to be addressed as Sir till he teaches at the school. At the most you can address someone like that for a couple of years after his retirement. The students I had taught have become doctors, engineers and lawyers. A few of them have become administrators and ministers." Sir stopped after saying this. I was still not able to understand what he wanted to say. He slumped to a chair after saying all that in one breath. He had gripped my left hand with both of his hands as if this was his last effort to reach the last step.

I could see everything like pictures. The windows of the village school where the woodwork was missing, the table, blackboard and the duster. Ananda *Mastre* stood inside the classroom wearing a white dhoti and a *panjabi*. He had a book of *Gita* or *Bhagabata* in his hand instead of a cane. There was a smile on his face instead of a *paan* inside the mouth. He was indeed an image of joy. My thoughts were interrupted when Sir turned towards me all of a sudden. Light from the veranda was reflected on his face. I had the impression that a ghost was hanging from a tree. I could imagine by looking at him that the times must have been tough on him all these years. I could not muster enough courage to ask him about it as I had turned my back on the village after joining the civil services. I used to send some money to father once in a while earlier. But even that relationship was severed after I married Anita Sanyal who was undergoing I.A.S. training with me. Ananda *Mastre* had asked one day in the class, "Boys! Do you know the meaning of happiness?" Before anyone else could say anything, I had volunteered, "Sir, happiness means a large house, a long car and a beautiful wife." Everyone had laughed looking at me. Two of the buttons on my shirt had come off and the thread was visible. Looking at my sunken stomach through that gap, Ananda *Mastre* had clasped me to his chest and said, "You are wrong, Saura. That is only material happiness. The real happiness is there in the soul and the mind. You find it through love and sacrifices." I had not been able to appreciate what Sir had said that day. I was putting my books and notebooks inside my tattered schoolbag. It was as if I was tying a knot around the present and getting ready for the future.

XXX

I have not been able to know till today as to what happiness really was. I have everything with me now that I had mentioned inside the classroom that day. But happiness was far away from me. Perhaps in an unreachable area. My wife was posted at a place that was four hundred kilometres away from my place of posting. She never had any psychological bondage with me before we got separated at a physical level. My son and daughter were away from us both physically as well as psychologically. There was only a financial link between us. Both of them were good students. Sir had said one day, "The son becomes happy because of the good deeds of his parents." I do not know where my parents are at present. I had helped Sir to sit down on the drawing room sofa. After he had had a glass of water, he asked, "Where are your children, Saura? Call our daughter-in-law. I am here since the morning. But I don't see anyone." A train ran over my head making a thundering noise. Everything became quiet after a while. Time had perhaps stood still. My present was moving between life and time like a pendulum. "Sir, what is Sumana doing now?" Sumana ... Sir looked at me with a steady gaze and lowered his face.

XXX

The night passed somehow. Time had turned into waves. Life was a sea. And the beach had extended from the north to the south. As my memories rose to the sky of clouds, my present was lost somewhere in the sky on the other side of the horizon. I recalled the promise that I had extracted from that girl studying in class ten named Sumana. "Sumana! I am leaving my parents in your charge." I had never enquired if she had looked after my parents. I too had forgotten their presence. I had also forgotten the scant relationship that I had had with the girl. My illiterate father used to wait on a narrow path of the village with a hurricane lantern in hand waiting for me to return from my tuition. My mother used to clasp me to her chest as she covered me with her dirty sari and told me stories about the old female demon in order to induce me to go to sleep. These were the people who had made all kinds of sacrifices for me. Did my I.A.S. qualification mean anything before their sacrifices? They continued to remain in darkness just like the space below a lamp. Their long sighs could be heard on the other side of the wall of my social status. But no one could see the way they disintegrated in the fire of my status. They were going through all kinds of privations. But they had still clung on to hope. However, I did not have enough nights to spare for their dreams.

I applied for leave for the following day and started out with Sir in the morning. I was driving the car myself. Sir was sitting beside me. The night was over a little while ago. It was a golden morning. I lowered the glasses of the car windows and looked at the sky to my heart's content. The sky was familiar to me. I thought I had found myself again after an interminable wait. A smile appeared on Sir's face and vanished. The smile seemed to be odd on his face. But I kept on driving the car silently. I could not understand why I could not cross that low wall of morality after gathering a plenitude of wealth. The results of my B.A. examinations had been published after I had returned from the village. I had got first class Honours with Distinction. I could not make up my mind whether I would do post-graduation in Sociology or go for a job. How was I going to take coaching for civil services examinations? I had many bitter experiences only in order to survive. Not only for living but to keep myself alive somehow. I worked as a private tutor, a night-watchman and a shop assistant. Neither idealism nor altruism had come to my rescue. But I had never forgotten those advices of Ananda *Mastre* at any time, neither at weak moments nor when I had a good time. He said, "My son, never turn back. Don't bother about the hurdles that come in your path. You have only one objective. You must forge ahead. This capital city will provide a roof over your head and a ground beneath your feet." I did not have the time to find the definitions of sin and virtue. I had only dreamt about a beautiful, orderly morning. I had forgotten the stories and characters that were part of my life before the difficult night passed slowly. I became exhausted under the intense heat of sunlight as I climbed the ladder of success in the morning and silence surrounded me. The past moved around me like pictures. I stopped at a particular page as the pages flew one after the other. I recalled the marshy veranda of clay and the smell of the tattered loose end of the sari that were so familiar to me in my childhood. I recalled my asthmatic old father inside the low thatched house and the children reciting the mathematical tables under an asbestos roof beside the small hillock. The pages kept turning. I could again see two deep black eyes, long, serpentine plaits falling over the blue frock and her face swathed in smile. Time ran ahead of her like a deer. I extended my hand. But my hand never reached there. I braked hard in an absent-minded way. "What's the matter, Saura?" "Nothing, Sir! I thought someone crossed the road in front of me." "Why, there is no one here," he smiled. I said, "Sir, let us have some tea here." "Since when have you been drinking tea? There is nicotine in tea, don't you know? You don't get any sleep if you drink tea."

I had not taken any tea in deference to Sir's wishes. Wasn't Sir aware that times had undergone a great deal of change in the meantime? I wanted to have a smoke. But I resisted the temptation. As I started the car, Sir said, "The village is one kilometre away from this place. The school will come after we cross the bridge. Drop me there." I had not given any answer as I was somewhat absent-minded. I was looking around for my friends from childhood days under the huge mounds of earth. Many moments had been stored inside my chest which I had not been able to forget in spite of my best efforts. I was feeling suffocated with the fragrance of those sweet memories. My oppressed mind was looking for a level ground where I could stand and stare at the sky without a worry.

The place where I reached after covering such a great distance in my life was my beginning. The beginning and end of the earth always met at one point. My old father lay on a plank of wood. An old woman who resembled my mother had stuck to the ground like a lump of clay. Her hip bone seemed to have broken. She seemed to have been shattered after the man who had taken care of her all these days was a broken man. Father was calling out to someone at intervals. Mother lay on a mat on the marshy floor where I could never stand steadily. A bat flew away from behind the broken wall when the door made a creaking sound. I turned around and looked at the place where our cows used to be tied. The children of the village stood there surrounding my car. An adult woman stood on the other side of the door frame who showed me the way to get inside the house. I had become speechless as I was about to cross the door-sill. She went back inside the house. The river was still inside the black pupils of her eye. She was wearing a plain sari like the afternoon beach. She had a bunch of glass bangles in her hands. There was a *bindi* on her forehead. But the parting of her hair on her head was bare like the twilight sky. Still she looked like an angel. It was as if she had descended silently from the heaven and would return there after her work was over. Sumana ... a fragrant garden from the past. There was a dense forest around her ... of time and age.

A blue cotton sari, a red *gamcha* and a red sari were getting dried on a wire in the courtyard. There was a dense basil plant on a well-maintained *chaura* (a stone structure under which a lamp is lit every evening). There were drops of water on the leaves. They looked as pure as someone's tears. Father called out from inside the house, "Who is there? Who was calling?" Mother shouted, "Sumana! Sumana dear! Give a handful of rice to the crow. It is cawing since the morning. Is my Saura coming today?" There was a churning inside my chest. What kind of a life had I been chasing till now? All I could have got out of it was a slice of bare sky and some dreamy blue colour. I was going to lose this silent enchantment, a horizon covered with fog. I was going to lose this fragrant forest of white flowers, loads of dreams and a sweet bondage without any strings attached. I came out of my reverie on hearing my mother's voice. She was pushing firewood inside the hearth. The gruel pushed the lid over the rice pot and fell on the hearth. The voice of my father calling out to Sumana, the lamentations of my mother and a garland of dried-up flowers on Ananda *Mastre's* photograph hanging from the wall buried my epoch-making ambition with mounds of earth and destroyed my entity. I was once again overtaken by an intense desire to live. The bank of the river in my village, the forest of grass flowers, the islet of the river, the herd of cows, and the interminable waiting of two silent eyes under the mango tree on the edge of the village with two long plaits hanging from the head gave me a new life. My parents, Sumana and Ananda *Mastre* provided me with the inspiration to build a factory to produce human beings. I sent my letter of resignation the following day and decided to set up an ideal school with the money that I had saved. A new story started from this juncture. Sumana put a garland of fresh flowers on Ananda *Mastre's* photograph who had guided me to reach the morning that I had lost since a long time.

****

Tearful Repentance

Chandrabhanu had been standing before the university gate once again after thirty to thirty-five years. The size and the design of the gate had changed in the meantime. It looked a great deal more impressive than earlier. But its attraction had remained as just before. It stood there like an extremely benevolent friend with time as its witness.

It was perhaps beyond nine in the evening. There were memories of tiny grasses under the feet. There were dew drops of those lost days above his head. The old days were somewhat hazy. But bunches of fresh jasmines still hung from plants beside the gate. Many months and years had passed in the meantime like streams of water. But did time pass on its own? Prof. (Dr.) Chandrabhanu Mohanty would be welcomed inside the university the following morning through the gate in a beautiful ceremony. It would be his first day of taking charge as the vice chancellor. It is the same place where he had been conditioned for a prosperous future. He had been able to establish himself after going through all kinds of hurdles and struggles.

He had met numerous people along the journey. There had been friendship with a few people and enmity with some others. He had struck different kinds of relationship with different people in his long journey. He had lost a few people along the way while a few others had deserted him. The company of a few people, their love and affection, and the philosophies of their life had influenced him. But he had not been able to build any permanent relationships. He had been standing in the same darkness clinging to the memories of that incomprehensible and insurmountable past.

A boy had got down one day from a bus near this gate. He was wearing a pair of jeans and a half shirt. He had carried a zinc trunk with him. An airbag hung from his back. A few books and a few pairs of trousers and shirts were in the trunk. Some *chuda* (rice flakes), molasses, salty *khajas* and some sweetmeats given to him by his mother had been packed in the airbag. He had secured good marks in B.A. (Hons.) examinations. Therefore, he had easily got a seat in the hostel. That was all the resources he had in this unknown city.

He had met a boy the following day in the classroom who was studying with him till class five in the village school. They had not met after that. He had not been able to recognise him immediately. The boy came to him and said, "You are Chandra, aren't you?" He felt that he had found a dense gulmohar tree on a lonely desolate road when he heard his name being pronounced by the boy. He wiped the sweat sliding down his nape and held him tightly by his hand. He asked haltingly, "You are Amiya. Is that right?"

"You don't have to be so formal. Are you staying in the hostel?"

Chandra had flashed a smile at him. The smile lit up his handsome and slightly dark face like a bunch of fresh flowers. Amiya pushed closer to him and put his hand on his shoulder. He said, "Chandra! Your nose used to run in your childhood days. But you look quite handsome these days."

Chandra blushed. Amiya shook him by the shoulder and said, "You cannot afford to be coy in the university. I will show the city around to you this evening. Be there at the gate." He started his bike and sped away raising dust after him. He was able to see Amiya's smiling face in the dust. He would not perhaps be looking forward to the following day if he would not have found a childhood friend like Amiya in this unknown city. He would have spent the next two years somehow as he had come to study here and earn a living.

Malay, Sarat, Rajesh, Chinmay and the others accepted him as a friend within a few days without his knowledge like a streak of light piercing darkness. Someone was from Cuttack. Someone was from Bhubaneswar. Still someone had come from his village. But there was no one from his district Bhadrak or nearby areas in his department. The room in which he used to live in the hostel had its face towards the road inside the university campus. The rows of trees in front of the road looked familiar to him when he sat before his table. His eyes crossed the road and reached the place at times where groups of boys and girls sat beside each other. He kept his books aside and looked at himself in the small mirror hanging from the wall. He straightened the collar of his shirt and combed his hair. He looked outside again. But he felt restless. He went back to study again.

Amiya proposed one day to go for a movie. He said that they would have their dinner at a hotel later and move around in the city for a while after which he would drop him at the gate. As he dipped his hand into his pocket without being aware of it, Amiya pulled him away. It was late in the night by the time they returned. Chandra was walking with long strides. He had to turn left after walking some distance. The hostel would be visible from there. He thought he had wasted a great deal of time that day. His eyes had dashed against another pair of eyes out of the blue. He had the feeling that the image of a goddess had appeared for a moment before vanishing again. He could neither move forward nor could he retrace his steps. He had stared in that direction till someone had closed the window. It was quiet everywhere after that. He waited for some more time. Was there a guest in Prof. Satapathy's house? He could still see the white sari and the two beautiful eyes even after reaching the hostel.

Classes, seminars, picnics, etc. went on as usual and they realised one day that they had completed the first year and come to the second year at the university. They were in the final year of their postgraduate studies. He had come from his village without any friend. But he saw life at close quarters and his compassionate friends at this place. He might not have been equal to his modern and ultramodern lady classmates in status. But he had been able to carve out a niche for himself in the student community. His objective had become quite firm and specific after silently fighting all the adversities of life. Father arrived at the hostel the day his results were out. He said, "Chandra! Get ready to leave for the village immediately. There are problems at home." Amiya had arranged a party of the students in his honour that day. He had topped all the semesters in the fifth year. Tanya Singh, the most modern and beautiful girl of his class who drove to the university in her car every day, had requested him, "Hey Chandra! Are you coming today or not?" Rajesh had snatched a hundred rupee note from his pocket after Tanya sped away in her car. He said, "You miser! You have to buy cold drinks for everyone today."

He had not been able to tell Rajesh that that hundred rupee note would have seen him through for the following ten days.

Father said, "What are you thinking about? The bus is at twelve. It is already a quarter past eleven." He did not have the opportunity of informing anyone. What would Amiya do in the evening when he found him missing? What would Tanya think of him? His mind had ceased to function. As he looked outside sitting inside the bus he thought that he should have informed Amiya in the least. He glanced at his father. But he was sitting with his eyes lowered.

The scene before his eyes had changed after he reached home. His mother was lying with her eyes closed. She continued to lie like that for a few days before closing her eyes forever. The doctor had not been able to diagnose what was wrong with her. Father covered a sari over her pale face and emaciated body. Chandra stayed in the village for fifteen days before returning to the hostel empty-handed. He reached the hostel at ten in the morning and lay down on the bed. His roommate Sanjay rummaged through the contents of the airbag which Chandra had pushed under the bed. He asked, "Chandra, haven't you brought any sweetmeats with you this time?" Chandra started crying loudly at that moment. He had realised that his childhood days, his dreams and his fickleness had gone away with his mother. All his friends surrounded him and tried to cheer him up. Even Tanya had caressed his hair fondly and consoled him. Amiya could not stop himself from pushing his mouth closer to Chandra's ears and whispering, "You are a lucky devil! If my mother ...."

Everyone had burst out laughing. He had tried to keep himself under control from that day. Life was perhaps like that. His mother was not going to return again. But he had to think about the other people around him. He recalled his father's wilted face. He made him sit over his shoulder till he was a grown-up boy. He relieved him of his schoolbag on the way back from the school. He used to fall asleep before nightfall. Mother woke him up by sprinkling water in his eyes. She opened his books and notebooks. Father sat beside him and stared at him. Chandra could see the entire sky in his eyes. The moon rose from the other side of the window by putting all his thoughts to rest. It had become a part of his sorrow, happiness, wishes and emotions in the past few days. It had promised to show him the world outside by holding him by the hand. He could not explain his relationship with Ananya to Amiya. The same was the case with Rajesh. Girls like Tanya could not even think in their dreams that someone could waste his invaluable moments like that.

He did not have the courage to lose anything else after his mother passed away. Therefore, he had not informed anyone about this forbidden world of his. He used to share his dreams and love with Ananya very carefully. The tranquillity of an invaluable relationship dazzled in his eyes. His dream might recede far away from him if he extended his hands. Chandra did not want to let her know about it.

The classes had started. It was the day when the new professor of Sociology was to be welcomed.

He had no idea how long he had stood there. The sound of horn had brought him back from those enchanting moments of the past that were full of promises. He had turned his back on those days before the headlights of the car fell on his eyes.

He was driving himself that day. How the city

had changed! Prof. (Dr.) Chandrabhanu Mohanty had received many honours after working for long years in the universities outside Odisha. He had once again returned to the same place crossing all the hurdles of time where a girl had sat covering herself with an upper garment of helplessness and extended her hand unknowingly to hold his hand. The emotions shining in some corner of his eyes had poured down like the skies of *Sravana*. He had taught her to laugh in spite of all her miseries. He had not just consoled her but held out promises for the rest of her life. She had considered him to be superior to all other human beings. But she would not have known whether he was fit to be called a human being in the first place. Even a bird can live safely in the sky or in the hole of some tree. But Ananya? What would she have done when she would have come to know that all the students of the South Hostel had vacated the hostel a few days ago? Would she have stopped waiting for him? She might have stood holding the railings of the window and stared outside for a number of days. What would she have done after that?

Arrangements had been made to welcome Prof. (Dr.) Chandrabhanu Mohanty, the new vice chancellor. Gates had been erected from the gate till the vice chancellor's quarters. Everything was spick and span in the office room. The teaching faculty, students, office bearers of the students' union, etc. greeted him with bouquets one after the other. But there was a heaviness in Prof. Mohanty's heart. He was experiencing a mild pain in his chest. He had pressed down the left side of his chest with his hand without being aware of it.

"What's the matter, Sir? Aren't you feeling well?" Everyone seemed worried.

"I am feeling slightly uneasy. It's nothing. The

professors' quarters stood over there. Prof. Satapathy used to live in the quarters in the south-east corner. Who lives there now?" The members of the staff were looking at each other. About whom the vice chancellor was asking? Which Prof. Satapathy?

Chandrabhanu came back to his senses. His smiling eyes ran over the students. He left his chair and came close to them. He said with a smile, "I am also an ex-student of this university like all of you." The students had given him a thunderous applause. The echo of their clapping was hitting his chest like a hammer. That day would perhaps never come again the day Chandra had stepped out of the gate of the university with stones loaded on his soul.

Amiya knocked on his door in the morning. He said, "We will give a surprise to the new professor. What do you say? You will sing a song, Chandra. A song from your village. Sanjay said that you sing well. You sing regularly looking at Prof. Satapathy's window."

Chandra became somewhat grave and smiled after a while. "Are you out of your mind? Songs and me? No way."

"Come on! Don't try to show off!"

"We will see about it." He went to the bathroom with his toothbrush.

Amiya said from behind, "Listen to me. There is good news for you. Tanya Singh is going to dance Kathak today.

"So she also knows how to dance? I had thought that she only makes others dance."

Amiya pushed closer to him and said, "That's true. But you know better."

Chandra became quiet. He entered the bathroom and bolted it. He was scared to think if a beautiful sky would ever come into his life.

Kumar Sir, the new professor, had praised his songs a

great deal. He had sung one song after another on the request of the students. The girls had made most of the requests. Rajesh shouted in a loud voice, "He is a Chhupa Rustom." It was eleven in the evening by the time the programme was over. His friends had surrounded him. Like a streak of moonlight on the clouds covering his mind. All of them had gone till the gate to see Tanya off. Chandra stood there till she started her car. Tanya's face looked dazzling because of too much happiness. She liked Chandra. Chandra was not only a brilliant student. He was also a very good singer. This had made her a great deal sentimental. Chandra was tracing his way back to the hostel after Tanya's departure. The first floor window of Prof. Satapathy's house was completely open. The loose end of the white sari was swaying in the breeze. A thin ray of light had come out of the window and lost its existence after some distance like the regrets of life that were yet to be fulfilled.

Chandrabhanu had turned into a real hero at the university. Someone addressed him as Chandra, some as Chandra Bhai and still someone called him Chandra dear! Chandra and Tanya were the centres of conversation in the canteen, common room, outside and near the gate. Their singing and dancing had been appreciated by everyone. Tanya was very happy.

A man standing in darkness can see the world with a fixed gaze. But a man living inside the world cannot see the darkness. He had understood that it was not his job to watch or judge the moon, the sea, the jungle of grass or the fragrance of flowers. Tanya and Ananya were two contrary characters. He could see Tanya's love for him. He had already drowned in the depth of Ananya's sorrow. However, he had to achieve the aim of his life in spite of all this.

Every human being leaves some mark or the other on this earth after they leave it. They do so either knowingly or unknowingly. Prof. Satapathy would have decided on a poor, meritorious and obedient student like me to take care of his daughter who was going to have an untimely end. Therefore, he did not mind if I visited his house at all kinds of odd hours. I sat with Ananya for a while after discussing my lessons with Sir and returned from his house after having dinner there. The hope of getting something after losing a great deal in life had made him quite weak before me. He could see a thin ray of moonlight in the confused life of his daughter because of my poverty-stricken life. He had confidence in me that I loved Ananya. But there was another facet to my life too. It was my high ambition in life. However, I had not let them know about it. I was applying to different colleges for a job while staying in the hostel. I registered my name in the employment exchange too. I realised that I needed an address at the university from where I could collect any letters that came for me. I knew that Prof. Satapathy would live in his quarters for at least three more years. Therefore, I had asked him if I could use his address for the purpose of correspondence. He had thought that I would at least be able to meet Ananya more frequently using this as an excuse. He had happily agreed to my request.

He was not certain the other day whether he would go to Prof. Satapathy's house. But he had found himself at his doorsteps. The door was open. Chandra had entered the house without a thought as on any other day. Ananya's mother called him inside. He sat alone for some time on Ananya's bed. Ananya's photographs hung from the walls of the room. The photographs were with her parents, husband and daughter. There was a smile on her face in each of the photographs. He examined each photograph minutely. Ananya's eyes looked withered like the petals had dried up before a bud could bloom into a flower. Ananya had come inside the room with her mother and young daughter. She had worn a pale yellow sari that day and stuck a *bindi* on her forehead. She looked different from the other days. She looked beautiful and a great deal of dreams seemed to be floating inside her eyes like clouds. He was scared. He had met Prof. Satapathy before returning. He had been able to see a ray of light in Sir's eyes clearly.

None of his letters had come in the address of Prof. Satapathy. But he had received a letter from Ananya for the first time after leaving the hostel.

Prof. Rajkishore Raj, professor of Anthropology, had invited the vice chancellor for dinner on his first evening in the campus. He wanted to decline as he did not feel well. But he had agreed to come out of courtesy. He had assured him that he might be somewhat late. But he would certainly come.

It was a duplex quarters. There was a small garden in front. There was a row of deodar trees behind the quarters. He could not recall having seen such large trees in the campus earlier. A great deal of change had come about in the past twenty-five to thirty years. The departments had moved to new buildings. New hostels like North, South, East, West, Northeast and Southeast had been constructed one after the other. Prof. Chandrabhanu opened the gate and came out. Prof. Raj's quarters could be seen at the turn of the road. He walked on the left hand side road for a while to stretch his legs. Moonlight had lit up the entire campus ... on the trees, on the roads, on the quarters, everywhere. It had also fallen on him. He felt somewhat light-hearted. Chandrabhanu walked ahead restlessly. He stumbled over a rock. He had checked himself before he could fall down. The past stood before him blocking his path. Those deodar trees on the south east corner stood even today. They had grown wildly because of lack of care. He raised his eyes to look up. The window was open even today. The screen was swaying in the breeze. The moonlight had filtered inside the house through the open window. There was a constriction in his chest. The sky looked dark to him in spite of the moonlight. Many years had passed in the meantime.

He had not been able to eat properly. The professor couple had fawned on him. But he had remained absent-minded throughout the dinner.

He had chatted with them for a while before returning on the same road gathering the jumbled pages of memory for a long time. He changed his clothes and came to bed. The past was running backward before his sleepless eyes.

Amiya, Rajesh, Chinmay, etc. had found some job or the other for themselves. He had heard that Tanya had registered for her Ph.D. However, he had joined a college in Koraput district to fulfil his needs. Father was not keeping good health. It was difficult for him to manage on his own in the village. His father believed that he had to get married immediately as he had already got a job. Chandra didn't like the girls his father had paraded before him. He told his father that he had not been able to create any status for himself yet. And how could he marry of his own free will and that too the widowed mother of a young girl? His farmer father did not have such a large heart to compromise with such a terrible reality. Therefore, he had given precedence to his career. He had forgotten his father's wish, his friends from the university, Tanya, Ananya, everything. He did his Ph.D. on *Adivasi* people's life and became a Reader in the

Government College, Jeypore. He followed it up with post-doc studies and finally made it to University of Delhi after a long time. He had met life anew there. He was surrounded by heaps of books and groups of students from morning till night. He was regularly invited overseas to act as a visiting faculty in foreign universities. He had finally reached the place where life had begun for him after going through many lanes and by-lanes.

Prof. Chandrabhanu had been staring at the past. The thin ray of light that was looking for a way for itself inside darkness brushed against him. He was feeling agitated and perplexed today. He was also agitated and perplexed about his uncertain future that day. Ananya's attachment with him and Prof. Satapathy's confidence in him were gradually frightening him.

The sound of the university clock disturbed his train of thought. He was trying to recall a few lines of her letter that he had lost deliberately amid the emerging morning and the chirping of the birds on the other side of the window. He lay on the bed with his eyes closed covering himself with a sheet of silence. He was completely alone now. He had run ahead by himself one day in this manner. He had left all other things behind him. Why did the fragrance of that wilted flower preserved in his memory bother him once again at this age at the end of all his quests? His eyes had closed with the morning breeze. A few pages turned over.

"Has anyone been able to enclose time in his hands?" Ananya had said softly. Chandra kept quiet for a while and said, "Why not? May be I cannot do so with time. But I can tie you and time with my life and walk holding your hand."

Ananya looked at him for a while and then looked beyond the window. As she looked outside, she said, "A white sari is stained quite fast, Chandra. That stain does not come off easily once it sticks to the sari."

Ananya had continued, "There was sympathy for me in your eyes when you had come to me. You had not been able to know at the time that human beings were helpless before time and society. I had enjoyed sharing my grief with you and it had gradually become burdensome for you. But your attraction for me and my fondness were parallel to time. I had been able to understand that you were apprehensive about our future with you. I had understood without you saying anything about it that I won't be able to bring the slightest light to your disappointed eyes. I was only a momentary attraction before your great ambition. You could not tell me that I was nothing but a dream for your uncertain future. Your absent-mindedness after the last semester had made me understand that the untimely gulmohar flowers were likely to fall down at any time. The society pulled away the coloured sari from the body of a guileless young woman at one moment. But the person in love has to cross many rivers, hills and skies of the society before she can wear a coloured sari once again. You did not have that kind of a mind or courage. I didn't want to stain your love and promises by telling you all this. Therefore, I had turned my back on you. Father blamed me, my fate and him along with you and left this world leaving me behind. It was an absolute truth that you were going to achieve your high ambitions one day. You do not have the capacity to understand that everything else is immaterial before a little bit of love, some emotions and silent surrender. I will remain as a fragrant moment on your path in the morning. It is better that we do not get directly separated from each other. You had sought permission from father for your letters to come in our address. But not a single letter had ever come in your name as long as father lived inside the campus. It was only your beautiful pretension before my father."

The vibration of his mobile had put a sudden stop to his thoughts.

It was his first day at the university. He was supposed to go around the departments. The professors and readers of the departments would accompany him. Prof. (Dr.) Chandrabhanu Mohanty had reached his office hiding all his miseries and regrets. The faculty members were waiting for him beforehand.

"Sir, it is not possible to go around all the departments in one day."

He answered absent-mindedly, "I can at least make a visit to my department today. I mean, the Department of Sociology."

The classes were going on. The students were happy to see the vice chancellor with his entourage. The fact that the vice chancellor was meeting the students personally had also created positive vibes. He had asked there once again, "Dr. Satapathy was a professor of Sociology during our times in nineteen eighty-four or eighty-five. He was a very good teacher. Where is he now?" He became somewhat withdrawn after that. The eagerness of his mind was bothering him. A girl came to him and touched his feet. "Sir, Prof. Satapathy was my grandfather and he is not alive any longer." "What? When did it happen? I am sorry." The girl said, "It's okay, Sir."

The vice chancellor looked at the girl's face and asked, "He had a daughter ... her name was perhaps Ananya. I think she had only one daughter."

The girl looked straight at the vice chancellor's face and said, "Yes Sir. She is my mother."

"Oh, I see!" Prof. Chandrabhanu asked very carefully, "How is she? And how is your father?"

"Sir, my mother is a teacher. And my father ...."

He acted as if he did not want to hear the name of her father.

The vice chancellor had turned towards the other students before the girl could say anything. He changed the context and said enthusiastically, "I was also sitting in this classroom like you people. I used to sit on the front bench. My roll number was twenty-two."

One of the students said very boldly, "Sir, Chandrika also has the same roll number."

"Who is Chandrika?"

"Sir, it's me." The vice chancellor had looked at the girl affectionately. The beautiful face of Chandrika was dazzling like a trustworthy morning filled with self-confidence. Someone seemed to be telling him from inside those resplendent eyes, "I could have bound myself by your promise and gone on with my life till the end. I had a family. I had lost my husband before I had the opportunity of getting to know what family life really was. I had looked forward to a new life with the assurances of father and was introduced to you. You used to come to our house almost every day and your affection for me was increasing constantly. This had added colour to my life and I had been able to do away with my indifferent lifestyle. My father Prof. Satapathy had suddenly become sanguine about my future and my daughter's present. He considered it to be his good fortune that he was able to see you every day. He was becoming more and more confident that I would be able to live life anew with you by my side. He had allowed you to become friendly with me without any reservations. But all this had frightened you a great deal. You had said one day to me, 'Every person has to reserve a special place for him or her. Who knows when times might change?'

"I had been scared that the gulmohar tree standing beside me was shorn of branches and leaves. Its dense and green leaves and bunches of flowers were only dreams in my closed eyes. I had wanted to free you from this story of falling leaves in my life from that day. You had a sky to yourself and you wanted to fly. Time had made me aware of it before I had been able to understand what life was. I did not know the solution to all the problems in my mathematics book. But you had taught me the formulas. I had unwittingly found the formula for a strong frame of mind from you before I had fallen down and wounded myself. I had lived till then without any purpose and with the sympathy of other people. But the life I had led after being abandoned by you was more valuable for me. A river has to find its own way in order to reach the sea. Like you I have looked at life from a different angle and I have been able to find a secure place for myself. I have come out of the circumference of your wishes. Haven't I been able to establish myself between yesterday and tomorrow?"

The vice chancellor said absent-mindedly all of a sudden, "I want you to create a special place for yourself. Let the ground beneath your feet and the sky above your head belong to you."

"Sir, are you talking to me?" asked Chandrika.

He felt embarrassed as he tried to hide within himself. He said, "No, no. Do you live in the hostel?"

"No, Sir. I live with my mother."

"All right! All right! God bless you! My heartfelt regards to Late Dr. Satapathy and convey my best wishes to Ananya, i.e. your mom."

The tearful repentance that he had preserved inside

him for such a long time had flown down from his tired eyelashes. Prof. Chandrabhanu had been standing near the university gate and staring ahead of him. The road leading from the gate had stretched for some distance before disappearing from view. He looked back. A few deodar trees stood in front of that large house on the south east corner of the university campus. The half-open window could be seen through the gaps in the trees. A bird was picking up the twigs that had fallen down from its nest, that had flown away in the rains and was rebuilding it.

****

Old Age Pension

Kani turned on her side. She could hear the heavy breathing of Dhuruva's father in the darkness. Kani could never know whether he was asleep or awake by looking at his face. He slept immediately on hitting the bed because of the hard labour he did throughout the day. Where was the time to exchange pleasantries? Kani however kept on dreaming in spite of all the privations in her life. A neat and clean room, a twin bed made from the wood of a mango or jackfruit tree and a couple of pillows. Someone would be sleeping on the bed by her side who did not stink of sweat. A fragrant air would be moving inside the room. Kani would come to the bed wearing a clean sari after taking a bath. She would take out the tin of talcum powder from the shelf and powders herself liberally. She would comb her long and thick hair and plait it. She would switch off the light and lie on the clean bed. Her dreams came to an end when she heard Dhuruva's racking sobs.

Dhuruva's father turned on his side. Oh no! How he stank! Kani felt suffocated. She was afraid that he might come awake if she made much noise. Poor man! For whom was he slogging all day after all? Their son Dhuruva was still a kid. Dhuruva's father's dream was different from

Kani's dream. He wanted Kani to eat and live well. He was an uncomplicated man. All that he wanted was that his son would be properly educated and find a good job one day. He would wear clean trousers and shirts like gentlemen. He would not wear dirty and tattered dhotis like him. He won't sit on the ground like him when he went to someone's house. He would sit on a chair like other well-to-do people. There would be servants to serve him.

Kani wrinkled her nose, "You are a shameless man. You expect your son to become an officer! Find enough rice for three people first. You might then think about making an officer out of your son." Dhuruva held his father by his neck and said, "Father, buy me a fountain pen. I cannot write with chalks anymore." Dhuruva's father stood up straight. He picked Dhuruva up on his shoulder and showed him the sky. It was a clear sky. He pointed at the moon and said, "Look at Uncle Moon in the sky. You will go to your uncle's place. You will eat rice and milk there." Kani said between clenched teeth, "Your uncle does not allow you people to get up on his veranda since the day my father has passed away. And you are dreaming about going to uncle's house!"

The day turned into night. The night is waiting for the morning to arrive. Dhuruva's father had started daydreaming. He saved every possible penny and finally managed to put Dhuruva in the high school one day. He was in the seventh heaven that day. He called out to Kani from the doorstep and said, "Kani dear! Dhuruva's uncle's house is not very far away. You will see my Dhuruva will become an officer one of these days and your family members would be staring at him sitting on their front veranda. Take my word for it."

Kani raised her hands to the sky. Tears welled up

in her eyes. Dhuruva's father had been staring at her fair-complexioned body through the openings in her tattered sari. He was thinking that he would tell his son to buy an expensive sari for his mother the day he gets a decent job. Kani found him gaping at her and said angrily, "You cannot feed one stomach or find enough money to see him through school. Never come close to me. I am telling you!" Dhuruva's father smiled. The sparrow chicks were jumping around on the thatch. There was dust all over his head. His body was also dusty. Kani did not like him much. But she drank the watery portion of watered rice only after serving him a full bowl of watered rice. She did not have the time to think about herself in their poverty-stricken life. Still Dhuruva's father silently admired Kani's intelligence. She worked in other people's house from morning till evening. She washed utensils in someone's house. Or she massaged someone's baby with oil. She carried food from those people's houses and gave them to Dhuruva to eat. She didn't earn as much as Dhuruva's father did. But she still managed to provide enough food to the family one time a day. The parents had one meal a day. Their only concern was that their son would get two square meals a day. He would go to the school wearing clean clothes.

Dhuruva was even more capable than the dreams of his parents. He memorised all his lessons. He waited for the daily *The Samaj* at Hari Sahoo's book shop in order to keep himself abreast of the developments taking place in the country. He read the newspaper after the departure of all the customers from Sahoo's shop. He kept staring at the sky night after night. He chatted with the moon. Kani got scared at times. But Dhuruva's father had pinned all his hopes on his son.

XXX

The old man was no longer able to see properly these days. He groped around in the dark when he walked. It did not matter if there was a lamp in front of him or not. The sun as well as the rainwater entered his house through the holes in the thatch. He was afraid that the damp wall might crumble anytime. They had sold away almost all their bell metal utensils for the treatment of the old man's asthma. They could have managed things for a few days. But this had continued for years at a stretch. Their indigence was no longer alone. It had entered their house with family and friends. He could no longer think of admitting Dhuruva to the college after he passed matriculation.

Schoolteacher Sudhakar Sir said, "Dhuruva will get scholarship. He can study further if you can contribute something more. There is no one as intelligent as him in this village or state." Dhuruva's father started daydreaming once again. Kani started working in three more houses in order to arrange some milk for Dhuruva. Her eyes turn into sockets. The thin legs of Dhuruva's father became unsteady. But Dhuruva managed to stand straight. Perhaps the ground beneath his feet was not hard enough. But his legs were getting stronger. He was forging ahead.

XXX

Several days had passed in the meantime. Kani was drawing lines on the wall with a piece of brick since the day her son left for the city. The lines went on lengthening and the wall came to an end. They were not able to know whether their son's studies had come to an end or not. Dhuruva's father could no longer recall when he turned into a tottering old man. He was a young widower with a son when Kani had been brought to his house as a bride to be married to him. He kept on running all the time looking at

Dhuruva's face. He also made Kani run by making her hold his son's hand. At times, the son ran ahead and the parents followed him behind. Sometimes, it was the opposite. They had no idea where their son had reached. The parents had been left way behind. It was a dream for them now even to see the shadow of the son. Dhuruva's father was about to go blind looking for his son all the time.

The people of the village advised him to apply for old age pension from the government. The old man could not look at Kani's face. Kani never said anything. But the old man felt as if she was growling at him all the time. Kani brought home the bacon. Both of them were likely to die if she slept for a day without working. But Kani kept on working grittily. She ensured that food and medicines were available to them.

XXX

Was there a festival today? The people of the village had got together at one place. Government vehicles had gathered on the main road of the village. Pitch roads had been built in all the villages under the *Pradhanmantri Sadak Yojana*. Arches had been put up on both sides of the road. The old man had stared at everything sitting on his veranda. Kani had not as yet returned from work. He had a small front yard. A few people were looking at his low thatch. The old man asked, "Who is there? Who are you looking for?" He was not able to see very far. He thought that the government people had perhaps come to hand over his pension. He had gone to the office along with Kani and lodged his complaint. Did the government consider his case? Why else would so many people gather in front of his house? He was getting asthmatic attacks at odd hours. Kani had forbidden him to move around. Who could he ask? The road in front of his house was full of people. No one could hear his voice. The old man tried to straighten his stick and get up. Where did Kani go?

"Why are you calling me? Haven't I turned into an old woman yet? Do you expect me to keep running till I drop dead?" The old man became quiet. It was true that she was all skin and bone. The old man looked at her and said, "How much more can you work?" Kani said, "Save your sympathies. You wasted all your money on your first wife's son when you should have taken care of me. Why take pity on this barren woman at this age? You had got me as a slave so I would nurse you at your old age." She gulped down what she wanted to say at the end. She ran away to the backyard with dilated eyes. She had a harsh tongue. But she loved Dhuruva more than his father. Everyone in the village was aware of it. Someone seemed to have poked him with a stick of fire when he heard Dhuruva's name being mentioned. He closed his eyes and said, "No! I don't have any son." The old man looked outside and blinked his eyes.

Kani was talking to someone with her veil over her head. Had that landlord Pradhan come with the mortgage deed of his homestead? He seemed to be arguing with Kani. The amount he owed towards principal and interest must be an astronomical sum by this time. He would not be able to get his homestead released in even ten more lives. Where was he going to seek shelter with Kani at this age? He thought that the landlord would materialise before him like a demon any moment now. He was going to throw him out of his house. The landlord's peon Raghu would throw his son's trunk away. The old man shouted, "Hey! Don't touch that trunk. You can take everything else except that. My Dhuruva will return tomorrow if not today. His books, notebooks, pens, etc. are inside that trunk. Don't you know me? Do you think I do not have anyone just because I have become an old man? You think you can throw me to the street! This is the homestead of my ancestors. I have only one son. He may not have come home till now but he would arrive someday to offer *pinda* to me."

Kani came running hearing the old man's voice. She asked, "Why are you shouting in such a loud voice? *Sarpanch* Sir has come."

"Why has he come? You haven't said anything to me about it."

The old man stood up straightening his staff. The *sarpanch's* responsibilities seemed to have increased manifold. The biggest job in his hand was to repair the dilapidated house of the old man. The roof had to be thatched. A mixture of lime and cement had been applied as a coat on the broken wall that looked like a flicker of a smile on a lachrymose face. There were garlands of marigold on the thatch. The barricade had been removed from the front and a bamboo arch was being put up. The *sarpanch* extended a new sari and a pair of dhotis towards Kani and said, "Take them, Maa. Have a change of clothes." The *sarpanch* was addressing Kani the maidservant as Maa. The old man looked confused.

The headmaster of the school spread a newspaper before the old man and said, "Can you recognise the man in the photograph?" The old man looked indifferent to his surroundings. He wiped his eyes with the loose end of his dhoti and examined the photograph minutely. Kani carried a bucket of water from the well in the backyard of their neighbour's house. She took out a clean towel from a box. A few drops of tears from Kani's eyes fell inside the bucket. Like a pearl of hope on life. The illiterate Kani had taken a vow looking at the crying face of Dhuruva the day she had stepped into the house. A son was a son. How did it matter if he was a stepson? She had been happier to be the mother of a young boy rather than becoming the bride of an elderly father. She had no love lost for Dhuruva's father. She was the daughter of indigent parents. She had taken a vow not to look at her father's face again when he had given her away to a married man. She had no idea when her hair had turned grey as she and Dhuruva became close to each other. She kept everything good that came her way for Dhuruva. But Dhuruva started growing wings gradually. He lost his way and flew away somewhere.

Kani came out of her reverie when *Sarpanch* Sir called him. The police vehicle stopped in front of her house. Two or three other vehicles were following it. The schoolchildren showered flowers on the vehicles. The vehicles started moving forward buried in flowers. The *sarpanch* rode in the last vehicle along with the old man and Kani. They reached the school veranda. The children sang the national anthem. The chief guest was to deliver his address after the headmaster's address. The voice of Sudhakar Babu, the retired headmaster, was drenched in emotions, "I have taught each son of this soil who has grown up eating the rice produced in this village. I have caned them whenever I have felt it to be necessary. But I had no idea that Dhruva Biswal who has been born and brought up in this village is a space scientist from the USA. I never knew that he has been honoured as the National Space Scientist by the Government of India. He is a son of this village. He is dear to all of us. I bless him and pay my respects to his parents as they have dedicated their illustrious son for the cause of the nation. He has made our country proud by making it famous in the world. I hope he will make similar efforts to create many scientists from our village. We wanted to set up a state-of-the-art laboratory in our school since a long time. We can achieve our goal if you kindly lend us a helping hand. You can be the guide of this village and its children. You have brought glory to this land."

Dhuruva's eyes were turning moist. The days of the past seemed to be crossing him in a disorderly manner. He was feeling somewhat helpless in the beginning when he left home and went to the city. He became absent-minded when he recalled how he used to sit on his father's shoulder on his way back from the school. The aroma of hot rice and a curry of Malabar spinach (*poi* leaves) and prawns in mustard gravy cooked by his mother reminded him of the days he had spent in the village. But he had not been able to find any time to look back when he had forged ahead. The huge sky seemed to have kept him enthralled. He kept moving inside planets and constellations. He had distanced himself from his roots. But had he forgotten everything about the past? To whom was he going to furnish an explanation today? The person for whom he had dreamt of touching the sky with his feet rooted to the ground had turned into a bare tree today. The chief guest had stood up hiding all his mental agitations inside his eyes.

The audience broke into rapturous applause as the chief guest held the microphone. The old man and Kani had got up on the stage with the help of the *sarpanch* before he could say anything. Before the chief guest could reach the old man, the latter turned his back on him and shouted in a loud voice holding on to the microphone, "*Sarpanch* Babu! I have no idea why you have brought me to this place. I am a daily labourer who has been waiting for a better tomorrow for ages. I have no one to call my own except for my wife who has been working in other people's houses at her old age in order to provide me with two meals a day. *Sarpanch* Babu has dragged us here. I will narrate my miseries and everyone present here will hear me. My miseries have become a part of my life and I have learnt to live with them. I have only one request for you. Please prevail upon the government to ensure that I get my old age pension. I would like to take my medicines regularly as my asthma is getting out of hand. Kani would like to wear a new sari if anything would be left over after it. I have nothing more to say."

****

Basanti *Khudi*

*K*hudi (father's younger brother's wife) had an untimely death. Gitu had gone to the village during the Dola holidays. *Chaiti Punei* (the full moon day in March-April) passed two days ago. It was a month and two days from *Dola Punei* (the full moon day of February-March) to *Chaiti Punei*. Gitu had no idea what the matter was with *Khudi*. Of course, she had not been able to talk to her after returning from the village. She was either at the temple or busy with some chores or the other whenever she rang her. Gitu too was busy with her own family. She had not been able to find the time to talk to her. Finally, *Khudi* passed away.

When she had left the village, *Khudi* had asked her, "My dear! I need something. Will you give it to me?" As she packed her children's clothes in a suitcase, Gitu asked, "What is it? Please tell me." *Khudi* said, "No, let it be. I will tell you when you come here the next time." She sounded somewhat absent-minded. Oh dear! Gitu could not ask her anything and she too didn't volunteer any information. What was it that she lacked?

Madhu *Dada* (father-in-law's younger brother) took good care of her. She considered her sisters-in-law (husband's brothers' wives) to be as good as her sisters.

Grandfather used to fawn on her all the time. She was the most pampered among his three daughters-in-law. She did everything at home sincerely. There were ten children in the family. One of the brothers of Madhu *Dada* had five children, another had three and the sister had two children. But Basanti *Khudi* was the mother of all the ten children. Madhu *Dada's* sister had became a widow two years after marriage. Her elder son was one year old at that time and the younger one was in the womb. The younger son is now fifteen years old. Madhu *Dada* and *Khudi* had assumed her responsibility from that day. Madhu *Dada* didn't do much at home. *Khudi* looked after everything. Her sister-in-law would have most likely forgotten that she was a mother of two children.

Gitu's train of thought was disturbed. The river was at the turn in the road. It was visible from a distance. Kharasrota River was always full with water. She had been staring at the river with tear-filled eyes. She came out of her reverie when Sambit called her. She had travelled the last one hundred kilometres without speaking a word. Sambit said, "What could be done? Everyone will return when age catches up with them." Gitu asked in a broken voice if *Khudi* was old enough to die. The sun was getting drowned in Kharasrota River's water. The sun's reflection could be seen on the water. Sambit opened the door of the car and stepped outside. He looked at Gitu's lachrymose face and said, "Who is as fortunate as her? She passed away while her husband is still alive."

Gitu looked at him from the corner of her eyes. This was her husband. Sambit was staring at the river with his back towards her. He was waiting for the boatman who would ferry them across. *Khudi* loved him the most among all the children in the family. She considered him to be a child even today. She fulfilled all his wishes immediately. How could he accept *Khudi's* death so easily? Sambit took the car inside the boat. Gitu sat in the back with her son. She had pulled her veil over her head and kept staring at the river whose bank could not be seen. Tears were welling up in her eyes. Sambit started the car.

The bamboos were being joined together and tied with coir ropes to make the bier ready by the time they reached home. There were people everywhere. All the people of the village seemed to have gathered there. Gitu entered the house pulling the veil tightly over her head. She went inside *Khudi's* bedroom. The room was empty. The bed was unmade. The fragrance of *Khudi's* body and the smell of the coconut oil that she usually applied on her hair brushed against her nostrils. She returned to the courtyard where *Khudi's* lifeless body had been kept. Madhu *Dada* sat at her feet like a pillar of an old house that would crumble if held tightly and bring the thatch down. The grief rising from Gitu's chest turned into stone on beholding Madhu *Dada's* unperturbed countenance. *Dada* went away to the backyard without telling her anything. He turned around when Gitu broke into a wail. The women gathered around her and started crying. All their friends and relations had arrived after getting the news. *Khudi* was dear to everyone. It was almost evening by the time everyone had reached. *Khudi's* distantly-related brother-in-law shouted from the front door, "Deck up Basa befitting a woman whose husband is still alive. Apply some *alta* on her feet. It's getting late."

There were three brothers after Sambit. Everyone was there except the youngest brother-in-law. The two sons of the second uncle changed their clothes and got ready to carry the bier. But *Khudi's* feet had turned stiff. The barber woman said, "Ma, how am I going to apply *alta* on her feet?

Please come here." She covered *Khudi* with a white sari with red borders and applied a large spot of vermillion on her head. When four people tried to lift her, the brother-in-law said, "How come she became so heavy?" The women started crying and the musicians started playing the musical instruments. *Khudi's* body was lifted. Madhu *Dada* walked ahead throwing cowries behind him. All his meditations, prayers and dreams vanished as people around him chanted *Ram naam satya hai*. As the procession receded into the distance, Gitu cleaned the courtyard and the front yard before going to the well to have a bath. Her younger sister-in-law Nayana followed her to the well and said, "*Apa* (elder sister), the well will be defiled. Let us go to the pond to have our bath."

Instead of responding to Nayana, Gitu asked, "What was the matter with *Khudi*? Why didn't you inform me anything? I would have cooked something good for her during her last days." There was a tremor in her voice as she spoke the last line. She seemed to be having a feeling of guilt. "Forget it, *Apa*. Nothing was the matter with her. Please don't discuss this matter with anyone. She had an exchange of hot words with *Dada* yesterday in the evening. I was able to hear a few words. *Khudi* was sobbing and *Dada* was trying to placate her. Before we were aware of anything, *Dada* came and informed us that *Khudi* had passed away." Gitu was startled, "What do you mean?" "What can I tell you? *Khudi* drank a whole bottle of pesticide. Dada had bought it the day before to sprinkle on the field of green grams." The clothes that Gitu had held in her hand slipped down to the floor. As she picked them up, she wondered what pushed *Khudi* into committing suicide. How could she commit suicide after so many years of marriage? Gitu was not able to sleep throughout the night. She could only see *Khudi's* wet eyes on her smiling face. Like a dry cloud was floating in the blue sky helplessly.

The morning came. Food seasoned with the bitter leaves of neem had to be cooked. *Dada* asked, "Gitu, will you people stay back or leave?" Gitu had the reputation of never having talked back to an elderly person in the family. But she lost that reputation that day. She said, "Why *Dada*, won't the funeral rites be held for *Khudi*? My husband has lit the pyre. How can I go away? Besides, why should I go away? *Khudi* had burnt herself every moment of her life in order to free every corner of this house from darkness. Aren't you going to light a lamp in a corner of this house for the deliverance of her soul?" *Dada* had stared at her in amazement.

She was the daughter-in-law of a brother who had separated from the family. And yet she had so much right on *Khudi*. However, *Dada* had lost his wife in order to assert himself over her. Sambit began performing the rites two days after *Khudi's* death. He sent a leave application to his office on Gitu's request and stayed back without a bother. He rarely had the opportunity of living in the village after joining in his job. He was now going to stay back for a minimum period of fifteen days. He had assumed all the responsibilities at home. Gitu could now realise that he indeed had a great deal of affection for *Khudi*. Gitu was cooking the food along with her sisters-in-law. She was able to see *Khudi's* solemn face when she served parboiled rice and *dalma* (a mixed curry of pulses and vegetables) that had not been seasoned on banana leaves. The people of the house sat down to eat after serving food for the departed soul. She had no idea that the unseasoned *dalma* could also taste so delicious. The eldest mother-in-law was no longer able to see properly. Something got stuck in her throat as she picked up vegetables from the *dalma* and ate them. As she wiped her eyes with the loose end of her sari, she started crying thinking of *Khudi*. She said, "The vegetable curry made for her tastes so delicious. It is so because she was such a transparent person. No one can forget the taste of the food that she used to cook." Gitu loved the village because of *Khudi*. There was no reason why she would come here again in the future.

XXX

It was *Khudi* who had held her tightly to her chest the day she had stepped into this house as a new daughter-in-law. She had tried to forget those days when she had grown up as a pampered child of her mother and aunt after being attached to *Khudi* at an emotional level. She too had been pampered a great deal by her mother and aunt. She had never found any difference between them. Her aunt used to put up with her tantrums even more than her mother. When she came to her in-laws' place, she had been able to find the same love and affection in *Khudi's* eyes that had assured her that there was someone there who would provide her with the same kind of comfort. A girl always looked forward to receiving love and affection from her near and dear ones. Just as a person did not hesitate to walk down an untrodden path on finding a speck of light amidst darkness, *Khudi* had seemed to her to be someone who was known to her since ages among all the unfamiliar faces in her in-laws' house. She had slept the first night on *Khudi's* bed. *Khudi* had given her to understand that a new bond could be forged with people at the in-laws' place if mutual trust and sincerity of purpose were there. The love and affection she had received at her mother's place paled in comparison with the love showered on her by *Khudi*. She followed *Khudi* like a calf following its mother. *Khudi* drew water from the well when she had her bath. She washed her clothes and dried them. She also collected them and brought them to her room after they dried up. She had come to know everyone closely within one week of her marriage and learnt that *Khudi* had no children of her own. That was the reason she loved children. She was the mother of all the children in the house. Was the shape of a mother any different from her? Her sisters-in-law noticed *Khudi's* excessive affection for her and said in jest, "*Khudi*! You will live happily till the end of your days. There will be someone to nurse you during your old age." *Khudi* smiled. She had teeth like pearls. She chewed so many *paans* every day. Gitu asked her how she managed to keep her teeth sparkling white. *Khudi* said, "I never took *paans* earlier. Your *Dada* gave me *paans* with *katha* in them at intervals and got me hooked to them in my old age."

Khudi would be around forty years of age at the time. But she conducted herself as a guardian of the house. As she uprooted the grey hairs from the head of Gitu's husband's aunt, *Khudi* said sitting on the veranda of the backyard, "There are ten children in this house. Am I still a young lass that I am going to dye my hair? It's different with you. You are a daughter of this family." Mother-in-law enjoyed the banter of the sisters-in-law as she dressed the spinach. The ninety-five-year-old grandfather-in-law and the ninety-year-old grandmother-in-law were hanging like ripe palm nuts from a tree at the time. There were a large number of people in the house. The responsibilities of the individuals were being shouldered by the wives, mothers or husbands in the most cases. But Basanti *Khudi* had the responsibility of the entire household on her shoulders.

She left bed very early in the morning and swept the floors and swabbed them with cow dung water. She heated pots of water on the hearth in the backyard. She made several kettles of tea for everyone during that time. Someone took tea without milk. Someone wanted milk in his tea. The old people had to be served tea with crushed ginger and black peppers. She went for her daily chores after that. She carried different kinds of vegetables from the garden in the backyard and kept them on the veranda of the kitchen. She changed her clothes and performed her *puja*. It was around seven or seven thirty in the morning by the time she was through with these chores. She plastered the hearth with clay and prepared breakfast for everyone. Someone wanted *chakuli pitha* (a thin, round and flat cake), someone wanted *chuda* (rice flakes) and curd, and someone else wanted watered rice with fries. *Khudi* had to arrange all this. Of course, other people helped her out as she worked. Gitu used to be scared in the beginning watching *Khudi* doing something or the other at all hours of the day. She often wondered about the meaning of a life like that.

Basanti *Khudi* was being given private tuition by *Dada* for her matriculation examination when the latter worked as the mathematics teacher in the village school. Halfway through the examinations she left her home with *Dada* never to return there once again. No one from her family had ever bothered about her after that. The matter went to the court for a few days. But things became quiet after that. Her father had never stood beside her since then. Nor had he ever forgiven Madhu *Mastre* (teacher) for the liberties that he had taken with his daughter. Mother-in-law used to say that he loved Madhu *Dada* like a son. *Dada* too had never dared to go to his father-in-law's house as long as he was alive. It was not as if *Khudi* had not regretted the mistake she had committed in the excitement of the moment. But she had compromised with the situation and had not allowed grief to overpower her.

When she went to the roof during the summer months to dry clothes, *Khudi* stared at the road in front of the house till it disappeared in the distance hoping that she would be able to catch a glimpse of someone from her family. She suppressed her grief somehow as she got down from the roof thinking of her father. A girl is supposed to think of the welfare of both her father's family as well as her in-laws' family. *Khudi* had stepped out of her house destroying the image of her family in the process. She had survived by upholding the prestige of her in-laws' family. She had never crossed the front door of the house from that day and stepped on the street outside. She had never spoken a word about her father's family in order to uphold the prestige of her husband. But her fate played tricks with her. She could never bear a child. She could never know how it felt to experience labour pain or the joy of motherhood. But she looked as if she had led a fulfilling life. She attended on all the women of the house when they were in the confinement room for the delivery of their children. She did the cooking on all festive occasions. She acted like a child with children and as an adult with the adults of the family. But *Dada* was always detached. It seemed that he felt reassured by leaving everything to *Khudi*. *Khudi* too never objected to anything. It was as if she had stepped inside this house only to make everyone happy. Her world consisted of the four walls of the house, *Dada*, the family members and the children.

Times changed and so did the situation. The brothers decided to set up their own families and got separated from each other. All movable and immovable properties were divided among the brothers. But *Khudi* had the same cordial relationship with everyone as before. From whom could she demand a share in the property? And why would she have done so? They were now living in different houses. But a large hearth was built in *Khudi's* small kitchen when the children came home in holidays. *Khudi* cooked for all the children in large pots. *Dada's* pension was exhausted long before the month was over.

Khudi made *badis* (small lumps of pounded pulses dried in the sun) all afternoon on summer days for her eldest nephew Sambit. He could not eat rice without *badi* as an accompaniment. Gitu had seen it from the day of her marriage. *Khudi* made different kinds of *pithas* for everyone throughout the year. Gitu made plans to come to the village in holidays only because of *Khudi's* love and affection. *Khudi's* memory kept burning from under the ashes like fire.

Sambit had carried three pieces of bone home from the cremation ground. He kept the bones inside a clay pot and covered it with a clay plate. A lamp flickered inside the room. The room was lighted with the dim light just as *Khudi* had kept this house lighted while burning herself. A bond of friendship had remained in place among the sisters-in-law because of her even after the house had been divided. The rice bowls were different. But the eldest sister-in-law loved mashed brinjal and fried spinach. *Khudi* prepared all this and kept them aside for her. The three sisters-in-law sat down together to eat in *Khudi's* bedroom. The sisters-in-law were held in high esteem throughout the village. Human life was strange indeed! One could live without everything that was dear to her. One could also live in the absence of her near and dear ones. Did everyone love life like this or did they believe only in the present? Life might prove easier to live if one could look at the world afresh instead of digging up the ashes after the past is gone. What was the definition of life?

His contemporaries envied *Dada's* good fortune. Had *Dada* really understood the value of the great sacrifices made by *Khudi* for his family? She had left the safe haven of her father's house at the tender age of fifteen on the assurances of an unknown man. Had *Dada* been able to discharge his responsibility faithfully? *Khudi* might not have had an untimely death in this manner if he would have done so. Sambit returned home at eleven in the night. Gitu found the quiet night hanging heavily on her. A solitary star was blinking in the sky. Light was certain to come after darkness. A beautiful morning would arrive after the night of distrust. *Khudi* might have seen a dream like this. Before whom could she have expressed her grief and misery? She had turned into stone bearing the burden of the mistake she had made at a young age for *Dada's* sake. But had he been able to understand the value of her deep love and unconditional sacrifice? *Dada* had invited the people of seven nearby villages on the eleventh day. A large photograph of *Khudi* had been placed on a chair in the drawing room. It had been taken a few days after she had stepped into the house as a new bride. She looked somewhat shy but contented in the photograph. Everyone was looking at *Khudi's* photograph as if they were looking at the face of a new bride. She looked like a goddess. A person leaves her mark in this world by her deeds. The rituals of the twelfth and the thirteenth day were to be observed. Gitu was scheduled to leave on the fourteenth day.

Gitu took her leave from her parents-in-law and sisters-in-law before coming to *Khudi's* house. *Dada* was sitting like a sage in meditation. The twin pillows were missing from *Khudi's* bed. Gitu felt like crying. *Khudi's* bed was always neat and tidy. Not even a fly or an ant could dare to get up on her bed. She was afraid some insect might enter *Dada's* ears while he was sleeping. How affectionate she was towards *Dada* in spite of her numerous other work! But *Khudi* was a dreamer. She lived with her emotions. She had lost a great deal in life. But her smiling face gave the impression that *Dada's* deep love for her was her biggest strength. Why did she lose her confidence in herself in that case? She had learnt several lessons from *Khudi* after her marriage that had proved invaluable to her in her later life. She had said, "Gitu, your family does not consist only of your husband. The husband's family is much more important than the husband. Your conjugal life can be happy and you will be treated with respect if you can win their trust and affection." Who she was going to hold responsible for *Khudi's* death? She had perhaps not been able to see the world as she had been immersed in it. But *Dada* had all along stood on the edge of the world. How could he turn his mind filled with emotions into a barren land? Had he done so knowingly or unknowingly? She said, "*Dada* ...." Her voice sounded strange to him. *Dada* opened his eyes. He stood up and walked ahead of him. Was he going towards death from life? Or had he got up from the deathbed in order to walk towards life? Gitu pulled her veil tightly over her head and asked, "How could a woman with such high self-esteem stigmatise herself for a second time in her life by committing a heinous deed like suicide?"

Dada moved to the cupboard with difficulty and took out a photograph from inside it. He handed it over to Gitu. There was a woman with a child in her lap along with *Dada* in the photograph. The woman's face resembled *Khudi's* face. *Dada* had given a very simple answer to Gitu's question. He said, "She is the younger sister of your *Khudi*. My son is in her lap. He is fifteen years old now." Everything was crystal clear to Gitu. *Khudi* had not been able to give a child to Dada for the continuation of his lineage. That was the reason ....

Gitu paid her respects to *Dada* and returned with Sambit in a trance till the river. She had been sitting like a lifeless entity in the car. The entire water of the river had risen to her eyes by the time she had reached the river. Looking at Sambit's sympathetic eyes, she had understood that he did not know the cause of *Khudi's* death or he did not want to discuss it with her. *Khudi* had perhaps done the right thing. She might have got some sympathy from someone by narrating the irony of her fate before him or her. But she had wanted nothing from anyone. Perhaps she did not have that much confidence too after she stopped believing that *Dada* would one day be defeated by the strength of her love for him. She came out of her reverie when Sambit asked her what was biting her. He said, "You are as emotional as *Khudi*." Gitu said, "What am I going to do if the ground slips from beneath my feet or if the sky falls over my head?" Sambit pressed Gitu's palm tightly with his left hand. Gitu's eyes were filled with tears.

It was raining hard with thunder crashing in the sky. Sambit had raised the glasses and driving slowly. The village was receding behind them. *Dada* was going away even further. *Khudi's* memory was flying around very near them as if it was sympathising with her grief.

****

A Lonely Bird

Sandipan dialled the phone. He might not call her again after today.

"You do not know how to behave with people. Do you know more than me? I have studied as much as you. And I get a higher pay packet than you. Do you think I like the way you conduct yourself with me? You are a man and I am a woman. Is that the reason why I should put up with everything?"

"What have you put up with? We have been married for two years. We haven't lived together for even two months. I come to you whenever I can manage to get a few days of leave. Have you ever come to me? And what did I tell you that it became too much to bear?"

"I do not have the time to engage in such a silly conversation." Simlin had disconnected the phone that day after saying that.

Age had caught up with her today. The past was unreachable now like the horizon. There was total darkness now at the place where coloured birds used to fly one day. The memories seemed to be blinking inside darkness like glow worms. One wanted to turn the pages of the past in darkness. It might prove to be difficult to do so in the light.

Sandipan was her intimate friend. They did not have the time to find out when that friendship turned into bond. They lived like machines with all those classes, projects and seminars. All their emotions and excitements were joined together through the cursor on the computer screen. Both of them had found placement at the same place after studying together for four years. Sandipan had stayed as a paying guest. Simlin had to live in the working women's hostel. It had taken them a few days to adjust with their routine life and the new office. Still both of them lived in the same city. It was only natural that they should become very close to each other. But their natures were as different as chalk and cheese because of which they often fought each other. It took them a long time once again to make up and have tea or coffee together.

The middle-class psyche of Simlin did not want to confine herself to a cage. Dreams used to fly like kites in the sky of the extremely conservative family of Sandipan. But the thread of the kite was in his hand. Yet both of them met in the cafeteria at the weekend without fail. They went for a movie and dinner at intervals. Simlin had moved to a two-bedroom flat with two of her colleagues by that time. Sandipan continued to live as a paying guest. Simlin proposed to go on an outing on Sundays. Sandipan had purchased a bike for the purpose too. There were minor arguments between them as they rode the bike. Simlin felt light-hearted on seeing the dense trees by the side of the road running in the opposite direction. She held Sandipan by his waist. Sandipan placed his hand on her hand. They looked at each other in the rear view mirrors. Sandipan wondered why Simlin behaved the way she did. Her nature was the opposite of her education and environment. The words turned vile the moment she started talking. And yet the two of them waited for each other on the last day of the week. The conversation began pleasantly enough. However, there were arguments over trivial matters in a while. The egos clashed. Simlin always worried about the future of her parents and younger brother. Sandipan was the only son of his parents. Her father was a station master and mother was a schoolteacher. They were middle class people. But the influence of an educated and genteel family was reflected in his nature and character. However, Simlin was just the opposite. She made several demands on her father as the daughter of an educated family. Those days were gone now. She thought about her father still. But she did not have the time to miss her father with tears filling her eyes. They worked for sixteen hours a day in the I.T. sector.

Where was the time to decide who was wrong and who was right? The entire world was in their hands except for their minds. First, she was an engineer with a management degree. She had a higher rating in the office than Sandipan. She received twenty thousand rupees more than Sandipan per month when they joined in their jobs. However, Sandipan was not in the least materialistic in money matters for some reason. He received a lesser pay than Simlin. But he gave the impression that his salary did not matter to him. There were times when she was exposed for her complex before Sandipan. Sandipan did not bother about this trait of hers. This was the biggest reason for Simlin's headaches. She wanted that Sandipan should treat her with a little bit more respect. Her parents-in-law should also have given her due importance as the daughter-in-law earned more than their son. But nothing of the sort happened with her. The mother-in-law waited for the daughter-in-law to come when there was an off-day.

She did not realise that she had to apply for leave. There was also every possibility that it might be treated as leave without pay. She might not tell it to her mother-in-law. But she argued that Sandipan should inform his mother about all this. Differences arose between them on this account and it led to arguments. She could not concentrate on her job for a few days after that. Dark rings appeared under her eyes. Everything went haywire. Life again became normal after a few days. But she thought that their affection for each other became less with each such argument. It seemed as if the top layer of colour on their love for each other was gradually coming off. Had they gone wrong somewhere? This perhaps happened when two people got married without matching horoscopes. She thought that they should have consulted an astrologer first before getting married. But Sandipan held an opposite view. The nature of the parents influences the nature of the children. Therefore, children must be first given moral studies. They should be made aware of our traditions and customs. Higher studies should come after that. Simlin dismissed all this calling it an orthodox mindset. She wondered how she was not able to know about Sandipan's middle class mentality in their long relationship. After wasting a few more weekends in this manner, Sandipan declared one day, "It's best that we should not go for a child. I don't have to tell you the reason. You must be able to understand why I am telling it to you."

"Disgusting! You or me?"

The days of the past roared towards her now like waves. They receded far into the distance when she extended her hands towards them. She recalled those old days very often these days.

What did he want from her? There was a time when she didn't have the time to look forward or backward. She could get anything she wanted immediately because of which she had not placed any value on what other people wanted. She was looking for life from the footprints of the past which she had left behind thinking it to be of no consequence. A small word from the past hurt her terribly like a rock today.

Everyone was sharing their experience in the past four years in the college at the farewell meeting. Simlin had said with a smile, "We had left school in this manner one day. Then came Plus Two. Now engineering is over. A new life will begin once again. Our working life. There is nothing to worry about it. We can also live without anything. Just as we continued to live after our childhood and teenage were over." Everyone had applauded vigorously for her positive and practical thinking.

Sandipan's speech was soaked with emotions. He said, "I find it very difficult to free myself from these moments. I cannot easily leave the hands of the people with whom I have maintained a relationship for a long time. The memory of these sweet days may gradually become faint with the passage of time. But I cannot altogether forget this college, the campus, the canteen and even Ramanuj, the canteen boy. I will remember my friends, juniors and teachers for as long as it is possible if my memory does not fail because of some reason." Tears had flowed down from his eyes without any reservation. Everyone had given him a standing ovation.

She was able to recall those days more frequently today after the passage of so many years. This had no value before her sky-scraping ambition one day. There was not a very long road between the beginning and the end. Time seemed to be running in the beginning. But it seemed to be moving very slowly towards the end. But the soft sound it made seemed like a mountain crumbling inside her chest.

Sandipan had separated from her at a physical level much earlier. But his face resembled that of a stranger by the time he was separated from her at a psychological level. It was Simlin who had first sent him the divorce notice. How would he have felt after tearing the envelope? He would have stood up. He would have gulped down a glass of water. She knew his nature. He would have slumped to a chair and closed his eyes.

It was his nature to take quick decisions. He had decided about his marriage in a minute. He had telephoned his parents the following minute and returned to his home. His parents had come to Simlin's house within fifteen days. The marriage was solemnised in the month following. They had gone to Singapore after that for their honeymoon. Sandipan was in Delhi the following week and she was in Kolkata to join in their respective jobs. Sandipan always said, "I have never had second thoughts in my life."

That was perhaps the reason why he did not have any second thought about this exclusive relationship. Even though his parents had protested mildly about it. When he had come to her house for the last time, he had looked over his shoulder once while tying his seat belt in the car. As his car raised dust and moved away, she felt like running ahead and standing before his car. He would have braked hard. The car would have come to a stop after brushing against her. Time had moved a long way today. Many years had elapsed since Sandipan had left her and gone his way.

Sandipan was expected to go back to Delhi by the morning flight that day. Unfortunately, his mother had a massive stroke that morning. He had gone to Odisha on getting the news. His mother, Simlin's mother-in-law, had passed away the following day. She had not been able to go there even after getting the news. She had reached her in-laws' place for the rituals. She had stayed there for a few days before returning to Kolkata. She was supposed to go to America for two months in a new project. She was hoping that Sandipan would certainly come to the airport to see her off. But nothing of the sort had taken place. Sandipan had not come. He had not even sent her a good wish message for her journey. She had waited till the last announcement was made for the flight hoping that he would give her a surprise at the last moment. Sandipan had come to Kolkata after two months. He had given no explanations for his lapses nor had he expressed any regret for it. His indifference had humiliated her. He had spoken only one word after a great deal of arguments and talking back and forth.

She had not wanted to make any compromises that day. Her excessive self-esteem had blocked her path without her being aware of it. She was eagerly looking for her lost relationship today in her advancing years. From which she had turned her face away a few years ago.

She checked her email every day in the office when she surfed the net. Sandipan might have written, "Come back, Simlin. It is me who is responsible for everything." She recalled Sandipan's last words. He had said, "We are perhaps not fit for each other." Did she really consider Sandipan to be unfit? Or didn't she have the ability of keeping her family together?

She was gradually crumbling inside her. She felt pity for herself when she looked at her reflection in the mirror. It was her habit to go to a parlour every week. It had turned into a ritual for her to buy a new dress, gold earring or a diamond ring when she received her salary every month. Sandipan made no objections. On the contrary, he appreciated her tastes. She had never bothered to find out what Sandipan wanted.

Sandipan woke up very early in the morning and went for a morning walk. He had tea by himself on his return. Simlin slept till late. She got ready immediately after getting up and left for office. She made breakfast at times. But she rarely had the time to eat it. Sandipan was just the opposite. Everything in time for him. He took leave from office and visited her once every two months. But she could never find the time to visit him. Sandipan too never told her anything about it. He had gradually reduced the frequency of his trips. He had perhaps waited for a good time to come failing which he had retraced his steps.

Simlin wanted to have some fun at his expense as Sandipan was making tea one morning. She said, "Aren't you likely to get a promotion in your job? You have been working in the same project for years at a stretch. Don't you feel like moving to a new company? You should otherwise pressurise the people in your office to move you to a high profile project." As he extended a cup of tea to her, Sandipan said, "Morning shows the day. My morning has gone to the dogs. When can I think of the day? Are you going to be the owner of your company by getting a series of promotions? All right! I will move to your company at the time and work under you. At least, I will be there before you all the time. I will know what family life is all about."

"Oh! You are really insufferable!" She poured the tea inside the kitchen sink and banged the bathroom door after her.

Sandipan sat in the balcony every day with The Times of India after finishing his chores in the morning. Simlin didn't even apply for leave when he visited her in Kolkata. He came nonetheless. Simlin prepared the breakfast the other day and left for the office. She returned from the lift when she remembered that she had to pay the house rent that day. She found on her return that cheques had been signed and kept on the table. Not one but advance cheques for the next six months. Simlin thanked him only perfunctorily and ran back to the lift. Sandipan was supposed to return the same evening. He had to go to Germany immediately after his return to Delhi. He had returned after four years. The divorce notice sent by Simlin was in his hand.

He had not looked at her face before leaving India. He had also stood that day with his back to her. He said, "You didn't want to see those people in their last moments who meant everything to me in my life. I could not have allowed my life to become meaningless by hitching my invaluable heart to a heartless machine like you. It's good that you snapped the relationship from your side. At least I won't feel guilty before my soul any longer. You prefer the sky when you have to make a choice between the earth and the sky. You love to fly. I want to remain in touch with the earth. Thus, we are at the opposite ends of the spectrum. You will look around for a place to sit when you become exhausted in the process of flying. You will know the value of this life that day. You will know the meaning of soul, kinsmen and kinship." Simlin said, "What nonsense? We never had any topic on soul when we studied engineering." Her mother had heard them and knew that day that did not have a future together. Her apprehensions were writ large on her face. But Simlin was indifferent to everything.

A person is not finished in the midst of darkness. The fear of darkness finishes people. But she did not even harbour any such fears. Her job with a fancy salary had blocked her path. Therefore, she could not see the future. Age and time didn't wait for anyone. There was not only a physical distance between them. There was the difference of yesterday and tomorrow between them. She knew that yesterday was not likely to return to her even in her dreams. But she had remained uncontrollable yesterday. She had no more dreams for tomorrow. She realised it after a long time. She had been lost in the wilderness of loneliness. All roads to return seemed to have been lost in the sea of time.

She was no longer held in esteem at her office as before. There is a great deal of difference between an unmarried employee and a divorced employee. She had also been able to understand that her colleagues no longer looked upon her as a respectable person. She had uploaded their marriage photographs in the Facebook after their marriage. A few days had passed in receiving phone calls and congratulatory messages from her friends. All of them had commented on Sandipan's personality rather than on her.

Simlin had opened Facebook amidst a great deal of curiosity and apprehension. The fragrance of sweet memories was moving around in her mind when she typed Sandipan's name. She found S. Das in Facebook and checked the status. But she was not able to know anything. That meant Sandipan had not married again. Otherwise, a photograph would have been there. A lamp of hope was burning faintly in some corner of her mind. She typed her name in friend request and closed her eyes. Age, time and social status were moving away to one side. The pages of memory were turning slowly.

She had taken a week's leave two months after their marriage and visited Sandipan in Delhi. Sandipan came close to her that day and said, "Simlin! Come to the office with me today. You can meet all our old friends."

She moved away from him and said, "Why? Haven't

your colleagues seen me?" Her voice betrayed her ego.

However, Sandipan had persisted, "Oh, come on!" He had booked the small Santro car before their marriage to give it as a gift to Simlin. He extended the car keys towards her and said, "This is yours. You will drive today and I will sit beside you." The sound of the computer brought her back from the past to the present. Sandipan had accepted her friend request.

She examined herself once again in the mirror that day. Silver strands were shining on her head. There were dark circles under the eyes. Her body and mind were exhausted. Still she had typed, "Can you forgive me?" She had uploaded her marriage photographs after writing it. She had not forgotten to mention the date and year. Nineteen years had passed in the meantime. Her eyes had been completely drenched bearing the sufferings of twenty years. She had received a message within ten minutes of uploading the photographs, "Nice pictures without doubt! Papa is looking very smart. But you look like my Papa's boss. My name is Sangam Das, son of Late Sandipan Das. My Mama is a simple housewife. She also likes your photographs. Have a nice time." All the branches from the tree had broken and fallen down without a sound by the time she had read the last line. She recalled Sandipan. His last words were, "It's true that you are a bird. But you are a very lonely bird."

****

The Will

The sisters-in-law arrived in the village one after the other after getting father's letter. The younger brother had already arrived with his wife by the time the elder brother and sister-in-law reached the village. The younger sister Ruby arrived late in the evening with her two sons. *Bou's* (mother) wait was over. The younger sister-in-law came out of the room and went towards the backyard when the elder sister-in-law entered father's room with the veil over her head. Father lay on his old bed staring at the roof. As the elder sister-in-law placed her head over his feet, father smiled and said, "So you are here? All right! Have a wash and eat something. You have travelled such a long distance." Father didn't know whether the elder sister-in-law heard him or not. He lay on the bed with his face towards the wall.

Bou called out, "Chhabi! Chhabi dear! Where are you? Your brothers and sisters-in-law are here." As I was making tea in the kitchen, I answered, "Yes, *Bou*! I am coming with the tea." I entered father's bedroom after serving tea to everyone and found that water was dripping from his bed. Had father urinated once again? I decided to put an oil cloth on the bed the following morning. "Father! Father! Get up! Let me change your clothes." "My God! How I am putting you into trouble!" Tears welled up in his eyes. The same was also the case with me. I said, "This is no trouble, father." Like an obedient student solving a mathematical problem being scared of the teacher, father stood up slowly holding me by the hand. I changed his dhoti after changing the wet bed sheet. Just like changing my daughter's school dress. The elder sister-in-law materialized out of the blue. She took the talcum powder from my hand and sprinkled it on father and the bed. She pulled the bed sheet a little further up his chest and told me without looking at me, "Won't you go back to your in-laws' place anymore? Since when have you been staying here? Of course, I had heard about it." I did not say anything to her although she was giving me a sarcastic smile. I gave father three tablets one after the other and gave him some water to drink.

I came out of the room. As the younger brother entered father's room, he said, "*Apa* (elder sister)! Have you come alone? What about Soubhagya *Bhai*?" I could get the sarcasm in his words and said, "His college is open. Besides, I am here for the past three months." There was a small change in the environment of the house by the evening when Ruby reached home. Her two sons were making quite a racket. I was cooking along with *Bou*. *Bou* wanted to cook what her children loved to eat. Everyone was sitting in the courtyard on low stools. *Bou* sat in the middle and served. Just like the days when we returned from school and sat down to eat. The elder brother loved *moong dal* with rice, fish curry, fried *badis* (small lumps of pounded pulses dried in the sun) and mashed brinjals. Ruby always wanted some mashed potatoes. I liked ground *badis*. *Bou* used to feed all of us in our childhood. We sat down around *Bou* in the kitchen after throwing our schoolbags away. The youngest brother Shubha didn't like to eat anything. *Bou* always kept a mango or a few *papads* aside for him. Where had those days gone! Looking at my absent-mindedness, the elder brother said, "What are you thinking about, Chhabi? Aren't you eating fish these days?" I said, "No, *Bhai*. I am no longer taking any non-vegetarian food. Soubhagya doesn't like them. I too gave them up gradually." The elder sister-in-law smiled looking at the younger sister-in-law. The younger sister-in-law stood below the veranda with the veil over her head. The younger brother turned around and looked at her. I was able to understand everything. But I didn't say anything. The younger brother extended the glass to *Bou* after drinking water and said, "*Bou*, why has father sent for all of us? He becomes ill now and then. But he recovers every time." *Bou* went to the kitchen to get some mustard oil without saying anything. She had put a potato in the hearth to burn. She mashed the potato with a few cloves of garlic and some mustard oil and gave it to the younger brother. She said to him, "You got an opportunity to serve your father because you came. He has turned into an old man. He wants you people to sit beside him at times. He wants you to press his feet at times.

"When you got tired after jumping around in the house in your childhood, your father found you sleeping at an odd hour on his return from school. Instead of getting angry with you, he caressed your feet. Have you forgotten all that? You are now grown-up people. Has your father ever beaten you or has he ever asked you for a share from your income? We just want to see you at intervals. What else do we need? Here, have a drink of water. Food has got stuck in your throat. You still have the habit of talking with food inside your mouth like a child." But the younger brother persisted, "What is wrong with father? Why is he lying on the bed? He is able to walk. Why doesn't he sit outside?"

Ruby asked me, "*Apa,* since when is father bedridden?" The elder sister-in-law said immediately, "He was standing up this morning. When was he bedridden? People are afflicted with diseases in the old age. Besides, old age is itself a kind of illness. What is there to worry about it? Your son will appear at board examination this year. Why did you come here without thinking about anything? How long are you going to stay here?" She looked sideways at me and said, "It's a different matter with Chhabi. As such, she stays six months out of a year at her father's place and the other six months at the in-laws' house." Ruby had stared at me like a kitten. I could see the helplessness in her eyes. But I had gone away from the place pretending that I had not seen anything.

The two brothers were sitting with their wives around father's bed as if they were engaged in a *kirtan.* Father stopped staring at the discoloured roof and finally started talking. He asked *Bou* to fetch a sealed envelope from the bottom shelf of the cupboard. *Bou* found it after a while and gave the packet to him. It had been sealed on all sides. What was there in the packet? The elder sister-in-law picked up the envelope in her hand out of curiosity and put it down once again. However, father continued to lie on the bed with his hands crossed across his chest like a sage in meditation. When she heard some noise in the kitchen, the elder sister-in-law said, "Chhabi must know about father's will. Otherwise, she would not be busy in the kitchen with such unconcern." Father opened his eyes while she was whispering in the ears of the younger sister-in-law. Everyone was quiet for a while. Father asked why Chhabi and Ruby were not present there. *Bou* caressed him on the feet and said, "The two sisters are cooking in the kitchen." Father smiled. "What cooking is going on today? What day is today?" *Bou's* eyes became moist. Human beings become so frail at a particular point in time in their lives. Father used to remember the days and dates like an almanac. *Bou* left the place and came near us. The sparrow mother was chirping and feeding its chicks in a corner of the roof. But she did not know that they would fly away once they grew wings.

I was straining the gruel from the rice keeping a pot near the hearth. Ruby sat beside me on a low stool. She called me faintly. I could not look at her face as I was afraid that the gruel will fall inside the hearth. She said, "The bed on which father is lying today would perhaps be empty tomorrow or *Bou* would be lying on it. *Bou* too would not be there after a few days." Ruby wiped her eyes as she said this. My eyes were also hazy in the steam coming out of the hot gruel. Father's children sat surrounding his bed like a pack of jackals around an unknown dead body. They gave the impression that they did not know each other. The elder brother was telling the younger one, "It's no easy matter for us to come twice a year with the entire family from such a great distance." Before the younger brother could say anything, the younger sister-in-law was saying for the benefit of *Bou*, "We keep running to this place at the drop of a feather just because we live a hundred kilometres away. We come when someone falls ill. Or they come and live with us. My husband is only a clerk in the secretariat. But he has to bear the entire burden of the family." The elder sister-in-law shot back, "Why, you had not paid a dime for Ruby's marriage! We had shouldered all the responsibilities at the time." Oh dear! Oh dear! What would father be thinking? He would be wondering, "Is this the family that I have raised? I had considered them to be my four walls. I had built the roof of my future despite all kinds of privations with the support of these people." I had made rice, *dal* and vegetable curry. I was preparing *Pohala* fish in mustard gravy. The elder brother loved them. I did not what to do although I was hearing everything.

Soubhagya had sent fish through one of our tenants in the village as my brothers had come. I could get the smell of my in-laws' family from the fish. I was feeling miserable as I had come to this place leaving my husband and children behind. Father was already an old man. *Bou* was ten years younger to him. Even then she too was an old woman. Father had retired since about twelve years. No one had ever seen them crossing swords with each other. We have never seen father getting angry with *Bou* because of the children. *Bou* had given us a decent enough education. She kept waiting for *Bhai's* return from tuition with a hurricane lantern burning by her side. The younger brother Shubha was a cricket player. He moved around the state to participate in cricket tournaments. Anyway, he had been able to get a job in the government because of being a cricket player. The elder brother was a professor in Delhi University. Sister-in-law did not come to the village even once earlier. What makes her come four times a year these days? Our backyard was being rarely used earlier. But its value had skyrocketed after Kalinga Nagar became a developed area. However, father was beside himself with joy when the elder sister-in-law came to the village. He went around the village telling everyone that his son and daughter-in-law were visiting him. That is why he needed something or the other every day. Had father been able to see the discoloured wall on the other side of the spider's nest that was his mind? I was getting lost in thought.

The elder sister-in-law had suggested to *Bou* that they should divide the property between the brothers. But *Bou* gave her only a smile. Sister-in-law had never bothered to find out how father was managing after his retirement. She had never enquired how they took care of their expenses. Father too had carried on the burden for as long as he could do it. But his shoulders had stooped now. And these people wanted to withdraw their support instead of reinforcing it. Smoke rose in my eyes and it caused Ruby's eyes to rain. Ruby said, "What's wrong with you? *Bou* had written that you were here for the past three months." Ruby knew that her *Apa* was different from all other *Apas* in the world. She had never seen her being greedy about anything from her childhood. Ruby always had the first choice when father bought saris for them from Cuttack for Ganesh Puja and Saraswati Puja. *Apa* was happy with whatever was left over. She always took care of their parents. Everyone loved her more than they loved Ruby.

Apa was in love with Soubhagya *Bhai*. Only she knew about it. She had never told anyone about it for fear that they will look down upon her. Soubhagya *Bhai* was coming to their house to teach her Mathematics before he joined as a lecturer in the college in the village. *Apa* was studying I.A. in the same college at the time. Ruby had never seen her talking to Soubhagya *Bhai*. But she knew that *Apa* used to have a bath and look at herself in the mirror after applying some talcum powder on her face just before Soubhagya *Bhai's* arrival. The waves of a sea seemed to rise high in her eyes at the time. Her face dazzled with happiness. Ruby broke into a smile as she thought about it. She examined *Apa's* face minutely. *Apa* was wiping a plate with a dry piece of cloth. There was a brownish ring around her eyes. The eyes seemed to be filled with tears. Had she picked up a fight with Soubhagya *Bhai* or was she here because of father's illness? Ruby called out to Chhabi in an indistinct voice. As Chhabi arranged her dishevelled hair, Ruby clung to her tightly. Ruby broke into a sob at the drop of a feather. Chhabi asked, "Did you have a bad dream?" Ruby said, "Won't you go to your in-laws' house?" "Of course, I will go. But can I leave father in this state?" "Don't you have any responsibility towards your husband and daughter?" As Chhabi served rice, she asked, "You are now talking as if you are the guardian of this house. Tell me one thing. Don't we have any duty towards our parents? How did we grow up? Take these plates and serve everyone. *Bou* is already there with the others." "*Apa*, what is father going to eat?" Chhabi said, "Father has given up eating anything these days. He will have a drink of sago or barley."

Bou's stomach was giving her more and more trouble by the day. I would ask elder brother to get her examined by a good doctor when father became well. Ruby had already left with the food. But my mind was full of all kinds of forebodings. Was she going to disbelieve her *Apa* like the sisters-in-law? No! There was no point in plastering her already polished mind with clay. Ruby said, "Get your plate, *Apa*. We will eat together with *Bou*." I gave her a smile. I said, "No, my dear. Father is going to have sago now. He will have three different medicines after that. Once every ten minutes. Go ahead and eat. Let me find out if father needs anything." Halfway through his meal, the younger brother asked, "*Bou*! Why did father send for all of us in such a hurry? Do you think that *Apa* would be cooking rice and fish here and we would be having a feast here every day while wasting our time? I am going back tomorrow. Let your daughter-in-law stay here if she so desires." Ruby interrupted him and said, "Do you know about it, *Bhai*? Father has urinated on the bed throughout last night." As she served rice, the younger sister-in-law asked, "Have you seen it yourself or was *Apa* telling you about it?" *Bou's* eyes became moist with tears. As I poured the curry in the younger brother's pot, I looked straight into his eyes. He could not face my gaze and extended his hand to pick up the glass of water. The elder brother was still not back from the marketplace. The elder sister-in-law was moving around the house grimly. Ruby continued, "*Apa* and I were sitting beside father throughout the night. The elder brother had come to us twice in the night. Father dozed off towards the early morning. He used to get up the moment we moved our hands away from his feet. He shouted, 'Chhabi! Ruby! Where are you going leaving me in this state?' We assured him that we were by his side. I was crying. I got him to stand up and changed his dhoti. *Bou* changed the bed sheet. Father called out to Shubha. He was looking for you too. But you were snoring as if you had remained awake throughout the night." All of us ran on hearing *Bou's* wailing from father's bedroom. She was crying hitting her head on father's lifeless body. The elder brother entered the house at that time. *Bou* said, "How unfortunate you are! You didn't stand beside your father even at the last moment." Everyone was crying lying on father's dead body.

However, I kept staring at the sky standing on the outside veranda. The coconut tree that father had planted was about to touch the sky. An owl sat on it looking at our house. With father passing away, we felt that the roof over our head was gone. Ruby was wailing, "Father, I have not been able to do anything for you. You have given us everything throughout your life. We have only run away from you in turn." Before the sky and the earth became one with everyone calling out to father, *Bou's* bangles were broken. She sat in the courtyard like a statue. In the same place where she had played cawries with father at the time of her marriage and where she offered *shraadh* to the ancestors. Father's dead body was lifted before my eyes. Father rose from the ground towards the sky on the shoulders of the two brothers, Soubhagya and the elder uncle. The house was cleaned after father left for his heavenly abode. The mattress and bed sheet were removed and the bed was washed. The daily chores began after that. Only the rituals changed. Food was cooked one time a day. Brahmins were fed. And so forth. The elder brother had invited everyone from the village for the feast on the eleventh day. The feast had been held on a grander scale than any marriage celebration. Everyone said that father was indeed a very fortunate man. He had such capable sons. The daughters-in-law were supervising everything pulling their veils over their heads.

But *Bou* was ruminating about the time that she had left behind in life. She was thinking about the intimate moments of the past. The youngest brother Shubha wanted to leave with his family after the rituals of fourteen days were over. There were no feelings or emotions on his face like a plain paper. As he bowed before *Bou* to take her leave, she said, "The roof over your head is gone. Things will be different for you people now." It was not clear whether he had heard *Bou* properly or not. He said, "Father said that his will is going to be opened after mother's death. Why did he make a farce by calling all of us here in that case?" *Bou* wiped her tears once again. She said, "You saw father alive because you came." The younger brother said quietly, "Inform me if you want to stay with me. I will come and take you to my place." The elder sister-in-law said, "We will decide about it later. Why should she leave such a large house and stay elsewhere? Won't we come here if there is a need?" *Bou* slept with her face pressed on the pillow after the younger brother left. Father used to love the younger brother the most. *Bou* felt really hurt that he could not easily accept the fact that he had been called to this place without any valid reason.

One can put up with things when your expectations do not come true. But it is difficult to adjust with things when something happens which is just the opposite of what you expect. That day passed somehow. The elder brother asked me the following morning as he was having his tea, "What about you, Chhabi? When will you go?" As I gave a sorbet to *Bou*, I said, "*Bhai*, I will go away to my house without a bother if you take *Bou* along with you. I haven't had the time to discuss the matter with you. There is an ulcer in *Bou's* stomach. I had taken her to Cuttack to get her examined along with Soubhagya. The ultrasound revealed the ulcer. *Bou* has become ill even before father. I had written to you. *Bou* too had written to Shubha. I was forced to stay beside her as none of you came." There were tears in the elder brother's eyes. It was not possible to know whether it was because of gratitude towards me or out of spite for sister-in-law. He moved to *Bou* and caressed her in the head. The elder sister-in-law found that the situation was getting out of hand. She said, "We would have taken care of things if something had gone wrong. Why did you have to bother your head about it? You are a married daughter. You have your own family. How could take a unilateral decision to leave your house and stay in your father's house?" The elder brother looked outside instead of looking at her.

Bou had an outburst before tears could come to my eyes. She said, "Is a sister any different from a brother? I have undergone the same labour pain while giving birth to each of you. I have seen the same dream while walking beside you in the house and the backyard. I had hoped that my children will grow up to be someone in life. They may not turn out to be Gandhi or Gopabandhu. But at least they will be like their forefathers. I feel very confident of myself when I find all of you together. Your father threw the staff away and stood straight. What happened to all those dreams of mine? My night has still not passed .... Your father lay in bed for three months. A huge man like him lay curled up like a carpet. But none of you had the time to come and see him. Even when you arrived, none of you washed his dirty clothes or placed your hands on him. Did all of you forget everything together? How much salary was your father getting as a schoolteacher? But had he ever deprived you of anything? He taught you himself as long as he was capable of doing it. All of you went for private tuition at a later time. He had done more for you than he was capable of doing. But you made excuses and stayed away from him instead of lending a helping hand when he needed you the most. My daughter stood beside her father at the last moment. She forgot her husband and child and slogged day and night because of which I am alive today to see you people." She wiped her tears glancing at the elder sister-in-law.

She gulped and continued, "Do you know how much money was being spent on medicines for your father-in-law? You are living at Delhi where you pay as much for water as you would pay elsewhere for gold. Half of the people in this village have become billionaires by selling land. Your father-in-law had never thought of selling his land and having a good time for himself." I could realise that she was experiencing unbearable pain while releasing her long sighs. But I had not said anything. I carried her medicine from the bedroom shelf and tried to give it to her. Ruby took the medicine bottle from my hand and helped her drink it. Ruby said, "*Apa*, I will take *Bou* along with me. I do not have any problems. My parents-in-law live with me. They will stay together. Go back to your family." *Bhai* was moving around in the courtyard restlessly. A frog stood with its head raised inside the hearth in the courtyard. The baby frogs arrived near the hearth in a line after a while. The mother frog came out of the hearth on seeing them and the baby frogs followed the mother inside the hearth. She was looking at the frogs minutely. The elder brother said, "*Bou*, how can I go away leaving you on your own? Come with me. You can make *badis* and mashed brinjals for me every day. You had told me only half the story of Lord Jagannath begging on the streets in my childhood. You did not tell me how He returned to the Temple." Ruby burst out laughing. She said, "*Bhai*, do you think you are a child?" The two children of Ruby held *Bou* by her hands and nagged her, "Grandma, tell us the story that you told uncle. Tell it from the beginning." *Bou* had turned into an image of stone.

XXX

Ruby led *Bou* to the bed and helped her to lie down. *Bou* lay there with bare hands and neck wearing father's old dhoti. She looked like a tattered bed sheet whose beginning and end could not be identified. The memories from childhood till now were entering the mind like a jumbled ball of thread.

XXX

It seemed to me as if time was going back. I could hear father saying to *Bou*, "Do you hear me?" *Bou* said, "What's it?" Father reclined in the armchair standing nearby. He said with a smile, "How about taking a family photograph some time?" I was around seven at the time. Elder brother was perhaps fifteen. How time passed! It seemed it had grown wings.

Father had been able to make little headway in life with such a large family to fend for. He had a child almost every year after his marriage like paddy was harvested year after year without fail. He had ended up as the headmaster of the upper primary school in the village. However, my father had been able to realise perfectly that the crop that he had grown had not ripened properly. *Bou* often said with regret, "Where did I go wrong in raising them? No one learnt anything from their father." Father's ninety-year-old elder brother and seventy-year-old widowed sister lived with us. Even *Bou's* mother lived with us after the death of grandpa as *Bou* was an only child of her parents. Father had provided shelter to everyone under his thatch. Tea and hot water had to be provided to the three old people every morning. Someone even had to be given a bath at times. *Bou* used to do all the household work along with cooking by herself. She also lit a hurricane lantern in the kitchen and asked *Bhai* to study there sitting beside her. Her far-sightedness had shown us the way for a secure future. She never expected anything from anyone. That is why father showered a great deal of love and affection on her even at this age.

Ruby and I came outside when the two children fell asleep. The house seemed desolate in the absence of father. Ruby said, "*Apa*, I will take *Bou* along with me if *Bhai* does not take her with him. You will see. I will take more care of *Bou* than what you did for father." I said, "You don't understand. There is no way *Bou* can go with *Bhai*. *Bhauja* (sister-in-law) used to ask either father or mother to come and stay with her with the excuse that she didn't have enough rooms for both of them in her house. Neither of them had gone to Delhi at the time leaving the other behind. Do you think *Bou* will leave the house and go there soon after father's death? Know something, Ruby? Father used to make tea every morning after his retirement. He also used to serve tea to *Bou*. *Bou* was ecstatic that father took so much care of her. She felt bad because father gave so much importance to her every need. Father used to say with a smile, 'You spent more than half of your life in serving the people in my house. I don't know if I will find the time to serve you or not.' *Bou* cried on hearing that. I have lifted all the screens of *Bou's* mind and dusted every corner in it.

"*Bou* cannot even live for a moment without father beside her. Have you seen *Bou* eating with father? There was such happiness in her face the day father picked up a fried potato from her plate and ate it. *Bou* said, 'Come on! Have you gone out of your mind at this old age? You eat my leftover food. You will send me to hell and go to heaven yourself.' Father said, 'I cannot live even in heaven without you. You will either come after me or go ahead of me.'" Ruby was crying. I continued, "No one can understand *Bou*. Why did father draft such a will? There are two sons. Everything would have been divided equally. But father would have thought of something." Ruby said, "I could not talk about it earlier although I wanted to do so. He was unsure about *Bou's* future because of which he might have taken a decision of this kind. Why did he draft the will? And what did he write in it? I have no idea. The sky was full of stars a little while ago. They are all lost in the darkness now. Only one golden star is shining in the east. A cloud has covered it. Let us go to *Bou*." *Bou* turned on her side. Her eyes were still swollen. The area behind her ears was wet. Ruby called her, "*Bou! Bou!*" There was no response from her. Ruby slept beside her. I slept beside Ruby.

I was thinking a great deal about Soubhagya. How broadminded he was! He had a mind like the sky. He took over the responsibility of looking after his parents, aunt, two brothers and two grown-up daughters and sent me to my house to nurse my father. Had I ever understood that man's psyche? The dam had broken inside my chest after getting *Bou's* letter and I had come running to father's place. Soubhagya had been able to understand my emotions and he had left me at our house. I could not go away leaving *Bou* on her own if *Bhai* did not take her with him. I knew that *Bou* would not be able to take care of her diseased body without any support. However, *Bou* went away soundlessly without waiting for anyone's sympathy or service. *Bhauja* was crying loudly. *Bhai* had been staring at the sky. That solitary shining star had become one with the darkness since a long time.

Bou had died on the fourteenth day of father's death. Therefore, her *shraadh* had not been observed with much pomp. However, the brothers had not cut corners while doing so. *Bou's* photograph had been placed near father's photograph. Tears were streaming down from Shubha's eyes. However, it could not be understood whether it was because he had neglected *Bou* during her last days or because he had not been able to see her when she took her last breath. But he seemed to have broken down. The younger sister-in-law had not been able to attend the function. Father's *Bada Bapa's* (father's elder brother) on was slightly older than father. Father used to respect him a great deal. Elder brother proposed that he should be invited home and the will should be opened in his presence.

A bundle of papers came out of it when the sealed envelope was opened. *Bada Bapa* was turning the pages. But father had not written anything anywhere. Shubha looked at elder brother's face and asked, "How do you know that this is the will? Look in the cupboard. It might be elsewhere." Shubha looked at me and asked, "You are here since a very long time. Don't you know anything?" I said that neither father nor *Bou* had said anything to me. *Bhauja* pulled her veil over head tightly and said, "Had father inserted only a bundle of papers inside the envelope and sealed it?" *Bada Bapa* said something that had the effect of an explosion. He said, "There is a smaller envelope inside it." Holding the envelope in his hand, *Bada Bapa* was saying, "When was your father doing all this?" Everyone leaned over the envelope at the same time. Ruby and I were sitting on the old bed of father. We had gone back many years in time. I said, "Father, weren't you a human being? Were you a god who had been born as a human being?" An old photograph that had turned yellow with time fell out of the envelope. The elder brother was examining the photograph minutely. Grandfather and grandmother sat on two chairs in the middle of the courtyard. *Bou*, father and *Bou's* mother sat on both sides of them. Ruby sat in *Bou's* mother's lap with her finger inside her mouth while Shubha sat on grandfather's lap. He seemed as if he was about to jump out of his lap. Elder brother laughed when he looked at the photograph. He said, "Ruby looks so fat in the photograph. Was she so hungry that she was chewing her finger?" A piece of bamboo had stuck out from the thatch. The bamboo would have pierced father's head if he would have moved back a little bit. Ruby looked at the photograph and said she didn't remember when they were living in a thatched house. The elder brother said, "Serve food for us. We are hungry." He ate sitting beside *Bada Bapa*. *Bada Bapa's* son did not have any children. He had one son. His name was Nira. He was a teacher in the village school. The daughter-in-law was a nurse in the primary health centre. *Bhai* asked *Bada Bapa* how many years ago *Bada Ma* (*Bada Bapa's* wife) had passed away. Something seemed to have got stuck in his throat. He said, "It's very difficult for either a man or woman to leave without the spouse at this age. Your *Bou* was a very virtuous woman." The ball of rice fell from elder brother's hand.

Everyone had packed their things by morning. They were bidding farewell to each other. Ruby would go with the younger brother. The elder brother and *Bhauja* would drop Chhabi at her in-laws' place and board the train for Delhi in the evening. The sun was overhead by the time younger brother arrived with two auto rickshaws. The people of the entire village had gathered in front of their house. Elder brother had been standing with the family photograph in hand. He clasped the three of us to his chest and started crying loudly. He said, "Shubha! Chhabi! Ruby! You haven't been able to see father's will yet." Younger brother wiped his tears and raised his eyes. Elder brother showed him the photograph and said, "Look at this. This is father's will. He received such a meagre salary. But he had kept so many people bound together by his love inside the four walls below the low thatch of the house. Can't we remain bound together in this manner as long as we are living?" The sky seemed to be crying loudly. *Bhai* called *Bhauja* to him and said, "I have a son and Shubha has a son. What are they going to learn from us?" The dam had broken for *Bhauja*. She was crying loudly like a child holding *Bou's* photograph in hand. *Bhai* gave the keys to the house to *Bada Bapa* and said, "Water the *tulsi* plant of *Bou* every day, please." *Bada Bapa* was wiping his tears. *Bhai* said, "All of us will come here in the holidays." His face looked to me like father's face as he carefully kept the photograph inside his bag.

****

Majhia Saantani

Majhia Saantani (the second daughter-in-law of an aristocratic family) made arrangements for *Saanta's* (the lord of a manor) dinner when the sky became dark. A Brahmin came every evening to light the lamp near the deities. The gardener carried wicks for the tutelary goddess of the village after that. *Saantani* was startled when she looked at the clock hanging from the wall. It was already eight o' clock. When would *Saanta* have his dinner? He was a strong man earlier. His teeth were strong. He could digest mutton curry with hot rice, raw onions, cucumbers from the backyard, everything. He was an old man now. He could barely eat two chapattis, half a bowl of milk and some vegetable curry.

They were three brothers. Elder brother had four sons. The youngest had three. Only the second brother was childless. Elder brother's wife was dead long since. The youngest brother was an officer in the capital city. His wife too was an officer. Everyone loved the second *Saanta*. Everyone in the village addressed his wife as *Majhia Saantani*. They did not have a child of their own. But the children of the entire village gathered every day in front of her house. Ganesh Puja was celebrated in her house. Khudurikuni Puja was also held there. Their house was never lonely because of those children. The children used to call out to her the night before the Khudurikuni Puja, "*Saantani*, come and stand guard over us. We will pluck the lilies from the pond." She asked her servant to make turmeric paste for the children the night before the Raja Sankranti. Why did she do all this? Who did she have to call her own? *Saanta* felt sorry for *Saantani* for her plight. But the children of the village filled up her house throughout the year. She did not have a child in her lap. But her house was always crowded.

Someone from the village dropped in at their place occasionally in the evening. Otherwise, *Saantani* was engaged in conversation with *Saanta*. She was the daughter of a *zamindar*. She talked about the good times she had spent at her father's place. She talked about the time she had spent with her sisters in her childhood. *Saanta* too listened to her with rapt attention. She treated her sisters' children like her own children. *Saanta* often felt guilty looking at *Saantani's* lachrymose eyes. He recalled his childhood. He had found a Naga monk sitting on a mat in their house as he returned from the school one day. The sharecroppers, servants and the cook were standing below the veranda. His father Jagannath Tunga Samanta sat at some distance. His mother had stood there with the veil pulled over her head. The Naga monk had the horoscopes of the three sons in his hand. It did not matter whether the prophecy made for the eldest brother would come true or not. But different things were ordained for him. The monk had told his parents, "Your second son will be the father of one child. He will die a pitiable death. No one will come to know about it." The mother loved her second son the most. She grieved silently when she learnt that he was such an ill-fated boy. He was the son of an aristocratic family. His mother could not compromise with the fact that he was going to die in this manner.

Years passed. The aristocratic and wealthy family gradually became impoverished. The eldest daughter of the *zamindar* family was the second daughter-in-law of the *Saanta* family. But she was childless. Her parents-in-law passed away in grief one after the other. The three brothers divided the ancestral property among themselves after the death of their parents. The second brother built a four-roomed house on the land he inherited along with a kitchen and a storehouse. A deities' room was also built. What could they have done with more rooms? There were just the two of them in the house. They used one of the rooms as their bedroom. Another room was used to keep the crops, vegetables and fruits from their fields and the backyard. The children of *Saantani's* sisters visited them in the summer holidays. Guests visiting them occasionally slept in the drawing room. *Saanta* and *Saantani* were beside each other throughout the year. The people of the village held them in high esteem. The girls of the village learnt songs of lamentation from *Majhia Saantani* before they got married. She also taught them how to conduct themselves at their in-laws' house, "Serve food to your parents-in-law first. The husband's brothers are to be served next. Sit beside the plates that you have served for you and your sisters-in-law (husband's elder brother's wife and husband's sisters). Eat only after they start eating. Press the feet of your parents-in-law at bedtime. Go to bed only after they retire for the night. And so forth." *Saantani* was quite proficient in all kinds of household work. The girls of the village learnt everything from her. She recited the *Bhagabata* in the evening and the children of the village listened. At times, the girls did the recitation and *Saantani* and other elderly women of the village listened to them while dozing. *Saantani* had forgotten her own grief in this manner while finding pleasure from these activities. A beautiful girl was born to *Saantani* when one year of her marriage was to be completed. But the girl passed away after completing just one year. The husband and wife became heartbroken. Night followed day as usual. But they had lost interest in everything in life. *Saanta* had only one sister called Basudha. She had two sons. Finally, she allowed her *Bhauja* (sister-in-law) to adopt her elder son. *Saantani* took every care to raise the child properly. He finished studying in the village school and joined the high school. The husband and wife were busy with the boy from morning till night. They took care of his every need. Time passed gradually. Their son studied in the city while living in the hostel. *Saanta* mortgaged a few acres of land and took care of his expenses for four years. They were confident that the son would get the land released when he got a job.

The son started working. He also married a girl of his choice. Shyamasundar Tunga Samanta compromised with everything for his son's happiness although he had been shattered. He wanted to move with the times. But he had not been able forgive his son for the inter-caste marriage. He was from a *Saanta* family. He was the cousin brother of a king of a princely state. He could not accept a *Kayasth* girl so easily although he had remained quiet because of the ways of the world. The son and daughter-in-law stayed in the village for a few days before going away to their place of work. They came to the village once a year at the time of Laxmi Puja. The son and daughter-in-law reached late in the evening when the Puja was about to be over. They stayed the night and returned to the city early in the morning. They had school-going children. The children could not miss school even for a day. The old man and old woman had understood their attitude towards them. Time never waited for anyone. *Saanta* had already mortgaged half his land and sold the other half by the time his hair had turned grey. *Saanta* had sold almost three-fourth of his land and a pond by the time his son had completed his studies and built his house in the city. Now he was left only with his homestead land, the four-roomed house, three *gunths* (one *gunth* is one-twenty-fifth of an acre) of backyard and a well besides the ten acres of land on which crop was raised. Forget about getting the mortgaged land released, the son was after him to sell off the rest of his land. The daughter-in-law said that the land in the village was of no use. She wondered why the old people continued to live in the village. Couldn't they provide them with two square meals a day? She said that the first floor on their house at Bhubaneswar could be easily constructed if the land in the village was sold off. She said all this for the benefit of the old people. But *Saantani* had cautioned *Saanta* not even to respond to her.

The daughter-in-law had a great deal of affection for her father-in-law rather than mother-in-law. She never forgot to present two Khurda *lungis* (a piece of cloth worn inside the house by wrapping it around the waist), a red *gamcha*, a tin of coconut oil and a tin of *zarda* from the city every year to her father-in-law. *Saanta* had given up wearing Shantipuri dhotis since a long time because of lack of money. But *Majhia Saantani* was always dressed as a *Saantani*. When she stepped out of the house, she was always dressed in her finest silk and ornaments with a large spot of vermillion dazzling on her forehead. People passing by on bicycles or bullock carts got down on the street to pay their respects to her when they saw her. *Saantani* chatted with them for a long time about their welfare. Time passed in this manner. *Saanta* had said this morning that he was going to have *chakuli pithas* and mutton curry for lunch. *Saantani* always did his bidding. He had not eaten mutton curry since a long time. *Saantani* had cooked the mutton curry herself. A great deal of oil was floating on the gravy. A few potatoes had been cut into two pieces and added to the curry. She had made thin *chakuli pithas*. She arranged everything for *Saanta* and closed the front door of the house. *Saanta* kept on humming the song *Barijaki tu manaru maana mari de* under his breath. He kept on humming this one line all the time. As she made the *chakuli pithas,* she kept looking at *Saanta* through the opening of the kitchen door. She was afraid he might get up and wash his hands. She carried two *chakuli pithas* with her and quickly moved to the veranda where *Saanta* was sitting on an armchair. But *Saanta* did not respond when *Saantani* called him. The mutton curry was getting cold. He was not going to eat it if it became cold. She shook *Saanta* not knowing what to do. His body was cool to the touch and he slumped to one side of the armchair. "Wake up! What makes you sleep at this odd hour?" shouted *Saantani.* Naba, the labourer, came running to her and said, "*Saantani, Saanta* is no longer there." Not being able to comprehend him, she asked stupidly, "Where could he go?"

Their nephews and daughters-in-law came running. Friends and relations were given the news over the phone. One of the nephews rang Ramakanta, *Saanta's* adopted son. *Saanta* had chosen to adopt his sister's son while his elder brother's four sons were beside him. Therefore, there was no love lost between them. As such, they did not have any money with them. Whatever little they had, there was also no hope of getting anything from them. Therefore, the nephews did not show any interest. How was the dead body going to be removed? Who was going to do it? Their friends and relations arrived late in the evening. The bier was made ready and carried to the cremation ground. The question now was who was going to light the pyre. The adopted son of *Saanta* was not ready to shoulder the responsibility. How could he attend office without shaving for ten days? He could not stay in the village for ten days on leave. The nephews were also not willing to do so. The person who was enjoying *Saanta's* property was not willing to light the pyre. Why would they observe all the rituals for ten days? Why should they shave off their carefully groomed hair? One of the nephews finally agreed to light the pyre. But he demanded an acre of *Saanta's* land for the purpose. Anyway, the cremation was over and the daughter-in-law gave *chuda* (rice flakes), curd and molasses to everyone to eat. Then came the next phase. Who was going to take the gold bangles that were to be taken out of *Saantani's* wrists? They weighed five *tolas*. The necklace she wore weighed three *tolas*. There might be more such in the chest. *Saantani* could hear her daughter-in-law crying and saying to their neighbour that she was a lonely old woman now and it was not safe for her to keep all these ornaments with her. The adopted son returned to Bhubaneswar the following morning with his two daughters. However, his wife had stayed back to supervise the rituals. *Saantani* lay on the old bedstead with bare hands and bare neck wearing *Saanta's* used dhoti. She had kept staring at *Saanta's* photograph hanging from the wall. She was not able to see *Saanta's* face clearly as her eyes were filled with tears. The past days were running before her eyes.

It was almost evening by the time her palanquin was taken out of the iron gate of the *zamindar's* house. The women of the household were crying their hearts out. The eyes of her sisters were filled with tears. The arrogant face of her father *Zamindar* Jagmohan Harichandan had wilted with the grief of sending his daughter away to her in-laws' house. Not a leaf shook on the trees that day. It was extremely humid. She left her father's house. The goddess-like image of the second daughter-in-law and the gold ornaments she wore had dazzled everyone's eyes. She had tried to live life anew because of her husband's intense love and affection for her. Time passed gradually. She turned into *Majhia Saantani* from the second daughter-in-law. But that was that. She had reached the same place from where she had started. She was alone earlier. She was alone now. She had forgotten the agony of being a childless woman because of *Saanta's* ardour for her. She had not been able to become a mother from being an aunt even after adopting her sister-in-law's son. She had cajoled the child such a great deal to address her as Maa instead of aunty. Still she had done everything possible to make something out of him. But did he turn out to be a good human being?

Saantani had held the first anniversary of *Saanta* with a great deal of difficulty. The son had sent five thousand rupees. They had not been able to come as the daughter-in-law had to undergo eye surgery. Twenty years had passed in the meantime. She had been on her own. She was doing her own chores herself. Her sharecroppers were faithful to her. They had not tried to cheat the old lady. They gave her paddy for the entire year. They sold the rest of the paddy and handed over the money to her. *Saantani* took care of all of her expenses with that money. The wives of her four nephews lived beside her. Everyone was facing financial difficulties. The third nephew had an untimely death. Therefore, *Saantani* was closer to her than the other daughters-in-law. She was an old widow. But the daughter-in-law had become a widow at a young age. People tried to take advantage of her. Her two children were quite young. However, she managed everything with a great deal of patience. Her husband used to work in the *tehsil* office. The money that she received as pension along with the earnings from the crops in the field were sufficient for her to manage her family. Times were somewhat different. But *Saantani's* house was still full of people. The children of the village sat beside her for a while when they came to gather flowers. The girls listened to *Saantani* reciting the *Puranas*. She had become frail. Her vision had become weak. But she still spoke as sweetly as she used to do earlier. The house could not be thatched every year. The clay walls of the house got swollen with rainwater. Snakes and frogs moved around the house. Monkeys had a free rein in the backyard. Who was going to look after the old lady if something went wrong? Her neighbours discussed the matter among themselves and informed her son. They said, "The old lady is having hallucinations in the night. She might fall off the bed sometime. She might also give up the ghost while sleeping in the night with her door closed. Come to the village. Otherwise, make some arrangements for her." Her daughter-in-law said, "Our daughters are already married off. We have no further worries. Sell off everything in the village. Come and stay with us." *Saantani* had tears in her eyes on hearing the daughter-in-law's proposal. She might get some rest now at long last. She was not able to do the household chores and cook for her. She thought she would get to eat some delicious food now. She might feel better with the daughter-in-law's nursing. She made arrangements to sell the ten acres of land. She locked her house and gave the keys to the wife of her nephew. She said, "Keep an eye on the house. The soul of your uncle resides in this house. Light a lamp in the evening. Don't allow the *tulsi* plant to die. I don't care what happens to all this after I am gone."

Saantani cried as she took leave from everyone in the village and sat in the car. The cement veranda in the front of the house, the banana trees, the boundary wall of the Jagannath Temple, the paddy fields, etc. moved to a distance. She fell asleep on the way without being aware of it. When she came awake, she looked around for her bag where she kept her *paans* and the money bag that she was holding in her hands. The bag containing the *paans* lay at her feet. The daughter-in-law slept beside her without a worry in the world with her money bag in her hand. The bag contained the forty thousand rupees that she had received by selling her land. She had never laid eyes on that bag since that day. She had already spent a month at her daughter-in-law's place. She had become exhausted in the process of listening to homilies from her daughter-in-law during this time, "Don't sit there. Don't spit there. Eat at regular intervals. Do not go to the drawing room when a visitor is there. Don't eat too much. You will have indigestion. Who is going to nurse you? After all, we are not getting any younger." And so the harangue continued throughout the day. *Saantani* already looked ten years older in the last one month. She kept awake throughout the night and thought about the days she had left behind. She was reminded of *Saanta's* smile, his *Barijaki* song and how he took care of her every need. Her vision had become blurred. But the past days were alive in her mind. What was she going to do? Would she go back to the village? She could hear *Saanta's* soft footsteps in the house in the village. That house was still waiting for her. But she had sold her land off. How was she going to live if she returned? She had held her money bag in her hand on the day she had left the village. She had not seen the bag again in the past six months. She didn't also have the courage to ask her daughter-in-law about it. Her daughter-in-law had taken away her gold ornaments at the time of the marriage of her daughters. She had been left with nothing except the homestead. *Saantani* had been staring at the sky lying in the courtyard. She didn't know what day it was. The sky looked very dark. A solitary star could be seen blinking far away. *Saantani* sat up. She recalled that *Saanta* had bought a pond at the edge of the village the year their daughter had been born. Bipin *Mastre* (teacher) was asking her last year, "*Saantani*! Please let me know if you would like to sell the pond. My youngest son was no good at studies. He is busy with village politics. He could breed and rear fish if we could have the pond. It is worth at least forty to fifty thousand rupees. Its area is almost half an acre. I can buy it with my savings." Her eyes lit up. The desire to return to the village became stronger. She could sell the pond to Bipin *Mastre*. She would have some money with her. Oh yes! She would return to the village!

It was noontime. *Saantani's* childhood friend came running when she found a car stopping in front of *Saanta's* house. The people living on the street came and got her down from the car. They made her sit on the cement veranda. They also took down her belongings from the car. The driver bowed to *Saantani* and left. The news spread rapidly throughout the village. *Saantani* had returned to the village. The village people gathered in front of her house. *Saantani's* throat was parched. The thatch had flown away from the roof at several places. The clay walls had not been plastered since ages. The inner veranda could be seen through the holes in the walls. Two cats lay on *Saanta's* armchair. How was she going to drag her worthless life till the end? The house was empty. Who was going to give her a glass of water? What was she going to eat? She could barely move her limbs. Everyone looked at her with questioning eyes. What was she going to say about her son and daughter-in-law? Why had the old lady returned to the village once again after selling off her land? *Saantani* lay down on the veranda thinking about all this. A hand picked her up before she could lie down on the floor. The hand arranged the unkempt hair on her head and extended a glass of water towards her. The old lady caressed her face. She shouted, "Second daughter-in-law!" and broke into a loud wail. "No, no, *Majhia* Mama! Please don't cry. I am with you. You have two grandsons. Your nephew had taken one acre of land from you after lighting uncle's pyre. That land is still with us. Can't we feed ourselves from the earnings from that land? Come, please come with me." *Saantani* asked, "Where are the keys to my house?" "Why do you need the keys? Let that house remain closed. Uncle's soul is moving around in that house. The keys are lost. It's all for the good. No one will open the locks as long as you are alive." *Majhia Saantani* stood up straight with the help of the second daughter-in-law.

****

A New Morning

"The morning is so beautiful."

" Didn't you ever see a morning earlier?"

"Of course, I did …."

"Come. Let us have tea together."

"Let *Bhauja* (sister-in-law) get up."

"She sleeps late like you."

"I have given up that habit since long." Gitu had stared far into the distance.

"When will *Bou* (mother) and *Nana* (father) get up?"

"*Bou* is not keeping well these days. She would be awake but lying on the bed. *Nana* would be watching the television. He watches programmes on the television from morning till night."

"*Bhaina* (elder brother), *Nana* is indeed fortunate that he has a son like you. *Bhauja* is closer to him than you are. Am I wrong?" Samir smiled at Gitu.

"How long are you going to stand there? Get a chair from the dining table. Sit down here beside me." Gitu stared at Samir silently.

Sudha stood with the tray in hand.

"*Bhauja*, have you got up so early in the morning?" Gitu was pulling a chair from the dining table. Samir picked it up from her hand. Gitu said, "*Bhauja*, you sit there. I will get another chair for me."

Samir felt somewhat disturbed on looking at Sudha's solemn face. Sudha stood there keeping the tea tray on the parapet. She had not taken her seat although a chair was empty.

"Why don't you sit down, *Bhauja*?"

"You sit down. No one needs to tell me to sit down in my house." Gitu's eyes softened. Samir was not able to look at Gitu.

Sudha picked up a cup from the tray and extended it towards Samir. She asked, "How long will Gitu's case go on?"

No one had answered this short question of Sudha immediately. Gitu sat with her head lowered. But Samir had raised his head and looked straight at Sudha. He could see the loathing in Sudha's eyes for Gitu.

As he finished the last drop of tea from the cup and extended it towards Sudha, Samir said rather firmly, "It will be over when it will be over. How does it matter? Gitu will stay here now in her father's house with her family."

Gitu stood up. Her eyes were filled with tears. Taking Sudha's hands in hers, she said, "*Bhauja*, where can I go? Do I have anyone else except you people?" Sudha had released her hand and left the place before Gitu had finished talking.

The morning was in its full glory on the still waters of Kathjodi River. Gitu was disintegrating inside her looking at the layers of soft sunrays. Her twenty-five-year-old frame shook mildly with helplessness.

Bhaina left after having tea. *Bou* had been unusually quiet since yesterday. *Nana* was indifferent as always. He never bothered about his family. He never tried to find out what his children needed. She had spent seventeen years of her life in this house beside *Nana* and *Bou*. *Bou* was unconcerned when they left for school in their childhood. *Nana* took the least interest in their studies. Still she had been able to get a first class in matriculation examination. *Nana* and *Bou* did not seem to be overmuch happy when the brother and sister performed well in their examinations. She lived a life of her own. Sometimes she yearned for a bit more affection from *Bou*. She wished *Nana* would praise her before other people for doing so well in studies. *Bhaina* too stood first in his class every year without ever going for tuitions. She had purchased a *rakhi* for *Bhaina* that year for the first time looking at her friends in the college. His friend Nandan had come to their house with *Bhaina*. She had stood carrying a *rakhi*, sandalwood paste, vermillion, *arua* rice and *chhena poda* (a sweet) in a tray. *Bhaina* had a bath and changed into fresh clothes. She didn't know *Bhaina's* friend. Therefore, there was no question of her tying a *rakhi* on his wrist. Nandan had extended his hand forward as she tied a *rakhi* on *Bhaina's* wrist. She fed the sweet to *Bhaina* and bowed down to him. But *Bhaina* stopped her midway and said, "Hey Gitu, when did you learn all this? You never tied a *rakhi* or touch my feet earlier."

Gitu smiled and said, "You have forgotten it, *Bhaina*. You had yourself told me about it. I was young at the time. But I remember about it."

"What had I said?"

Gitu said, "So you don't remember. You said, 'I don't need a *rakhi*. You will tie a *rakhi* and then ask me for money.'"

Nandan asked, "Samir! Have you now struck a deal not to pay any money?"

Bhaina said, "My Gitu is very touchy. Don't say anything like that to her. Don't you have another *rakhi*? Why don't you tie one on Nandan's wrist?"

"I had carried only one *rakhi*. For you."

"All right! All right!" Nandan said and ate the sweet in Gitu's hand.

Bhaina said, "You have to give her a *rakhi* gift now that you have eaten a sweet." Nandan had looked straight at her for a while. He said with a smile, "I will certainly give her a gift. But not for *rakhi*." There was something in his smile which had created ripples in the mind of the seventeen-year-old Gitu.

A smile was on her lips. She came out of her reverie on hearing *Bhaina* calling out to her.

"Yes, *Bhaina*."

"Have you been standing here since then? Come with me." Samir extended his hand towards her. Gitu said, "You go ahead. I am coming with the tea cups."

Gitu was still entwined with her thoughts. Nandan stood before her once again.

Gitu was getting down the stairs that day after her classes. Nandan was coming up the stairs. He stood in front of her and held her by the hand. Gitu was highly uncomfortable looking around her. The students were coming up and getting down the stairs in groups. Everyone must be watching her. She freed her hand from Nandan's grip and said, "Nandan *Bhai*, what are you doing here?"

Nandan had stared at her without saying anything. Gitu had not yet seen the world properly with her own eyes. She could now see the picture of a beautiful morning. An orange-coloured ball was rising slowly. The first rays of that ball brushed against her young mind. She had not been able to know when a tender leaf of love had sprouted inside her. Nandan *Bhai* was the childhood friend of her *Bhaina*. He was in some foreign country for a long time. *Bhaina* said that he now worked as the director of an educational NGO. But would *Bhaina* be happy if she developed a relationship with Nandan *Bhai*? She had returned her face from *Bhaina* and looked at her parents. They might agree to this relationship.

Bhaina had been sitting near her study table the other day before she came there to study. Gitu was scared that *Bhaina* might have known about what had happened in the college. What would he be thinking! He might very well say, "Oh dear! Are you going to the college for this reason? Didn't you feel ashamed of yourself? What is the difference between *Bhaina* and his friend? Don't we all love you at home that you looked forward to being loved by an outsider? This is the age for you to study. You have to first stand on your own feet ...." *Bhaina* always spoke to her in this vein. Gitu returned to get a glass of water for herself on seeing *Bhaina* near the table. *Bhaina* had asked her nothing about her studies or friends that day as he did on other days. But he had sat beside her table quietly for quite some time. What was biting him? Why didn't he say anything if he thought about Gitu's present or future? They had not eaten together that night as on other days. She had gone to the kitchen after *Nana, Bou* and *Bhaina* had eaten. She didn't feel like eating anything. A light was burning in *Bhaina's* room. *Bhaina* was certainly aware of her relationship with Nandan. Gitu came to her bed without eating anything. She had fallen asleep sometime in the morning hours. She saw a terrible dream as she slept somewhat fitfully. A girl whose hands and feet had been tied lay inside a large cage. Someone was carrying that cage in his hands and walking on the street. She could not see his face. Another man came and blocked his path. The first man threw the cage into a river when his path was blocked. The girl came awake inside the cage. The river was full of water. The door of the cage was locked. The girl let out a loud shriek, *"Bhaina ... Bhaina ... Bhaina ...."*

Samir came running from her room. "What's the matter, Gitu? Did you have a bad dream?" She jumped from the bed and held *Bhaina* tightly. But she had not been able to tell him anything about her dream. *Bhaina* stood beside her for a while before giving her a glass of water to drink. He said, "Drink it and go back to sleep." *Bhaina* went out of her room. She recalled the dream once again with her eyes closed.

Nandan *Bhai* had stood near the college gate the following day. He held something in his hand. Gitu tried to avoid him and keep walking. He had held her hand tightly and pulled her towards the gate.

Bou, Nana, Bhaina and she herself ... their life was so beautiful together. Time passed slowly. *Bhauja* (elder brother's wife) came home in due course. She was Sudha, *Bhaina's* childhood sweetheart and sister of his childhood friend Aranya. She often felt that there was much dissimilarity in the characters of the husband and wife. But they gave the impression that they knew each other for ages.

She said to *Bou* the other day after dinner, *"Bou,* I am going to the roof for a while. It's a moonlit night." She rarely went to the roof as she was busy with her studies all the time. Her first year examination was over. *Bou* was watching the television. Without looking at her, she said, "All right. But come back quickly." She had leaned against the railings of the roof and stared ahead of her. The moon was playing hide and seek with the clouds. A face flashed among the stars and vanished once again. She was startled to find that Nandan *Bhai* was standing close to her. He was examining her minutely. He pushed closer to her and said,

"Your *Bhaina* will never give you in marriage with me. Do you know that or not?" She did not know how to answer this question. He continued after a while, "How much do you love me?"

The pages were flying around before her eyes. It was perhaps the age in which such things happened. A silent compromise was what was needed among all kinds of obstinacy. It was perhaps important to run after everything that was unreachable and make it your own. Did such thoughts come only to her or to everyone as old as her? She thought more and more about Nandan *Bhai* and his intimate overtures when she slept beside *Bou* at night. *Bou* looked at her only as a responsibility. But she had been looking forward to receive love and affection from someone. She had lost her heart to Nandan *Bhai*.

It was her second year in the college. There was a long way for her to go. She seemed to have achieved everything in life once she had acknowledged Nandan *Bhai's* love for her. The noisy world around her had become absolutely still that day she had turned her back on *Nana's* prestige, love for *Bou* and affection for *Bhaina* and crossed the threshold of the house to move outside. Her world that had begun from her house had stretched to a deserted island. There was no way she could return from there.

Nandan *Bhai* had taken her to the railway station from the college. They bought two tickets and got into a general compartment. They reached Puri at six in the evening. He had purchased two garlands on the way.

He pointed out Lord Jagannath to her from afar. They were standing with a garland each around their necks. Gitu had covered her head with her wrapper to shield herself from the curious eyes of the onlookers. Nandan *Bhai* carried two red bangles from the temple of Goddess Laxmi and gave them to her to wear. She came inside the hotel room and looked at herself in the mirror. There was vermillion on her head and red bangles on her wrist. She blushed.

Nandan *Bhai* said, "Gitu! You become my wife from today." The following morning appeared magical to her. She forgot her childhood days, *Nana, Bou, Bhaina* and her own identity during the course of that one night. She lost herself completely in the unknown emotions of Nandan *Bhai*. After spending a few days and few nights on their own, she had come to Nandan *Bhai's* home in Kolkata as his wife. She came to know that day that it was Nandan *Bhai's* hometown. *Nana* and *Bou's* face danced before her eyes a few days later. She thought even more about *Bhaina*.

What would have happened in their house the day she didn't return home from the college? *Bhaina* would have made the rounds of his friends in a frenzied state. What would *Bou* have done? She must have cried a great deal. How would she have faced her relations? How would *Bhaina* have shown his face in the office and before his acquaintances? Should she go back home? Should she request *Bou* to accept Nandan *Bhai*?

The days passed slowly. The nights became scarier than days the day she found that there was an invisible wall in the middle to stop the light inside and outside her life. She was scared out of her wits. She had already crossed a great distance of time by that time. She had insisted on going back home that night before Nandan *Bhai*. There was no word of sympathy from him. Instead, he had abused her in filthy language that she had never heard earlier in her life. Someone banged on the door at this time. Gitu had sat up in fright. A new chapter began in her life from that day the moment Nandan *Bhai* opened the door.

Gitu got down from the roof and came inside the

room of *Nana* and *Bou*. *Nana* was holding the remote in his hand. He was changing channels every minute. *Bou* lay on the bed with her eyes fixed on one point in the roof. She potrayed no feelings or emotions. She sat down at *Bou's* feet. *Bou* moved her feet away. She looked at *Nana*. She could see both fright and loathing in his eyes at the same time. She came outside walking slowly. The house seemed deserted to her. *Bhauja* had changed the decor of the house completely in the past six years. A double sofa, divan and dining table stood in the drawing-cum-dining place. There were matching screens, the marriage photograph of *Bhaina* and *Bhauja* and a few photographs of their son below it. A family photograph of *Nana, Bou, Bhaina, Bhauja* and the son was in the middle of the drawing room wall. *Bhauja* stood behind *Bou* and *Bhaina* stood behind *Nana*. Her grandson was in *Bou's* lap. She imagined herself standing in the empty space between *Bhaina* and *Bhauja*. Their first family photograph hung there earlier. Her elder uncle had taken that photograph with his new camera. *Bhaina* stood behind *Nana* and she had stood behind *Bou*. *Bou* was smiling. She had kept her hand on *Bou's* shoulder. Where did those days go? Her childhood days breached the banks of her eyes and flowed down.

Bhaina came inside shouting 'Gitu, Gitu!' He had come to a sudden stop finding her standing on the veranda. She had come out of her reverie on hearing *Bhaina*. *Bhaina* stood before her with his back to her immersed in his misery. He was trying to find enough courage every moment to face *Bhauja's* derision. He came close to her and said, "Listen to me, Gitu. Put your room in order. Your room had turned into a storeroom after you left." Gitu was gulping down her tears. She moved towards her room without saying anything. It was the room of her dream. Her study table, book shelf, double bed, cupboard and her photographs were there all right. But layers of dust had gathered on everything. Her invaluable life and time had been lost in the dust.

She had slept soundly after many nights in her own house under *Nana* and *Bou's* protection and the assurances of her *Bhaina* that was spread out like the sky. That moment entered her subconscious mind slowly once again. She had not even imagined it in her dream.

The person she had seen that night after opening the door was the closest to her till that day. But she had been startled to see the woman that day.

It had been a long time since she had returned to *Bhaina*. Now she had the responsibility of looking after *Nana* and *Bou*. She helped *Bhauja* in getting her son Pupun ready for school. She helped *Bhauja* in household work after *Bhaina* left for court. All her dreams had been shattered and turned into stones. But a small bud of self-confidence was blooming into a flower inside her and indicating the arrival of the morning. *Bhaina* returned from court the other day and said, "Gitu, many other cases have been clubbed with your case. We don't know how long it will take to get the case disposed of. Do you think you will spend your time in this manner doing household work?" She had stared at *Bhaina* in amazement. Was *Bhaina* going to send her away to that place once again? Where she had gone till hell after stepping out of an aristocratic family.

Bhaina had sprinkled a handful of assurances like moonlight on her cloudy mind, "Fill up the forms this year to appear at the Plus Two examinations. I had kept all your books and notebooks in the bottom shelf of the cupboard in your room hoping that you would return some day." Samir's voice was choked when he said that.

Gitu had closed the door of her room and cried for a long time after *Bhaina* went away. No one had ever returned after going to hell. She might have done something virtuous in the present or past lives.

There was sustained applause inside a prominent auditorium in the town that was so well-known to her. The applause died down slowly and the hall became absolutely quiet as the girl picked up the microphone to bare every page of her life before the audience, "After I put up with the mental trauma for a long time, a time came one day which showed me the picture of a beautiful sky. The coloured sky of the setting sun on one side and the solemn features of the sky on the other had taught me to fall in love with me. Mine was not an ordinary past. I didn't know how to wipe out the stains that had stuck to my mind and body. I had to pay a great price for love when I had not understood the meaning of love. The people who had used many other bodies like my body as a profession were educated people. They hoodwinked the society and sowed the seeds of sin in their debauched gardens. After wasting my objectives, age and time in running after a false dream, I would have perhaps been lost in that hell. But the dove that was sobbing inside my mind started flapping its wings one day in search of an open sky. I gathered enough courage the following morning to lodge an F.I.R. against my so-called husband Nandan *Bhai*. I had pressed the calling bell of my father's house soon after.

"I had tried to find a solution to my problem by myself. I had not expected that the people in my family would come forward to comfort me and help me out. But I had set my life in order once again with a silent objective when a few green grasses grew on the barren land of my past. With the help of *Bhaina*, I cleared Plus Two examination. I also completed my graduation and post-graduation in

Sociology. I gathered the broken pieces of an image that had been shattered in a severe cyclone and tried to recreate the image with the solemn vow that I was not going to be lost in my past.

"The lustre of a new morning had appeared and faded from my depressed eyes and lachrymose face the day *Bhaina* informed me that Nandan and his associates had been punished with rigorous imprisonment for fourteen years.

"Love and attachment have a particular attraction for a young girl. But I had not understood anything and jumped into a bottomless sea out of momentary excitement. I have paid a very heavy price for my folly. I realised that there was such a huge desert inside me but there was also a beautiful beach near it. All forbidden areas had moved away from me by that time.

"Trafficking in women has been spreading like a pandemic in the twenty-first century. No one enters such a contemptible profession of her own accord. Numerous women get into this profession without realising what they are getting into. My first duty is to bring these helpless women back from the hell they are experiencing so that they can join the mainstream of the society.

"I had formed a unique temple of life called *Prayas* with the active encouragement of *Bhaina*. Every member of this organisation is like a soldier. They have the responsibility of freeing others from this contemptible profession besides defending themselves. The organisation also tries to find a new life and employment for these women according to their capabilities. Working directly against the anti-social elements who masquerade as masked noble men in the society is one of the chief objectives of this organisation."

Her last words had been lost in the rousing applause

of the spectators. The hall reverberated for a long time with the clapping of the people. Simultaneously, she could hear the loud banging on her door that night.

A woman stood outside wearing a gorgeous, coloured sari, ornaments all over her body and thick red lipstick on her lips. She was a prostitute who had introduced herself as Nandan *Bhai's* mother. She had not been able to believe it. Nandan *Bhai* hurried out of the room leaving her to face the music. Two or three people barged inside her room and closed the door from inside. The story after that was quite long. She realised that she had been utterly deceived by Nandan *Bhai*. Her so-called husband Nandan was an educated anti-social and pimp who presented himself as a successful businessman. Many half-educated, unmarried girls like her had been exploited by him earlier. She had stopped living from that day. She was only dragging herself around as per Nandan's wishes.

She could see a vast body of water before her where she could not see the banks. There was only a boat without oars with her. And an unknown sky full of black clouds over her head. She had left behind a sky on the other side that had numerous familiar stars in it. A new sun was slowly rising in the sky of her depressed eyes. The spectators present in the hall rose in unison to give her a standing ovation as she got down from the stage holding *Bhaina's* hand. Her *Bhauja* Sudha had extended her hands towards her with tear-filled eyes. As she slept peacefully that night with her head in her *Bou's* lap, *Nana* placed his hand on her head and said, "This is the reason why man wants to live amid life's struggles. What is more important than the embrace of love? Who is closer than the members of one's family?" The sun was rising in the deep orange-coloured sky.

****

The Sky at Dawn

The night had passed and it was morning. She had not seen the dawn since a long time. Pallavi was feeling very depressed looking at the languid morning. There will be light everywhere in a while. Even the morning star will hide behind the white clouds. The sun too will rise in the cloudless sky wearing its golden crown like every other day. Everything and everyone on the earth will have a sunbath. Life will come alive with the appearance of the sun. Pallavi pushed closer to the window and opened them. Soft breeze moved around the house. Her hairs started flying around. She ran her hand over her face. The stains of the emotions of the previous night still stuck to her face like dewdrops. She had cried throughout the night.

What had she lost? Had she been shattered because she had lost someone? The sunrays had fallen on the bed through the windows. She looked outside. The sun will move to the other side of the horizon in a little while. But she would be waiting as before. She would be staring at the road that had stretched before their house. She would prick her ears to hear the sound of the gate being opened. She was convinced that Pranab would certainly come back. She had complete faith on their kinship of years. Their conjugal life was based on love and trust for each other. The ties of this world were snapped in allegations and distrust of the moment. But it became very difficult to join them once again. Had her bondage with Pranab become loose? They had married after falling in love with each other. How unrestrained was their love for each other! Where had the flow of the flood waters come to a stop? Pranab's personality and winning smiles even turned his enemies into friends. He was always well-groomed and well-behaved. But everything was different now. He was finding every excuse to point out Pallavi's deficiencies these days. She was feeling helpless in the face of this untimely change in him. Her eyes were covered with clouds. She gulped down the grief that was emerging from inside her and stood up. She was as lonely as the moon. She was close to everyone. But no one belonged to her. She had spent twenty-four years of her life with him. She had looked at the world with his eyes. Her tastes and interests had been fashioned after his. Still she had not been able to win him over. Pranab went away leaving her alone on the way. He allowed his world of twenty-four years to float away aimlessly in the blue sky for the sake of momentary happiness. It was getting quite hot. The leaves of the plants had started wilting. Pranab, her son Nishant and daughter Pratikshya were bound to her by trust. The children lived in the hostels for their studies. They were meritorious students. Pranab was a senior officer. She had thought that she had a fulfilling life. But the fire lay under the ashes. She was scared to think about it. Pranab had been creating trouble at home for some time without a valid reason. But the embankment of her patience had broken that day a long time before the flood came. The phone started ringing and someone pressed the door bell at the same time. Before she could decide which was more important, the telephone stopped ringing. But the door bell continued to ring nonstop. She still hadn't her bath. The maid had not come too. Pallavi looked down from the balcony thinking that the maid might be at the door. The gate was half open. But no one was visible. A woman's shadow could be seen on the other side of the glass door of the drawing room.

Who could be at the door at this hour? She didn't have any friend at this place. She opened the door and looked at the visitor questioningly. The ultra modern woman standing before her dazzled the eyes. The colour of her hair was close to the complexion of her body. She looked like an aggressive woman. She had been actually frightened by the derisive smile on her lips. She had asked gently, "Who are you looking for?" The lady threw a barrage of questions at her. "This is Pranab's house. How are you related to him? Is he there at home or not?" And so it went on. Pallavi thought that she might be one of Pranab's acquaintances. Therefore, she wished her with folded hands and invited her to get inside the house. The lady barged inside the house like a storm of dust in summertime with her high heels clicking. She looked around her and sat on the sofa with a thump. She threw another unexpected question at Pallavi, "This is Pranab's own house, isn't it? Who else lives here?" Pallavi had shaken like a doll of wood. She replied, "I am Pranab's wife. We have two children who study elsewhere." Pallavi gave her a frightened stare after saying that. She was afraid she might say that she was closely related to Pranab or that Pranab had married her earlier. Such things were not very strange these days. Everything was possible before one took the possibilities into consideration. Still she could not mistrust Pranab. But what relationship he might be having with this strange, ultra modern woman? The lady was perhaps noticing the change in her demeanour. Taking advantage of her absent-mindedness, she asked, "Where is Pranab now? I mean, where is he today?" "He is not at home. He is out on tour for the past three days." The lady came out with an explosive sentence after that, "I know his daughter. She is two years junior to my daughter and they are also roommates." Pallavi felt reassured. Her daughter's friend's mother had come. She should at least serve her a cup of tea. She came to the kitchen for it. She returned with two cups of tea. She placed the tray on the table and relaxed in a corner of the sofa. The lady had picked up a cup soundlessly. Pallavi too could see the ever-smiling face of Pranab in the steam rising from her cup of tea. Many things were going through her mind. All wives were suspicious no matter how educated they might be. The lady continued to sit there with her face lowered. She was wondering how she was going to broach the subject. She broke her silence suddenly and said, "I haven't come to your house as a guest. I haven't also come here because our daughters are friends. On the contrary, I have come here to unmask a perverted character close to you. What is going to unfold before you could not even have been imagined by the director of a play." Who she was going to talk about? Had her daughter Pratikshya done something untoward? She stood up in a state of agitation. She said in a choked voice, "Please tell me." Pallavi was eager to know which aspect of her life had remained covered by grey clouds.

The lady's voice hit her like a thunderbolt. It was enough to shatter her mind's temple. But Pallavi had trusted Pranab implicitly all these years. How could she believe that he could play with her emotions in this manner? But the firm and implausible words of the lady banged against her ears like the restless waves of the high noon. She thought she was standing over quicksand. She and her future were going to be engulfed by it anytime. The lady went out like a storm of dust, just the way she had barged into her house. There was nothing but a black void around her. Her parting shot went as follows, "Think about the matter. I have no objection to anything. The seed of love which Pranab has sown in my daughter's mind has to be reared in your house. I do not have any personal opinion in the matter if my daughter has no objection to remain as Pranab's second wife. We should share in their happiness." Her heart broke into a thousand pieces and fell down from her chest. How was this possible? Can a fifty-year-old man like Pranab be maligned by someone in this manner? Someone has certainly been conspiring against them. Pallavi did not even have the strength to find out if there was any truth in the matter. She had never known any world without Pranab. Who could she ask about it? How could Pranab fall in love with a young, unmarried girl when she had spent twenty-four years of her life with him in this house on one bed? A girl who was just two years older than his own daughter!

The lady had left quite a while ago. It took her some time to recover from her depressed state after which she went to have her bath. She cried to her heart's content in the bathroom. She performed the *puja*. Pranab returned before evening. As usual, he started complaining against her for no reason. Pallavi too had flared up that day which was against her nature. Pranab had scattered around like hot lava.

He had returned just the way he had come. He had taken all his clothes and important papers with him. The last words that he had said while leaving the house had left her twenty-four-year world bleeding all over, "I do not want to live with you any longer, Pallavi. This house, my bank balance and the two children all belong to you. I am not returning here again." How Pallavi had spent the last night by herself in this house! She had been exhausted in the process of arranging the heaps of memories of the past twenty-four years. There was not a speck of dust anywhere. But everything had gone haywire this morning. She finished her daily chores in the morning and sat down for *puja*. Pallavi was in a hurry. The maid was about to finish her work. She had to take her bath and perform the *puja*. She finished her chores and sat down in the deities' room. The seat of Lord Jagannath, Balabhadra and Subhadra was in the middle. Lord Ganesh sat on the left and Lord Hanuman on the right. She had remained with thirty-three crore gods and goddesses in this house. But the lord of her life was in someone else's house today. She had worshipped all the gods and goddesses of this house with flowers of memory. She was often reminded about the first day that she had stepped into this house after marrying Pranab.

Her eyes were filled with tears and she had been filled with grief. She was getting separated from her parents and siblings for all time to come. She had got down near the gate of this house with trembling feet hiding her grief-stricken face under her veil. Her parents-in-law, sister-in-law and brother-in-law had welcomed her warmly. She had been overwhelmed by the rousing welcome she had received from each member of this family. Her mother-in-law had brought her to this room to bless her. She had taken a solemn vow placing her head at Lord Jagannath's feet that her life would be dedicated for this house. She had carefully guarded the prestige of this house since that day. She had been abandoned by her husband today. Still she had not been able to leave this house. She had looked at all the deities with a great deal of faith. She finished the *puja* and lay down in a corner of their bed. Her frame was shaking with grief. She was reliving her married life in the diffusion of time.

The night arrived with soft footsteps that day after all the rituals of marriage were over. Everyone was worried on account of her. Her sisters-in-law had decked her up. Coloured flowers had been strewn on the snow white bed sheet. She was getting exhausted with an ardent desire to lose her carefully preserved maidenhead as the fragrance of jasmines moved around in the air. Pranab had entered the room with soft footsteps. He was wearing a silk *kurta*, pyjama, a gold chain around the neck and a pair of glasses with a gold frame. She was rediscovering his strong personality. A familiar fragrance seemed to be spreading from her mind to the body and thence to her blood. She was trembling with an unknown tremor. There were numerous untouched flowers in the spring of the nineteen-year-old. Pranab had opened each petal with a great deal of care. He had lost himself in the forest of her dense hair on that first night. There were tremors inside her chest even now like that first night. Pranab forgot everything and went away leaving her to fend for herself. She could even now recall the day her daughter had been born. Pranab had felt the searing pain in his heart every time Pallavi had screamed in labour pain. He had run till the door of the operation theatre. His eyes were filled with tears. He had held Dr. Patnaik by his hand and entreated, "Please save Pallavi. I do not need a child." Everyone in the family had been overwhelmed at the intensity of his love including Pallavi's parents and parents-in-law. Mother-in-law had given him a hug and said, "It's no easy matter to be a mother, my son. How Pallavi is suffering to give birth to your child! All husbands should remain indebted to their wives as they should be to their mothers." He had forgotten all his misery when his daughter had cried out after her birth.

The same Pranab had made her sit today on a boat without oars. How long was she going to float on the boundess sea? There was the taste of salty water on her lips. It was not of the sea but of her tears. Pranab's night dress still hung in the wardrobe giving her a ray of hope. He would return. He had considered a momentary excitement to be a necessity. He will come again inside the pre-determined lines when the cause of this misery became a burden on him. He will feel sorry for his wife and children. Her children had run from one corner of the house to another and grown up as if time had grown wings. Everyone had flown away like cuckoos. She was the only one sitting here guarding the nest that she had built with her own hands. A long sigh escaped her. But she had still not lost faith. After all, that was the basis of this Creation! It was already evening. The telephone rang slicing the silence of the lonely afternoon. Pallavi came back from the world of dreams. Pranab's eager voice could be heard from the other side before she could respond, "Pallavi! Pallavi!"

She was trembling with indignation. She broke into a sob. She was not aware when she had replaced the telephone. The depressed voice of Pranab seemed to be shaking in repentance. Oh dear! Was she such a narrow-minded woman? Would she destroy their harmonious married life of twenty-four years relying on the irrelevant allegations of an unknown woman? She felt ashamed of herself and felt that all her energy was getting sapped. As such, women were weak-willed. She did not believe when people spread rumours about Pranab's character. But she had not been able to ignore the strong words put forth by that lady before her in her own house. Pranab had gone beyond the vow he had taken at the time of his marriage. There could be no smoke without a fire. But she was not going to measure the magnitude of truth in this allegation. She was also not going to make an effort to do so in order to bring ill-repute to her family. Therefore, the only way out was to wait.

The day was coming to an end on the other side of the window. The evening seemed to depress her. Life was strange indeed. One keeps getting new experiences every day. Several changes in direction come in life as a person passes through the stages of youth, adulthood and old age.

She had never separated herself from Pranab in her subconscious mind. She caressed him like a child when he lay down on the bed. She became absent-minded while arranging his unkempt hair. He pulled her to his chest with such affection. Her children were grown up. But she still flew around like a young maiden inside Pranab's mind. But a sudden change came about him. He became suddenly detached and grave going against his nature. He was absent-minded all the time. He started shouting at her for no reason. Pallavi knew that a man looked around for an excuse to hide his weaknesses. She knew that his indifference was only a false pretence. But what was his weakness?

What a huge difference was there in the environment of a few days ago and the environment of today! She had lived as a new daughter-in-law in the house as long as her parents-in-law were alive. They had not given her any responsibility except looking after the children's studies. Therefore, she had ample time in her hand to be close to Pranab. They went on long trips during holidays. She had visited many places inside and outside India. They had even gone around the four *dhams* in the later years. She had seen him from very close quarters. He was an uncomplicated man with an empathetic soul. She was greatly troubled by her fond memories. She could not remember when he had made her unhappy. At times, he got angry with the children because of their studies or because they were careless in money matters. All said and done, her life was a flower garden without any thorns. Her home was no less than a heaven. Pranab was the second child of his parents. He was highly educated and was held in esteem in the society. He was also the head of an ideal family. He was bound by the excessive love and affection of his parents and Pallavi's complete sense of surrender to him. The bondage had perhaps become somewhat loose after the death of his parents. Had he become wayward because of it? No! Everyone said that happiness was transitory. She had no idea when a ship of sorrow had dropped anchor at her port. She had not tried to look at the other side of the sandbank of trust. How could she have seen the scene of such a contemptible story behind the huge personality of Pranab?

Pallavi moved to the window. Life without Pranab was like a vacant sky. The moon was there in her life. Stars blinked eagerly in it. They were free birds in the authorised prison of social bondage. They flew freely. But they returned to their nest in time. But Pranab was beyond her bondage today. He was far away from her love and affection for him. A husband and a wife are supposed to have a relationship for several lives with the holy pit of fire as their witness. But a husband has certain rights over the wife in the present life. Did he think that gave him the right only to assert himself over his wife? Would he have forgiven her if Pallavi would have done what he had done? Perhaps not! She was familiar with Pranab's nature. The rumours doing the rounds about him seemed to be true in the context of his leaving the house in a huff. She could not also forget the words of the lady. The warning of the lady reverberated in her ears just as stray dogs barked at night out of fear that something untoward was going to happen, "You are going to approve of the night that Pranab has spent with my daughter. Otherwise, I am going to unmask him before everyone for the kind of person he actually is." Oh dear! How she had suffered! The half moon was trying to come out from behind the clouds. She had stared at the sky on the other side of the moon with frightened eyes. There was only darkness there.

What else could this life be other than the result of indiscreetness? He might have strayed somewhere in order to forget the depression brought about by his absence from the family for days on end. That did not mean that he would go forth to start a relationship with a twenty-two-year-old girl and devastate his family of twenty-four years. What would his daughter think about it? Was his son going to forgive him for the treachery he had played with his mother? Such a mistake could have been forgiven in the case of an adolescent. However, she still did not want to admit that Pranab would conduct himself in this manner. No! She was in the wrong too. She could have discussed everything judiciously with Pranab. She could have found out what made him invite this disaster on himself. Pallavi struggled with remorse. *Bhajans* could be heard from the nearby temple. The sufferings of life dripped from the voice of the devotee. Tears started streaming down from her eyes. She had still not lost hope. She was a wife and a mother. She was closer to them than anyone else. Who would forgive them if she didn't do it? A strange magnanimity overtook her. She had herself spoiled everything in her life because of her suspicions. She went away to the nearby temple to relieve her mind of stress.

She had been looking forward eagerly to the following morning. Pranab had come back home. He had slumped on the sofa in an exhausted state like a broken image of failure and frustration. Creased lines of suffering were apparent on his humiliated countenance. He was full of excitement the day he had left home. But now his body had become flaccid. Pallavi stood beside him with a cup of tea in hand. He raised his dolorous eyes and stared at her. He took the cup of tea from her and gulped it down as if he had been thirsty for a long time. Pallavi left with the tea cup. She kept his towel in the bathroom as always and asked him to take his bath. She informed him that the children would arrive today as the Dussehra holidays were beginning from the following day. Pranab was still in a state of confusion. He continued to sit on the sofa for a long time. Time passed slowly like a handful of dry sand was slipping from his grip. The half moon of the previous evening had come out completely from behind the clouds showing its sympathy to the doleful evening. Pranab had slept throughout the day hiding himself under the quilt. The rainy season was already gone since long. But the sky was still overcast. His silence provided credence to the story of the past few days. Pallavi stood leaning against the bed. What was she going to tell her fifty-year-old husband? Pranab turned on his side on hearing her footsteps. Pallavi had broken down completely before tears could come to his eyes. She said, "Tell me the truth. I have surrendered myself completely and sincerely to you in our conjugal life of twenty-four years. Where did I go wrong? The stream of my full blown life has flown only for you like a mountain stream. I had lost the invaluable identity of my life in the intensity of your love. But I had never been so perplexed. Our natures were so different. Still I had lost myself completely in you. What did I ever expect from you in return? I was not able to imagine my entity without you. Is that the reason why you ignored me? You should have trusted me once. You should have given me some indication about this disgraceful chapter of your life. I might have thought about a remedy before my life became unbearable for me. You have asserted your rights over my body. Have you never read a single line from my mind's pages? Your Pallavi has not only considered the transparency of a moonlit night as her own. She also has the capability to face the darkness of a new moon night.

"Just think for a moment as to what your daughter would have thought of you. Could your son have forgiven you? How are they going to welcome their future if the beginning of their lives is like this? Forget it, Pranab, if this new relationship is only a momentary lapse on your part. Don't forget your reputation in the society that you have built up the hard way. Try to understand that your children hold you in great esteem. Have faith on yourself. I am not asking you to pay me a price for my invaluable years that I have surrendered to you. But tell me, Pranab! Are lust, anger and delusion greater than this noble love? One can blindfold himself and dream. But he has to face humiliation and dishonour when the eyes open. One cannot find love so easily. You look younger than your age. That twenty-two-year-old girl is after you because of your innocent looks, your high position and status in society. But do you think she can share in your happiness and sorrow and walk beside you till the end of her days?" Tears were streaming down from Pallavi's eyes. Pranab shrank into himself with her gentle rebuke. She continued, "Your daughter is twenty years old. She still hangs from your shoulders. She hides her face in your chest. She cries when she finds grey hairs on your head. She shouts that her father is never going to grow old. Don't you remember what pleasure you derive at such a time as a father? Tell me, Pranab! How could you fall in love with a girl only two years older than her instead of showering your affection on her? I am still not carrying a grudge against you. To err is human. Misfortune enters our lives at our weak moments. You are a conscientious man. You still have time on your side. Whatever you want is to be considered to be our fate. Do not think that my tears betray my weakness. I can only make entreaties to you thinking that it is essential for you and me. But I cannot compel you to do anything." The sky was crying making terrible sounds. Pranab was crying for a long time clasping Pallavi to his chest.

The evening was in progress. The sky looked clear even though it was dark. The moon was rising from inside the clouds. Pallavi stood up. She groped in the dark and switched the light on. The room was awash with electric light. Her daughter stood near the door wearing a sari like a goddess from Greek legends. She ran to embrace her mother restoring faith in the grieving mother's heart. Pranab lay on one side of the bed like an exiled god. He thought that the dazzling resort by the side of the sea attracted only travellers. But the silence of the temple beckoned every pure soul. His daughter was saying, "Papa, it's my birthday today. Don't you remember it?" Pranab came awake from the terrible suffering of repentance into the joy of truth. His daughter had held her mother in an embrace. Pallavi was smiling in spite of all her grief. The sky looked peaceful. Moonlight had spread everywhere. His daughter was saying, "I love you, Papa. We need you only beside us." He could hear his son's voice from outside. He had a beautiful world to call his own. How could he have become a pauper amid the wealth of limitless love because of his momentary lack of judgment?

****

The Bedstead

That bedstead of *Bou* was dear to everyone. It was made of teak wood. There were several carvings on it and mirrors had been fixed on it. The length and breadth of the bedstead were the same. It was very strong. Ten people could sit on it comfortably during festive occasions with room to spare. The bedstead was there in our house since ages. *Bou* had brought it along with her from her father's place at the time of her marriage. Her father was a very rich man. They had fertile land by the side of a river. They lived in a six-bedroom building. There were other utility rooms too that had clay walls and thatched roofs. She was an only daughter. We were told that ten people had been engaged at the time to carry the things that she had brought along with her as dowry besides the bedstead. The girls of the entire village gathered in our house to look at the bedstead. *Bou* was held in high esteem by everyone in the village because of the bedstead.

Bou had five sons and two daughters. *Apa* (elder sister) was the eldest. The five brothers came after her. I was the youngest. *Bou* was held in great esteem by all the people of our village. She passed away on that bedstead while giving birth to an ill-fated girl like me. She died even before the umbilical cord was cut. I lay beside her dead body on the bedstead she had carried from her father's place. That bedstead had set her apart from the other girls and women of the village. She made *paans* sitting on it. She combed her hair sitting there. She fed nectar from her chest to her children sitting there. She had become a mother seven times in sixteen years lying on that bedstead. She left me on that bedstead by myself and passed away ....

XXX

Ghana Dada (uncle) had informed from Haladibasanta that *Nuabou* (sister-in-law) will arrive with a proposal for Sumi. My brother-in-law Raghu said that while plucking bottle gourds from the thatched roof with a bamboo pole with a hook. I was plastering the hearth in the kitchen. I came out with the piece of cloth in my hand. I asked, "What did you say? Who told you that? Does the boy have a steady job? How many siblings does he have?" Raghu smiled as he dusted a bottle gourd with his *gamcha* and said, "Why, are you going to give your daughter in marriage if he is an only son of his parents? Aren't you going to get your daughter married otherwise?" I shook my head and shrank into myself. I returned to the hearth just the way I had come out hurriedly. As I went back to plastering the hearth with the piece of cloth, I was looking for Renu of twenty-five years ago outside the door of Nari *Mastre* (teacher) of Kanakpur village ....

Shukadeva, the astrologer, might have prepared my horoscope the day *Bou's* dead body was carried to the cremation ground. I had been told that he had prepared the horoscopes of *Apa* and all my brothers. No function had been held for me after my birth. No one had ever thought of preparing any delicacies on my birthdays. I always regarded my father as a god. Even he had not bothered about me as long as I was in his house. I did everything for *Bada*

Bou (father's elder brother's wife). I made *paans* for her. I washed her clothes and combed her hair. I even pressed her feet every day. But she had never said an affectionate word to me. She called me all kinds of names while alleging that I had devoured my mother at birth. She said that I ate like a hog and whiled away my time doing nothing. When did I eat and when did I waste my time doing nothing? I slogged from the morning till night in the kitchen and around the house. I did my brothers' bidding. On top of that, I had the responsibility of cooking for everyone. I thought that I was much better off than father when I looked at his wilted face. *Apa* had got married when I was nine years old. I had slept one day that year with my face hidden in the warm lap of *Apa*. *Bou's* face in her photograph hanging from the clay wall seemed to be smiling at me. *Apa* used to break into a sob when the subject of her marriage came up for discussion in the house. She held on to me tightly. She had passed class seven. She hadn't studied any further as the high school was far away from the village. Father had given a decent education to my brothers to the best of his ability. He had seven children to take care of with the salary of a schoolteacher. *Bada Bapa* (father's elder brother) and *Bada Bou* had no children of their own. Therefore, they too lived with us.

Bada Bapa and *Bada Bou* slept on the bedstead brought by *Bou* after the latter died. *Bada Bou* said that the bedstead was too large for only father to be sleeping on it. Father slept on a single bed in the room near the backyard. The brothers slept anywhere it suited them. But *Apa* and I lay down on the old-fashioned bed of *Bada Bou* and missed *Bou's* bedstead. *Apa* wanted to talk to father about it. But she could not bring herself to do it. She returned from father's bedroom not being able to say that we should be allowed to sleep on the bedstead as it belonged to our mother. Father always had a light on in his room and he used to read something or the other all the time. He took watered rice in the morning and left for school along with the boys. But he always forgot to take me along with him. I felt as if he had cremated me too in the cremation ground along with *Bou*.

The two elder brothers married at the same time after several years of *Apa's* marriage. The eldest *Bhauja* (sister-in-law) had brought nothing with her except two boxes. She always bragged that her father was a very rich man. My brother was an ideal teacher. He had married without any dowry and was held in great esteem because of it in the village at the time. The ideal son of an ideal father. But my destiny had remained unchanged all along. The eldest brother and *Bhauja* had slept on *Bou's* bedstead on the fourth night of their marriage. I had touched *Bou's* bedstead for the last time that day as I placed a glass of milk beside the lamp that was flickering in the room. I had made the bed for them. *Bou's* eyes looked lachrymose in the faded mirrors of the bedstead. *Bhauja* had handed me *Bou's* photograph hanging on the wall as I left the room and asked me to hang it on the wall of father's room.

Time kept on passing. I entered the bedroom after cooking lunch for the day. Hot wind was moving inside the room through the window. I had dreamt father for twenty-five years after my marriage. I had dreamt about my brothers too along with that bedstead in my father's place. Father had promised to my father-in-law at the altar that he would give him twenty-five thousand rupees and a bedstead. The man who had asked for twenty-five thousand rupees had already passed away since fifteen years. Half of my hair had already turned grey waiting for the bedstead to arrive. My family still slept on a bed spread on the floor.

My husband was waiting for the day when his brothers-in-law would come with the bedstead. Therefore, he had never thought of acquiring a bedstead himself. My children were now grown up and capable.

Poor people are more miserable in this world. People from the boy's family would come the following day to see her daughter. It was a joint family. Where I was going to ask the guests to sit? What would they think of me? The village Haladibasanta was near Sujanpur, the village of *Bou's* father. Who did not know about the father of her *Bou* in the area? The old man Samal's granddaughter was going to get her daughter married. The guests would be coming to her house with high expectations. A silk sari does not lose its value even if it is worm-eaten. I was from an educated family. I had seen my brothers fighting each other for their individual interests. I had cursed myself for the same. I had not held anyone responsible for my miserable life. My mother had an untimely death. The responsibility of such a large family at a young age had made me prematurely old.

Three other brothers used to work in the city apart from the eldest brother. Father had mortgaged his land and paid a bribe to find a clerk's job in the civil supplies office for the second brother. He moved his family to the city after joining in his job and hasn't been seen in the village since then. The third brother got into the military after making a number of attempts. He had kept only a small part of his first month's salary for himself and sent the rest by money order to father. My father's eyes had been filled with delight as he signed the money order form and counted the money that the postman had given him. *Bada Bou* had curled her lips and said, "Forget it! This is not going to last for a long time. Just wait till he gets married." Those were prophetic words. *Bhai* (elder brother) married a non-Odia girl there without consulting anyone at home. Father had been devastated. He took to the bed never to get up once again. He didn't have any money with him. But he was held in high esteem in the village. Even that was gone. Fortunately for him, *Bada Bou* and *Bada Bapa* were already dead by that time. Otherwise, father would have been utterly humiliated.

Father had selected the eldest daughter-in-law himself. He had not asked for any dowry from her family. And they too had not volunteered to give anything on their own. Still the eldest *Bhauja* had a great deal of ego that she was the daughter of a rich man. As I was warming towards the eldest *Bhauja,* she had shunned me out of greed for that bedstead for as long as I was in my father's house. She knew that there was nothing else in our house except for that bedstead which would have increased her esteem in her father's house. Her attitude towards the members of our family had shaken all of us to the core. The household expenses as well as the expenses on father's medicines were met from the eldest brother's earnings. Only the rice was cooked for the entire family on one hearth. But each brother had a separate hearth so that delicacies could be cooked for their wives and children separately. The two youngest brothers had formally separated from the family after their marriage. I had been married by that time without a dowry. My father-in-law had agreed to the marriage without even seeing me only because of that aristocratic bedstead. He had thought that the bedstead would certainly come from Kanakpur to Haripur as the youngest daughter was always the closest to everyone in the family. The villages were nearby. My father-in-law always said as long as he lived, "Ten carpenters had worked nonstop for three months when the bedstead of your *Bou* was being made."

My mother-in-law's cousin brother had come as

the mediator to my father's house. He sat down on *Bou's* bedstead where I served him a glass of *dahi* sorbet. He had agreed to the proposal without blinking his eyes. Looking at the desperate eyes of my father, he had realised that we were as poor as church mice. But he said by way of conversation, "We have only one demand. We want a bedstead. No one demands less than one lakh rupees these days. Our son is highly educated. But he works in the farmlands. It would have been a different matter if he would be working somewhere. He wants to buy a pump to water the fields. Otherwise, I would not be asking you to give him twenty-five thousand rupees." No one knew whether father was listening to him or not. But he was running his fingers on the bedstead and trying to estimate how much it might have cost. Father knew that nothing would come out of this proposal too. But the gods had taken pity on him.

Banana trees had been buried in front of our house. The old altar had been painted with a bit of lime. I had worn a small quantity of ornaments that belonged to *Bou*. I had left home with tearful eyes carrying two boxes of household appliances and two tins of sweets. But I was certain about one thing. Nari *Mastre,* my father, might not give me *Bou's* bedstead. But he would certainly give a bedstead to her daughter who had never demanded anything from him so that she would be treated with respect at her in-laws' family.

The sun was moving from the east to the west. I lit a lamp at the *chaura* (a stone structure with a *tulsi* plant) and lit the hearth. I had three children. My brother-in-law had two children. My husband's elder brother's daughter had been married three years ago. All the three sisters-in-law live under the same roof and manage with one hearth. I know how difficult it is for three women to live together.

But I had faced greater hardship in my father's house. I have no complaints against anyone. I don't alienate anyone too. Everyone belongs to me. All the children are mine. If my daughter's marriage is settled at this place, I am going to tell my elder brother-in-law that he should at least give an expensive bedstead to my Sumi if not anything else. My eyes were filled with tears. I had an inferiority complex before my sisters-in-law because of the bedstead. I could not tell anything to my husband. There was constriction in my chest when I found my children returning from the school and lying on my brother-in-law's bedstead. It was a joint family of three brothers. It was not possible for one brother to spend money and acquire something for him alone. My husband was indifferent about these things. Still I thought I would tell my brothers that I would keep the bedstead for my own use if they gave it to Sumi at the time of her wedding. Won't her father and *Bada Bapa* buy a bedstead for Sumi?

****

Change

As i was getting up on the staircase, I could hear someone reciting, "*Shantakaram ... gagana sadrusham, meghavarnam shubhagam ....*" I thought to myself that people who had nothing to do indulged in such things. I opened the door to my room, kept my slippers aside and sat down on the bed. My gaze shifted all of a sudden to my son's study table. Several books and notebooks covered with brown paper, a number of other books and dried up flowers lay on the table. I felt irritated. I looked at my watch and recalled suddenly that Nandita had a class at ten in the morning today. I did not have anything to do after I dropped my son in the school. I could extract some money from Nandita today under the pretext of dropping her at the college. It was nine o' clock. I decided to have a bath and get ready. I entered the bathroom with these thoughts. I could hear sounds from the kitchen. There was an aroma of something cooking in the air too. I could hear someone closing the bedroom door. Had Nandita gone away?

Three rooms on the ground and the first floor of the house had come to me as my share in my father's house. The eldest brother and the second brother had constructed their bathrooms on their balconies. But I had to come to the ground floor for my bath. A bathroom had been constructed by father on the courtyard. Of course, that suited me fine. No one ever used that room.

I had to beg Nandita for money for everything I needed these days. Water did not come in the shower these days. Something must have gone wrong with it. The intolerant lump of clay that had gathered on my mind was perhaps washed away and cleaned as I poured water above my head with a mug. The parents of a friend of my son Sanjog had come to him last evening. But I had not come down from the first floor. Nandita was talking to them at the front door. My son gave them a notebook. As I dried my hair with a towel, I thought my son was telling his mother, "Mama, why don't you and Papa come to the school together at times like the parents of other children?" I got inside the bedroom hurriedly. Nandita had indeed left for her college. She had hung the keys outside the door as always. The assorted fragrance of incense sticks and potato curry hit my nostrils when I opened the door. I never had the time for the deities. As I had my breakfast, I thought I could perhaps have managed without a bath. I might not get another opportunity like this. Last month I had taken five thousand rupees from her for getting the television set repaired. I spent fifteen hundred rupees on it. The rest of the money was exhausted in Shibu's foreign liquor shop in three days. I had to borrow from some source now to tide over till the following month.

Nandita had perhaps left hurriedly this morning. The disorderly room seemed to be mocking me, "You don't have any work to do. You simply while away the time. You have had your bath early today. You can put one side of your disorderly world into order today." I didn't feel like eating. Nandita's photograph as a bride hung from the wall. The photograph of my son on his first birthday was beside it. A layer of dust had gathered on his photograph and his face was not visible clearly. I felt uncomfortable for some reason. Nandita was flowing away soundlessly like a river in a valley. She had no longer any emotions in her body and mind.

I never did any work ever since Nandita started working. I moved to my son's table wondering why all these things happened. Should I start cleaning from this place? I was startled out of my wits as I came outside to wash my hands. There were black stains everywhere on the walls. The iron rods from the roof could be seen. It seemed a ninety-year-old man lay there clinging to his dirty bed sheet. The pigeons had defecated everywhere. Birds had built their nests in the corners of the room. The pictures of the bride and bridegroom drawn outside my room at the time of my marriage had become so discoloured that it was difficult to distinguish between the bride and the bridegroom. When had all these changes come about? I was not able to recall the year when father died. The rooms had not been coloured since then. The smooth cemented veranda had cracked. It seemed it would swallow everything in the house through that crack. Oh! Why did my eyes seem to be so heavy? I got lost inside me when the mother and son left home. I had never thought whence I had come and where I had reached. On the contrary, my downhill plunge continued unabated. My inebriated mind revolted not against any particular person. As Nandita's silence went on increasing, my inferiority complex kept pace with it. I bashed her up after that till she bled all over and I lost myself in bottles of liquor. I do not know whether she cries or blames her fate after being thrashed by me.

Bhai's (elder brother) son passed engineering this year. *Bhai* had gone to the railway station to bring him home. I used to do this chore in earlier years. *Bhauja* (sister-in-law) did not talk to me these days. *Bhai's* son entered through the gate and went away to the first floor straightaway. Forget about wishing me, he gave the impression that he did not know me. My second brother passed me by like a stranger if I ever ran into him on the streets. His wife used to enquire about my welfare earlier. But she turned her face away from me in disgust on seeing Nandita's black eye once too often. But I had turned into an animal from a human being. I burned inside myself looking at others' families, wealth, vehicles and status, and comparing everything with my state. But I never looked at myself. I never thought that Nandita and my son suffered terribly because of my inhuman treatment of them.

Brush and canvas were not necessary to draw the pictures of being humane. The marks I had left on Nandita's clear complexion through my beatings had started frightening me in the daytime now. Nandita gave me ten rupees the other day to get a new bulb when the bulb burning in the kitchen got fused. I had flown into a rage on seeing a ten-rupee note in her hand. I held her by her hair and turned her around to face me. Her eyes were on fire. Something seemed to have pierced my foot at this time. I left Nandita and bent down to see an open pen. My son studying in fifth standard was sitting there holding the cap of the pen in his hand. The colours of Nandita's and my son's eyes were almost the same.

As my son watched the television the other afternoon, he said to his mother, "Mama, his father died today." "Whose father?" Nandita asked. "Mehak's father in the serial *Guddi*." Nandita said, "All right. Go and study. You have got your examination tomorrow." But my son had not moved from the television. He said after a while,

"Mama, his father didn't die just like that. He died in an accident. Mama, where is Papa?" I was entering the house a little while earlier. I had stopped in my tracks hearing my son. My intoxicated feet could not bear my load. My son continued, "Mama, Papa has taken his vehicle." Nandita's voice was not audible. My son had moved very close to the television. He shouted, "Mama, come and see. Mehak is laughing. Mehak is laughing behind his mother. I am also going to laugh like that when my father dies."

I heard a cracking sound followed by the sound of my son crying. I had been stunned. Nandita had perhaps used all her strength to slap my son. Was it meant for her son or was she cursing her fate. What did Nandita want in spite of all my ill-treatment? Did she want that I should remain alive? Didn't my son want that I should live in that case? The sky fell over my head in pieces. I was thinking of turning around and leaving the place. Where could I go? The words of Nandita from last night had stuck to the spider web of my thoughts like glue, "Why don't you take some more potent intoxicant than liquor? You can also go to sleep during daytime in that case. You beat me up and scold me in filthy language when we live in a joint family. How can a child study in this house?" The demon inside me had become still. I had realised it that day that a lamp burning silently had the capacity to burn its surroundings even with its last flicker.

Hanuman Chalisha and *Jagannath Sahasranama* lay on my son's table. A thin English book with the title *A Letter to a Son from a Father* also lay there. My son had perhaps written one line on the last page of the book after reading it. There was darkness all around me during the daytime. My son was grave most of the time. He had written: 'My father is an animal.' My son who had gone forth a few paces ahead of him didn't almost talk to anyone except to himself. He slept beside Nandita clasping her in his arms. As if a hawk would fly in from the sky and fly away taking his mother with it.

Nandita had stopped sleeping with her head on my chest since more than five years. She didn't want to have any kind of relationship with me. It could be said that I had married him forcibly. We knew each other earlier. Still she would not have perhaps taken the risk to spend her entire life with me if her father would not have died suddenly. She didn't have a steady job or source of income because of which she had to agree to my proposal. She was familiar with my nature. But she knew that no one would come forward to marry a girl without a dowry. My father was alive at the time of our marriage. We were all safe and protected under his shelter. We did not have to worry about food and clothes. Nandita had found a job in a private women's college three months after the marriage.

My father liked her the most among all his daughters-in-law. She took good care of my parents. She got along well with her sisters-in-law. She helped them in cooking on her return from the college. She gave them some present or the other when she got her salary every month. She taught the children in the evening. She played carom with them. She gave medicines to father at the right times. She planted vegetables and banana saplings in the backyard on Sundays. She watered the flower plants. I knew that no one gave me any importance at home although Nandita had a special place in everyone's heart. How could I have got a job? I had no relation with books after passing B.A. My relations had perhaps not informed her about it. Therefore, she had the hope that I would get some kind of a job someday.

She didn't want that we should have a child within

three years of marriage. But I wanted to be a father as quickly as possible. I was afraid that I would be viewed as a useless character otherwise. Father had organised the twenty-first day ceremony and birthdays after my son had been born. But Nandita started disintegrating inside herself when she discovered both my inner and outer shapes at the same time. I was spending more money than she was earning. She could not become friendly with everyone in the family any longer. She didn't look after my parents too. Her sisters-in-law misunderstood her. They thought she was behaving arrogantly because she was holding a job. I too joined them. She was going away from me at a psychological level. She started getting exiled into herself gradually.

My mother used to support me in everything after father passed away. The brothers separated from each other before my waywardness breached the banks. Three kitchens came to exist in the same compound. I did not have to worry about bread and butter. Therefore, it had not made much of a difference to me. We were moving on strung in the thread of time although layers of dust had gathered on us. I had no idea when flowers bloomed and when they wilted. I was alive with my wife's earnings just as the eyes of a dead man remained alive for some time after his death. The memories of the past were coming back to me once again today. I was standing by myself. The sea was roaring all around me. There was a void all around me. I had put the entire house in order. I had sat for a long time clasping Nandita's sari to my chest. Time was passing by. I began getting frightened with the onset of the night. I came towards light from darkness fearing something bad was going to happen. Where would I go? I went to the roof when I heard temple bells ringing. I was stumbling on my memories as I got up the stairs. How much more could she have put up with? She had become prematurely old because of the atrocities of her unemployed husband. A dry smile crossed her lips at times to hide her miseries. She might have even thought of committing suicide. But she would have decided that she would rather drag herself some more in this world rather than leaving her son in my charge.

I could hear my elder brother shouting in a very loud voice as I reached upstairs. I thought he was calling me. I turned around and ran downstairs swiftly. I had all kinds of misgivings. I had the premonition that I was going to get some terrible news when I reached him. I was beside him in just a few seconds. He had stopped talking to me for more than a year. We used to eat together for a long time till I grew into a young man. I used to insist that I would sleep beside him even after *Bhauja* had come to our house. I was in class six at the time. A huge chasm had been created between us when I started going downhill. There was no water in that moat. But it was so deep that it was not possible to reach the other side after getting down inside it.

Bhai and *Bhauja* were sitting in the courtyard. There was a carpet of flowers under the *Gangashiuli* plant near the well. I held *Bhai* tightly and began crying, "*Bhai*! *Bhai*! Why were you calling me so loudly? Nandita and my son haven't returned home since morning. Did you get any bad news about them?" I could see that he had been moved by my choked emotions. He freed himself from my grasp and said, "I haven't called you. Your soul would have awakened and called out to you. There is still time. Change yourself. Look back at your past. The time that is past might not return. But you can be your former self once again."

I was trying to hide my weakness resting my head on *Bhai's* shoulder as I looked towards the front door. Nandita was opening the shoes of my son from his feet near the shoe stand. My son had kept his hand on her shoulder and was saying something to her. I ran to them hurriedly. I took my son into my arm. I pulled Nandita to my chest. She was struggling to free herself as she was embarrassed by the presence of *Bhai* and *Bhauja*. I asked, "Where have you been since the morning?" Nandita had not looked at me. She had handed over two packets containing a cake and a shirt to *Bhauja*. She said, "*Apa*, it's *Bhai's* birthday today. Have you forgotten it?" *Bhauja's* eyes were filled with gratitude. *Bhai* came to me and ran his fingers through my unkempt hair. He said, "I turned sixty today. Don't you know it? However, my sister-in-law remembers the day. She has got a cake for me. What present do you have for me?" The second brother was going upstairs at that time holding a packet of sweets in his hand. He found us together and stopped in his tracks. There was a questioning look in his eyes. My son ran to him and pulled him by his hand. He said, "It is *Bada Bapa's* (father's elder brother) birthday today. He is now a sixty-year-old man. The second brother lowered his eyes. He took out a sweet from the packet and fed it to *Bhai*. I called out to him, "Give me one, *Bhai*." The three brothers stood there like a triangle. The sisters-in-law had stared at us. The children too ran down from their rooms. It was decided there that *Bhai's* birthday would be celebrated together. The cake was cut. The sisters-in-law got together and cooked *Bhai's* favourite dishes.

All of us were eating together at the same table after a long time. My sisters-in-law were serving. Nandita stood nearby. Dew drops on a moonlit night were flowing down from her eyes. She had been staring at me. She could not believe this strange turn of events. She had looked at me with trusting eyes just like a stream looks for an even bed after leaving the bed of stones. I was looking at my life hiding the fact from my brothers. I had closed my eyes thinking of Lord Jagannath after *Bhai* lowered his eyes. I made up my mind to give this change in me as a present to *Bhai* on his birthday.

****

Life of Promises

Many things barge inside the mind at different times. We think about the houses of sand that we built as children, our games of hide and seek, cooking rice in coconut shells, dolls' marriages and so forth. We like to think about these moments that have been lost to us forever. At times, we find an invaluable jewel from wilderness. Sometimes, we feel suffocated because of the problems hounding us. It is not possible to solve these problems. Therefore, we push them away into a corner of our mind. Those days keep reappearing before us again and again before the sun disappears completely from the sky. Their footsteps can be heard at all kinds of ungodly hours. They wake us up from sleep at the dead of the night. Those moments keep on dazzling like invaluable gems. We might return them not being aware of their worth. But we keep searching for them again and again.

Father had felt humiliated and returned to the village by the night train. He had got up inside the compartment after buying a ticket. He didn't even have reservations. I wondered if he had found a seat. Did he travel all the way standing or did he somehow manage to find a seat? I had not been able to think judiciously that day. I was fuming.

What did father take me to be? He had promised some childhood friend of his that he would get his daughter as his daughter-in-law. He didn't feel it necessary to seek my opinion in the matter. He had perhaps thought that his son was going to abide by everything he said without asking any question. When I flatly said that I could not marry the girl, his arrogant mind had crumbled like a house of sand that had been constructed without the use of cement. I said, "I am an officer in a bank. My wife had to be a postgraduate in the least." Besides, who didn't want to rise beyond his status? Was it absolutely essential that one had to see the whole moon from under the thatch? I have no idea what father would have thought of me that day. The tree would have been uprooted completely inside his mind and weighed a ton inside his chest along with the broken branches. But I did not have the time to think about these things. I had slept soundly for a couple of hours after father left for the railway station in a huff. I had come awake late in the evening. My mind became heavy slowly. Did father really go back to the village? I had been to the village later once for three days.

I was transferred to Kolkata Main Branch after a year. I took eight days leave to go to my village before joining in the branch. I had been to New Market to buy a few things for home. My younger sister was studying in the medical college. I wanted to buy a bag for her so that it would be easy for her to move between our village and Cuttack. I ran into Rudrajit, my friend from my college days, as I was about to enter the shop. We had coffee together.

He asked me, "Have you got married?"

"No," I said. "What about you?"

"I got married two months ago. Would you like to see her photograph?" He took out a black and white photograph from his purse. Three to four girls were sitting on a rock. Before I could ask him about his wife, he pointed at one of the girls and said, "This is your *Bhauja*. He pointed at the girl next to her who was somewhat short. She was fair-complexioned. However, her face looked solemn in the photograph. He said, "This is Bijayini. She is the best friend of my wife Tikili. She has completed post-graduation in Political Science this year." I showed a little more interest. He went on, "Her father is a very rich contractor of Bhadrak. All her siblings are settled in life. She is the youngest daughter of the family. They are looking for a groom for her in real earnest." He was smiling as he said that. I was looking at the photograph sideways. Before he replaced the photograph in the purse, he waved the photograph once again before my eyes.

"Find out about the nature of the girl from Bhauja. She looks like a good-natured girl. I will go to the village tomorrow. Send the proposal to my father through someone. I have no say in the matter. They have to finalise everything."

Rudrajit laughed as if he did not have a care in the world and said, "You like her. Don't you?" I smiled at him by way of an answer. I bought a few things from New Market and returned. I had to catch the train at seven in the evening the following day. I had made reservations earlier. The entire day was spent in packing my bag and putting everything in order at home. I switched off the fridge and cleaned it. I covered the television set and closed the doors and windows of the bedroom and kitchen properly.

I had been to the village once for three days after father had returned from me. Maa said that father was not keeping well. He was looking for a groom for the younger sister. She had another year to go to complete her MBBS.

But father was not bothered about it. He wanted to get her married as quickly as possible so that his responsibilities would come to an end. He had not broached the matter of my marriage. He didn't also give me to understand that he had left my place one day after being miffed with me.

Many years had passed in the meantime. I checked the calendar and found that father's *shraadh* was four days hence. He had passed away since twenty-four years. Maa fed the poor and organised a *kirtan* on his *shraadh* every year. I came outside when I thought about Maa. Father had passed away four days after the Vyaasa Purnami. Maa had been to *Bhai's* (elder brother) place. *Bhauja* was about to deliver a child. Father died in the village. *Bhauja* had a son at Mumbai. The happiness of having a grandson was drenched in tears. Maa returned to the village along with *Bhai*. Her mother stayed beside *Bhauja*.

I came to my bed on seeing the light burning in the kitchen. I was filled with grief. What had I done! I had gone against my father's wish and ignored Maa's helplessness in order to give my assent to Rudrajit's proposal. Rudra had sought father's permission only as a matter of formality. Father had said in a depressed voice, "We are a lower middle class family. I do not know if the girl can get along with the members of my family. Besides, I have made bricks this year for the construction of my house. I had thought of getting my son married after the construction of the house."

How helpless my father was! He knew that his promises meant nothing to his son. But he had tried to assert himself. I had studied in the village school. I had developed a lower middle class mindset. I wanted to oppose father openly. But I had not been able to bring myself to say anything to him directly. However, Maa had been able to understand everything after seeing me. She didn't allow father to speak a great deal. She told my childhood friend Rudra that we were prepared to hold the marriage in the month of *Asadha*. I could easily see that father was against the proposal. But I knew that he would not be able to go against my mother. Maa had the entire responsibility of the family on her. She was an only child of our maternal grandfather. She had studied till class five during those days. She had memorised the *Bhagabata* and the Ramayana. Her family was wealthy too. There was a narrow river between our village and grandfather's village. A boat ferried people during the rainy season. We walked through the river to the other side during the summer season. Our grandfather had a mango grove. His pond was full of large fishes and prawns. What attracted us the most was grandfather's house. It was not a thatched cottage like ours. It was a one storey building. Steps had not been constructed to go to the roof. But a bamboo ladder had been kept near the house that was used round the year. We used that to go to the roof. We stared far and wide from the rooftop. We didn't feel like sitting on our cemented veranda with a hurricane lantern by our side to study after our return from grandfather's place. I had flown around on grandfather's roof from my childhood. The birds flew above me. I flew at a somewhat lower height like a wingless bird.

Father passed away in his sleep a few days before my marriage. We had to shift the marriage date by a year on seeing the condition of the house and Maa's state of mind. Maa introduced me to Hari Uncle during that period. He was father's childhood friend. Father used to address him as *samdhi*. They were returning on bicycles from another village one day after seeing a *jatra*. The two friends had promised to each other by the side of a river that they would get their son and daughter married when they grew up. Everyone in the village stopped the two *samdhis* from that day on the way. They asked, "Why Hari Babu! How old is your daughter now?" My father Madhusudan Gantayat had three sons out of whom two were already married. There was a difference of ten years between my age and the age of Hari Uncle's daughter. Still father had depended on me to be true to his word. My educational qualifications and Hari Uncle's daughter's qualifications ran like two parallel lines. I had come to the village six months after father's death. I had decided to take Maa to me. I didn't like to live by myself any longer. Had father passed away because he was peeved at me? My elder brothers led happily married lives. My sister was busy with her studies. Maa and I had different kinds of miseries.

I stayed in the village for eight days. The day I was supposed to return, Maa said, "Why don't you make a round of Hari Uncle's house and have a chat with his daughter? Show some respect to your father's wish after his death." Maa was not holding anything back. She was not making a request. It was an order from her. I had already been to Bijayini's house a few times in the meantime with Rudra. She was not extraordinarily beautiful. But I liked her. What attracted me the most was her father's social status. Her mother took all the important decisions in the family.

I compared her mother with mine. A swift stream seemed to be flowing between their natures. They could not be brought together under any circumstance. My mother wore a plain sari. She had a veil over her head at all times when she talked to other people. Her head was covered even when she slept. Bijayini's mother wore a matching blouse with her sari. Her face was always solemn and she looked like a highly educated matron. Our mother never asked us to study. She pointed to the teacher in the village school and our servant boy Raghua and asked, "Who do you want to be when you grow up? You will be an officer if you study well. Otherwise, you will end up as a servant boy." Maa could not see much ahead of her. I felt that Bijayini's mother was a much more farsighted woman.

I would feel uneasy if I did not sleep well before the morning. As such I have high blood pressure these days. The times flowed before me when I closed my eyes. Sometimes, we wanted to relive the times that have been lost to us.

I had not paid any heed to mother. I believed that there was no need for me to go to Hari Uncle's house. I had already taken a decision in the matter. The proposal given by Rudra was a challenge for me. No one had perhaps married such a highly educated girl in our village. My elder brother was a cardiac surgeon in Nanavati Hospital of Mumbai. But *Bhauja* was just a graduate. Father had fixed that marriage. Maa's distantly related brother had come to our village to find a groom for his brother-in-law's daughter. He had perhaps heard that my elder brother was studying medicine at Cuttack. Father had liked the girl before Maa took a decision in the matter. It was a middle class family. They were two sisters and a brother. The brother was also studying medicine at Cuttack with my brother. My brother had not even seen the girl. My younger sister Bindu had accompanied my parents to the girl's village. The pitch road had turned around before two kilometres from their village and come back to our village. Father finalised everything the same day. The marriage was to be held after two months. I was studying B.Com. at Ravenshaw College at that time. I had seen *Bhauja* on the day of the marriage. *Bhai* had seen his wife four days later. Dr. Arvind Gantayat, the famous cardiac surgeon of Mumbai, had hitched his wagon with an unknown girl because of father. It was obvious to see that he led a happily married life when one looked at his contented face.

I didn't know what life was. The ladder of arrogance leading to the building of my dreams had broken before I had come to realise what life was. The reason was that my wife was not under my control. I could no longer climb to the roof because of my wife's strange nature. Her unruly nature had proved too much for my orderly lifestyle. She could not do anything at home without a servant to assist her. She was an aggressive and intolerant woman by nature. Maa could perhaps read the story of helplessness writ large on my face while looking at me. She didn't tell me anything. But I could know that she ignored me silently. The man who dreamt was always unsuccessful in his life. I had thought that I could spend my life happily if I married an educated and beautiful girl. But the road went on lengthening for me. Time never came to and.

I came from Bengaluru that year with my wife and son Samyak for Bindu's marriage and reached the village at three in the afternoon. The wedding was to be held after two days. My wife started for her father's village with my son the same evening. She told my mother that she would meet her family members and come back before the wedding. My younger sister Bindu (Dr. Bandita) came and stood before me after her departure. She looked straight at me and said, "Bhai, you might have become a rich man after marrying into a rich man's family. We feel that way. Aren't you sleeping in the nights these days? Why are there such deep dark rings under your eyes? Is your wife more beautiful than the other two sisters-in-law? Does she have anything more than them?"

The second brother lived in the village. He worked

as the principal of the college that had been established there with father's efforts. His wife was also a lecturer in Odia in the same college. I looked outside. The altar could be seen through the window. Banana trees had been dug into the ground around the altar. I asked Bindu, "Who is drawing pictures on the altar with rice paste?" Bindu said, "The second sister-in-law and Hari Uncle's daughter Gita." I stood up. Bindu was keeping a few things inside the cupboard. She asked without looking at me, "Where are you going?" I said I was going to stretch my legs outside. As I passed the altar, the second sister-in-law said, "Sidhu, isn't Biji giving you anything to eat? You have turned into a dark-complexioned man." I was standing there facing the altar. The girl was drawing pictures on the pitcher with her face lowered. Her drawing was flawless. The pictures seemed to appear by magic. I called sister-in-law. Both *Bhauja* and Gita raised their heads. I was startled. Her face was as flawless as the pictures she drew. She was beautiful! Her long plait was moving around on her back like a snake. She had raised her hands smeared with the rice paste. She was asking *Bhauja* to straighten her sari. Her thin lips trembled. It was somewhat dark near the altar. But I could clearly see a black spot in the middle of her cheek. She was wearing a yellow-coloured sari. It was an ordinary cotton sari. *Bhauja* straightened her sari. Her face was uncovered. She was so beautiful. There was darkness all around me.

Bhauja introduced us, "Gita! This is my younger brother-in-law. He is a manager at the State Bank of India." She stood up straight on the altar. But she had not looked in my direction. She looked like a wilted flower. I had no idea whether it was because of anger or humiliation. I had straightaway refused to marry her. She must know about it. Both of them got down from the altar seeing my mother approaching. She had drawn no more pictures after that. She washed her hands at the tap and stood on the veranda of the second brother's house like an image of stone. There was no expression on her face. The breeze was caressing it softly. My wife returned from her father's place the following day and I returned to Bengaluru with her and my son after Bindu's marriage. The days passed. Leaves had fallen from the trees and new leaves had sprouted in their place. There were times when I felt completely exhausted. What was the point in dragging oneself through life? The entire day hung heavy on me. What kind of future was I looking forward to forget all my ideals? There was no peace even after I was exhausted after running nonstop. I thought about father. And the short story about his ideals and promises, "I have made a promise to my childhood friend ...." But I did not have the time for such rot. I had gone a great deal ahead of the time when one listened to stories about kings and queens. Coloured birds were flying before my eyes from the village to the city. Familiarity bred contempt for me. I thought about that so-called proposal of Rudra. The colour of the reality for my wife Bijayini and the colour of my dreams were completely different from each other. I came to know it after my marriage. She was short-tempered, foulmouthed, irritable and suspicious by nature. There was nothing in her that could bind us together. Except for her looks. Lime had started coming off from the wall of my dream from the first day. There was not even a beautiful beach for my rapturous mind where I could sit without a bother after a hard day's work. She kept asking me to get something or the other for her every day. She insisted on me taking her to some place or the other every day. She constantly talked about her father, her brother, her sister and so forth. I was completely ignored in this constant refrain of 'I' and 'mine'. I didn't have those invaluable moments of the past in order to dream about things without a bother. My dreams began flying here and there like lost birds. I wanted to return to my past again. I thought about the times that I had left in the past. I could feel the tremors of father's long sighs about his promises reverberating inside my chest.

Maa was writing to me regularly even after she had turned into a very old woman. One day she had written, "The thatched houses at the back are crumbling. If you brothers could get together, you could demolish the old house and build a new one. Come to the village sometime." The last letter from her had reached me about two years ago. Maa had offered a *puja* to the tutelary goddess of the village after the daughter of the second brother was admitted to the medical college. The second brother has instituted scholarships for poor and meritorious students of the college in father's memory. He was organising football matches in the village. Father used to love football. The elder brother was a famous cardiac surgeon in Mumbai. Bindu was practicing with her husband in Mumbai. All of them had a close relationship. I was the only one who had been cast away. I went to the village once in four or five years. I stayed the night and returned in the morning. I tried to hide from myself. I prepared my answers before someone could ask me a question. I do not have to go to the village again once Maa passes away. I thought I was barging inside my brother's family. The second brother rang me one evening during this time. He asked me to come to the village without any delay. The line had been disconnected after he said that. I had tried a great deal to get through to him without success. My wife would assume her original shape if she heard that I wanted to go to the village all of a sudden. I had come by flight with my educated wife who wanted to keep herself away from my family as far as practicable. From Bengaluru to Bhubaneswar. I was ruminating about my childhood days all the way to the village. I played hide and seek with my brother hiding myself in the loose end of Maa's sari. We used to play strange games inside the pond till we went out of breath. Everything was flashing by before my eyes like pictures.

Did Maa pass away? Father had not even looked around for me when he had died. What if Maa would have gone away today? Would my mother's love for me remain as elusive moments of my life? The sun was setting slowly in Maa's eyes for a few days after father's death. But she picked herself up once again for her children within a short time. She spread her branches and leaves and kept guard over father's world. Her children built their nests in those branches. But they too flew away in a few days. However, Maa continued to stand there spreading her branches and leaves. I was myself responsible for this sad change in my life. Maa reminded me about it at intervals. Father had turned into a burnt tree trunk that had been hit by a thunderbolt after returning from me. He felt embarrassed to face Hari Uncle as he had not been able to keep his promise. I was returning to the village today after all my dreams had been dashed. Father had passed away earlier. Perhaps Maa too would have passed away before I reached the village. My wife was running her fingers on Maa's feet surprising me.

There were many *chappals* outside the front door. But there were not many people outside the house. I thought about Maa once again. No! Nothing would be the matter with her. The eldest brother ran to me in a dishevelled state on seeing me. He said, "Sidhu, Maa is perhaps waiting for you. She hasn't even taken a drop of water since yesterday. But she has been staring at the front door." I knelt down beside Maa. I laid my head on her feet and stayed like that. I said, "Maa! Maa! Get up." Maa shook her head slightly surprising everyone. I too shook a little bit with the movement of her body. I raised my head. Maa had been staring at me with a fixed gaze. She made an effort to say something. But no words came to her lips. *Bhai* gave her some water to drink. She was drinking it slowly. Just the way she had drunk the unbearable misery inside her chest throughout her life. The younger sister was measuring her blood pressure. *Bhai* was massaging her feet vigorously.

Maa had turned on her side the following day. A festive atmosphere moved around the house. Our servant boy Sarat caught two large Rohu fish by casting a net into the pond. The second sister-in-law was dressing the fish along with Sarat's wife. The eldest sister-in-law and my wife were cooking for everyone. *Bhai* stood near the front door. Maa found me alone and indicated to me with her hand to come near her. Maa's face was shining with the faint rays of the sun falling on it. She wanted to say something to me. I was not able to understand anything. The reason was that I had never tried to understand her throughout her life. Now she had turned unintelligible for me. A woman came inside the room at this time. She was beautiful. But it was obvious to the eyes that she was getting on with the years. Her face looked solemn and serious. She cleaned Maa from head to toe and sprinkled some talcum powder over her. Maa had been holding my hand tightly all along. I had an impression that I had seen the woman somewhere. But I was not able to place her. Maa's lips were shaking. The woman pushed closer to her and asked softly, "Would you like to say something,

Maa?" Tears were flowing down from Maa's eyes. I looked at the woman. She raised her head and looked at me. The black spot on her cheek reminded me about who she was. My father had one day promised her father, "She will be the daughter-in-law of our family.

I found myself saying, "You are Gita, aren't you?" My gaze shifted to her head as I said that. The parting in her hair had stretched like the afternoon sky. She wore two bangles on her wrists. There was a thumping in my chest. She smiled and said, "I have not married. Your mother had provided shelter to me after my father left this world." Maa spoke very softly, "Sidhu ... Gita." Both of us pushed closer to her. She looked at me and said, "Hari Uncle never looked around for a groom for her daughter because he had given his word of honour to your father. The girl was ostracised in the village. Your father never looked at your face again nor did he show his face to Hari Uncle. But Hari Uncle used to address me as *samdhan* for as long as he was alive." Maa's trembling voice was lost again. She could speak no more in spite of her best efforts. She had been staring at Gita with tear-filled eyes. Her face washed with tears looked even more beautiful than the moon on the full moon day. Maa had said no more.

Maa passed away the same night before we could retire for the night. The house became lonely. I had stayed in the village for three more days after the feast on the eleventh day. *Bhai*, Bindu, the second sister-in-law and the eldest sister-in-law were grieving as they were going to be separated from each other. It was as if Maa was the link among everyone. Gita had come the same evening to bid us good bye. Everyone in our family was close to her. I wanted to see her once again to my heart's content as she passed before me. She smiled and wished me with folded hands.

I asked her, "Are we going to meet again sometime in the future?"

"Why, you can meet me anytime you want to," she said and handed over a card to me. I had run to her before she could get down the steps. I said, "Gita ...." She looked at my face. I could get a full view of her. Her sad eyes and trembling body ... it seemed like time had passed by close to her but had not dared to touch her. I asked, "Are you staying alone?" She waited for a moment and said, "I don't have a house of my own." She had gone inside the house after that.

Night had still not fallen by that time. But the village streets had become dark. As such I had no relationship with the village. *Bhai* was afraid that our bond that hung from a thread might snap anytime after Maa's death. He asked, "When will you come again?" It was his job to tear the hearts of people and rejoin them every day. He had been able to know that there were no medicines for the pain I felt in my chest. *Bhai* held me tightly to his chest. My eyes were quiet like a deserted road. I was only breathing. *Bhai* said softly, "Sidhu, You refused to give her the prestige of a wife going against father's wishes. But she did not break down. She did her I.A., B.A. and M.A. in Political Science after being rejected by you. She will be collecting her doctorate degree tomorrow in the convention hall of Utkal University. She does not have anyone else to call her own. She wasted the invaluable time of her life because of the promise made to father. Is it not our duty to stand beside her at this memorable hour of her life?" I had not said anything. I had shaken as if the ground had slipped from under my feet.

I used to see dreams at one time. I lived because of my dreams. I was pretending to be happy even after my dreams flew far away from me. But this girl was pretending even more before my family members and especially before me. Was she really happy? After sacrificing such invaluable moments of her life without a valid reason? *Bhai* shook me by my shoulder and asked, "When is your flight? Will you come with us?

Gita had stopped in her tracks as she was passing by. She was perhaps waiting to hear my answer. But I was silent. There was no other way out for me except to keep quiet.

****

The Last Wish

It was still not morning by the time all the chores were finished. The morning was about to appear from out of the faint darkness just like the chick of a bird stared at the world outside with its beak out of the egg. Its eyes were still closed. But it was alive.

Abodha stood beside *Bou's* (mother) lifeless body tied to six pieces of bamboo sticks as the fire from the funeral pyre burst into a flame for the last time before going out completely. He had begged Sushil Bhai to allow him to lend his shoulders to carry *Bou* with three other people. "I am not claiming any rights over her. But do not deprive me from carrying her on my shoulders." *Bhauja* (sister-in-law) had pushed closer to Sushil Bhai and whispered, "Take *Bou* out of the house. Allow him to carry her after that. As such you have got cervical spondilitis. You are forbidden to lift or carry heavy things."

A burst of rain lashed us and disappeared immediately afterwards when we lifted *Bou* on our shoulders. The water dripping from the eyes had become one with rainwater. I had dedicated all the tears of my eyes to *Bou* since a very long time. *Bou* became somewhat restless on looking at my sickly body and depressed eyes. I didn't think that *Bou* was a human being when she poured some country ghee over my rice on the sly so Sushil Bhai, Anne and Rinku would not be aware of it. I had decided one day that I would never leave *Bou* and go elsewhere come what may. I was feeling even more helpless after taking such a decision. *Bada Bou* (father's elder brother's wife) served hot rice and *dal* for Sushil Bhai when he returned from the school. She sat beside him and nagged him to eat more and more. I entered the house at such times. I didn't have any idea what *Bou* did at the time. But she ran to me wiping her hands with the loose end of her sari. Her eyes became moist on looking at my depressed face. She asked me affectionately, "Has the teacher beaten you today, my dear?" She waited to hear me answer in the negative. I always said no even if I had been caned in the school. My hands moved to my back of their own accord. A ball of fire was lit in *Bou's* eyes briefly before it disappeared. I had a wash and sat down on a low stool to eat. *Bada Bou* was not there at the time.

Bou never sat beside me when I ate. She didn't nag me to eat more of everything. But my rice was never exhausted even after my stomach was full. She stood on the kitchen veranda and kept staring at me with a fixed gaze. She came out with a second helping immediately when a dish was exhausted. Anne was three years old at the time. Rinku was crawling on the ground. I was afraid Rinku would fall down from the bed. Therefore, I stood guard over him all the time. *Bou* got angry with me and said, "Finish your homework first. Otherwise, get your books here and study." *Bada Bou* had a grouchy face. But *Bou* had a beautiful face. I examined myself in the mirror and wondered if my face looked like that of father or *Bou*.

Someone was poking the heap of ashes with a stick. I was feeling a searing pain in my chest. The funeral rites will begin when three pieces of bone are taken home after cooling the ashes. Had *Bou* turned into a ghost already? Everything became clear when it became lighted all around. Sushil Bhai and Rinku were nowhere to be seen. Anne had a baby. Therefore, she had not come. But she lay crying at *Bou's* feet for a long time. I had no idea who had taken her inside. Someone should have sat with *Bou's* head in his or her lap. But no one volunteered. I asked Sushil Bhai if I should do it. He said, "Why should you do it? Won't Rinku do it?" Rinku stood there without saying anything. I looked at father with a ray of hope. *Bada Bapa* (father's elder brother) sat on his wheelchair. He heaved a sigh of relief on seeing me and said, "Abodha, sit there with her head in your lap." I felt I had come alive once again. Holding the lifeless body of *Bou*, I was going back in time. *Bou* came to our house along with *Bapa* (father). *Bada Bapa* had left me that evening in Saanda Math (monastery) of Shyamsundar Babaji near our village.

I was around six or seven at the time. I was yet to appear at class two examinations. I told *Bada Bapa*, "I want to go home. There is going to be a feast today." *Bada Bapa* asked, "Why is there going to be a feast?" I said, "It's my father's wedding." *Bada Bapa* looked very sad and forlorn all of a sudden. He had pressed my head against his bulging stomach. *Bada Bapa* had returned to the village after I went to sleep. I returned to the village after about a week. A new face had been staring at me from inside the veil through the opening in the door of the kitchen. *Bada Bou* said, "Abodha, this is your *Bou*." I found the word 'Bou' somewhat out of place. *Bada Bou* had put all kinds of restrictions on me. Therefore, I could not bring myself to go near *Bou*.

I had no idea what the woman called Bou served for me beside rice, *dal* and curries. But I didn't feel like going anywhere leaving home after that. I was following

Bou inside the house all the time. *Bada Bou* expressed her displeasure about it. But the woman she had introduced to me as *Bou* ran to me the moment I called out to her. I had a great desire to touch her. Time passed in this manner. Anne came first to our house followed by Rinku. But they had come one after the other within a few years of *Bou's* arrival at our house. Neither I nor anyone else in the family had been able to know when *Bou* had turned into my *Bou*. She looked after my studies in spite of remaining busy in household work all the time. I used to go for two tuitions. *Bou* ensured that I got my meals at the right times. She had prepared a timetable for me. Sushil Bhai had gone away to the city for his studies. Ours was a joint family. *Bada Bapa* and *Bapa* were two brothers. Grandpa and grandma had left this world one after the other. *Bou* had taken over the entire responsibility of the home by that time. *Bada Bou* was not keeping well. *Bada Bapa's* legs were paralysed. Father worked as a teacher in the school and he took care of the things outside the home. But *Bou* nursed *Bada Bou* without a grudge and did all the household work. Anne and Rinku were growing up gradually. But I seemed to have grown up overnight. I supervised our farmlands along with *Bapa*. I also had to take care of *Bada Bapa*.

I had seen the moon smiling on *Bou's* face the day I had passed matriculation in the first division. *Bou* insisted that I should be sent to the city for further studies. She said to Bapa, "Is he going to be a teacher like you in the village school? No! He is going to be an officer. He will sit in an office." I had no idea how far *Bou* had studied. But she was a farsighted woman. She asked *Bapa* to buy a long, plain notebook along with the book on mathematics for me. She spoke very little. But she achieved a great deal. She made Anne sleep beside her and told her stories from the

Ramayana and the Mahabharata. But she insisted that we should buy and read books on Gandhi and Gopabandhu. *Bapa* did not want to keep me at the village going against *Bou's* wishes. But I used to help father in many ways at the village. I did not want to go to the city leaving *Bou* in the village. That was the reason *Bada Bou* was angry with me. One day *Bada Bou* said to me, "You are a big boy now. Why are you rubbing against your *Bou* all the time like a cat? She is your stepmother after all. Has she given birth to you?" I thought that the heavy branch laden with fruits broke down on my head. I was bleeding all over. But *Bou* had not said anything in protest. *Bou* had not stopped me from going to the city. I thought throughout the night that *Bou* would be put into a great deal of trouble in taking care of two old and sick people and two small children after I was gone. I thought *Bou* might change her mind in the morning and ask *Bapa* to enrol me in the college in the nearby village. But I found the following morning that *Bou* had already packed everything for me. She had also packed *chuda* (rice flakes) and country ghee in a sack which I could use as a snack. I wondered if *Bou* was indeed my stepmother. Why would she take so much pain otherwise to send me away from her?

I had got a seat in a government engineering college through Joint Entrance Examinations before I passed I. Sc. with first class. I came to the village after the results were declared. *Bou* looked much older during the course of a few days. I had been able to discover the cause of *Bou's* misery within fifteen days. Sushil Bhai was not coming to the village. *Bada Bou* was crying constantly. Days and nights did not make any difference to *Bada Bapa*. *Bapa* was due to retire in a few days. The situation at home was going from bad to worse. Still I had taken admission in the engineering college. I had no idea how *Bapa* arranged the money for the purpose. I received money from him pretty late in certain months. Sushil Bhai had married a girl in the city without informing anyone. All of us had been hit by an untimely thunderbolt on getting this news. *Bada Bou* lost her speech on hearing it. She too lay on a bed beside *Bada Bapa* all the time. *Bou* had not lost her speech. But she kept on flying from one room to another in the house like a silent bird. What could she talk about? And with whom? She could not even take proper care of Anne and Rinku. *Bapa* did not have the time to console *Bou*.

Sushil Bhai had come to the village one day along with *Bhauja* many years after his marriage. I too had come to the village that day with my posting order. How could I have joined in my job without seeking the blessings of *Bapa* and *Bou*? I had scanned Sushil Bhai's face to find the love and affection that he had for me earlier. He was looking after his father-in-law's business. It was obvious to see that he regretted not being a graduate even after staying for so many years in the city. He was envious of me on that count.

But *Bou* had been able to understand that no one would be any longer capable of holding time in his hand. *Bhauja* did not like the atmosphere at our home. But she had only one objective in mind. *Bapa* and *Bada Bapa* owned acres of land by the side of the main road. The distance between the village and the city was not much. The villages were getting transformed into towns. Culture and tradition of the villages were changing accordingly. Sushil Bhai was the only son of *Bada Bapa*. *Bada Bapa* wanted that all the property would be divided equally among the children. He did not want to change the ideals of the family. *Bhauja* called *Bapa's* indifference as selfishness. He said to *Bou* that *Bada Bapa* had one son Sushil. Similarly, *Bou* had given birth to one son, i.e. Rinku. It would be proper to divide the entire property between the two brothers equally. Sushil Bhai and *Bhauja* did not bother about *Bada Bapa's* unhappiness. But they were scared of *Bou's* magnanimity.

The *asthi* (bones of a dead man after cremation) had been collected in a clay pot. Someone said, "Abodha Babu, let us go. We have to return to the village. Maa wanted to go to heaven from this Swargadwara." The sun god had risen to the sky over the sea. The reflection of the sun could be seen in the water. I thought *Bou's* hand was still on my head after she had left for her heavenly abode. I had never touched *Bou* when she was alive. But I was trying to wash all the sacrifices she had made during her lifetime with my tears when I had sat holding her in my lap. I had also held on to the pot of ashes as we returned home. I was going to immerse the ashes in the Ganges. Rinku was moving behind him when Sushant Bhai had lit the funeral pyre. I might not have any rights on *Bou's* body. But no one was certainly going to assert his rights over *Bou's* ashes. I had held on to the pot of ashes as if I was holding her hand tightly.

No one had seen *Bou* sleeping at odd hours. I am not able to recall what day it was. *Bada Bou* was shouting at Anne, "Go and call your *Bou*. It's already late. But she does not feel like leaving her bed." The words of *Bada Bou* hit my ears like drumbeats. Anne said, "*Bou* is ill. She has stomach ache." *Bada Bou* shot back, "And why shouldn't she have it? Her own son is moving here and there. She is sitting beside the hearth till the dead of night and getting fried for someone else's son. How can she eat at odd hours at her age?"

Bou had got up. The loose end of her sari dragged after her on the ground like an orphaned child. She said, "*Apa* (elder sister), please don't shout in such a loud voice. My son will appear at the matriculation examination." "How can he be your son? Don't give him so much importance. Otherwise, he will ask for a share in Sushil and Rinku's property. Let him remain where he belongs." I was not able to see *Bou's* face. But I could know from her depressed voice that she had been terribly hurt by *Bada Bou's* words.

I had been staring outside through the open window. A cow was licking its calf at some distance. My eyes became moist. Was I not my *Bou's* son? They were my *Bapa* and *Bada Bapa*. Why should my *Bou* be a stepmother in that case? *Bou* opened the door softly and came to sit beside me. Her face looked grim. But I dared not ask her anything. I wanted to ask if she was not well. *Bou* wanted to know if I had heard *Bada Bou's* words or not. I glanced at her and went back to solving problems of mathematics. *Bou* left my side quietly just the way she had come. The distance between her and me was growing silently as the days passed. But I was able to see her divine shape amid that silence. *Bou* was different from all other mothers in the village. I could see the moon in the corner of her eyes. She had preserved a huge world for me in the small opening in her closed lips. Her continued silence gave me the time to think about myself. I thought *Bou* perhaps wanted that I should go away from her. *Bou* had written me a letter for the first time after I left the village.

The driver brought the vehicle to a stop and said, "Sir, I need a cup of tea. I have been awake throughout the night. I feel sleepy." Everyone got down from the vehicle. There was no one else other than me and the body of my *Bou* that had turned into ashes. I recalled her words, "Do not drink tea. Don't touch cigarettes. Don't get into bad company. Your happiness is my only wish. Do you know the meaning of happiness, my dear? You will be known as a decent human being if you empathise with other people's miseries and rejoice with them when they are happy. You can become an important person in such a case. All the fish of a pond follow the biggest fish in it. You are the eldest son of your father. Anne and Rinku have come after you."

That was the first and last letter of *Bou*. Each letter in it seemed to be moist with her tears. *Bou* had called him the eldest son of the family. He would take on father's burden on his shoulders. The driver interrupted his thoughts, "Sir, please have tea." "No, I do not drink tea. *Bou* never liked tea, Nidhi Uncle." Nidhi was our sharecropper. His eyes had turned moist with the stupid words of Abodha. They had moved towards the village after that.

Sushil Bhai had performed *Bou's* funeral rites over the objections of *Bhauja*. I used to stand guard throughout the night over the lamp that was burning for *Bou*. My *Bou* was indeed a lamp herself. *Bou* had admitted Anne and Rinku to the village school after I went away to the city. *Bapa* did not have much money with him. He had also become weak-willed. *Bou* used to send me money by depriving Anne and Rinku of the necessities of life. Rinku often protested against it. The situation in the family was gradually distancing him from *Bou*. Anne was interested in other things rather than her studies. Still *Bou* kept waiting for better days to come and took everything in her stride. Anne decided to marry someone in the same village. It took five years for Rinku to pass B.A. *Bapa* could not stand up without holding a stick. *Bada Bapa's* world was confined to his wheelchair. *Bada Bou* was bedridden. She did not seem as if she would live for a long time. Sushil Bhai used to come once or twice a year to the village chiefly to quarrel with *Bapa* and *Bada Bapa* about division of property. *Bapa* had given a silent consent in the matter. But *Bada Bapa* was adamant and Sushil Bhai was not able to face him. I kept myself aloof after sending about half my salary every month to *Bou*. I did not know why *Bou* was always miserable. She cooked a variety of dishes when I came home. I fed *Bada Bapa* with my own hands. I pressed *Bapa's* feet when he went to sleep. I cleaned *Bada Bou's* bed. She lay on the bed all the time like a lifeless body. I heard *Bou* telling *Bapa* one day, "Why don't you find a bride for Abodha?" The thick branch of the tree laden with fruits had again broken down on my head on listening to *Bapa's* reply. I had not been able to hear what *Bou* was saying softly. I had left home the same day for my place of work with a new resolve. And after that ....

I worked at Bhubaneswar which was about one hundred kilometres away from the village. But my mind moved thousands of kilometres away from my own people. I was no longer going to the village although I was sending money to *Bou* every month regularly. *Bapa* decided against his wishes to get Anne married with the man that Anne had found for her. He had informed me about the date of marriage and the dowry to be paid to the groom's family. But he had not asked me to come for the marriage. I could not understand it. It was my sister's wedding but I could not attend it. I sent two lakh rupees towards the dowry and ornaments and saris for Anne. I still waited for *Bapa* and *Bou* to arrive and say to me, "Abodha, you have still not come to the village. How is your sister going to get married?" The days passed and it was the day of the wedding. The day passed and the evening came. All the possibilities of life had come to an end for me. Finally, I came to the conclusion that I meant nothing to these people. Not even to *Bou*. I was no longer myself after that day. I changed into a different man. I reduced the amount of money I used to send every month and stopped sending any money at all after some time. I had become exhausted in getting hatred, slights and humiliations from other people throughout my life. But *Bou's* silent affection for me had sustained me till now. Even that had been lost to me now. I had been flung away to a great distance with the passage of time. I no longer had time to look back. I have earned lakhs of rupees in my life. I have a huge building in Bhubaneswar. I have cars, drivers, servants and cooks. But I still feel suffocated. The pain in my chest rises to my eyes. I could not free myself from this inexplicable penury.

I had not been able to hide my helplessness. Therefore, I did not want to start a family. One day someone was wiping the sweat off my face in my dream with the dirty loose end of her sari. I grabbed the feet that were scurrying away after pouring some country ghee on my rice. I woke up shouting *'Bou! Bou!'* A cruel silence had stared at me inside the house. Everyone was running before me in darkness inside the house - Anne, Rinku, *Bada Bapa*, *Bada Bou* and *Bapa*. Someone still stood by my side after everyone else had left. I got up. I shrieked again, *'Bou!'* I drove down to the village early in the morning that day. I found people had gathered in front of our house. I felt scared. I went through the crowd and reached the bed in the middle room. *Bada Bapa* was blinking. *Bapa* sat on the ground like a burnt tree trunk. *Bou* lay on the bed and stared at the front door without blinking her eyes. Someone was reciting the Bhagavad Gita beside her. The women of the village were sobbing around her pressing their saris against their mouths. Anne was crying at *Bou's* feet. *Bou's* eyes became still for a moment as I entered the house and closed soon after. Everyone had kept staring at me.

I was getting ready to leave fourteen days after *Bou's* death. *Bada Bapa* handed over a packet to me filled with papers as I bowed to him. "What's this?" I asked. *Bapa* cried loudly. *Bada Bapa* said, "You have one-fourth share in all the property of this family." "How can I have a share, *Bada Bapa*? I am not even a son of this family." *Bapa* went inside the house. Sushil Bhai and *Bhauja* were about to leave after paying their respects to *Bada Bapa*. Anne came with her daughter in her arms and stood beside me. She said, "*Bhai*!" She had called me as *Bhai* for the first time in my life. I was startled. She said, "Don't you know about the last wish of *Bou*?" I looked at the photograph of *Bou* hanging from the wall. It had been taken when she had stepped into our house as a new bride. The word '*Bou*' escaped my lips indistinctly. *Bapa* was trying to stand straight with the help of his stick. He said, "Your *Bou* has written it on a piece of paper in the court. She has also written it on my soul, body and blood. She has written, 'Sushil is the eldest son of this family while Abodha is our eldest child. Rinku is his younger brother. Abodha deserves to get a larger share of our property. Our son and daughter will share the rest of the property.' You are your *Bou's* son after all! You are only her son! You had come to me by chance. But *Bou* had got you as her son because of her dharma."

"What is left for me now in this world, *Bapa*? What shall I do with property? From whom can I take a share? My *Bou* had not shared the loose end of her sari with anyone. How can I leave you people and go elsewhere?"

****

The Address Of Happiness

She had not left her bed even though it was evening already. She had not even lit a lamp outside the front door. She had kept staring outside through the broken door. She continued to sleep even after it was completely dark. She would have continued to lie on the tattered mattress if Sukibou *Khudi* (aunt) would not have banged on the front door with the hurricane lantern in hand.

"You haven't lit a lantern till now. Nor have you lit a lamp outside the front door. What's the matter with you? Aren't you well, *Bohu* (daughter-in-law)?" "No, *Khudi*. I was lying as I did not have anything to do. It's not as if I have a suckling baby. Who is going to eat if I finish the cooking early?"

Sukibou kept her dirty lantern beside the wall and sat on the veranda. "Get up anyway. We are destined to suffer. Can we get angry with anyone? Haven't you gone to work today?"

"No, I didn't feel like it. I work throughout the day. Still the mistress of the house gets angry with me all the time. She refuses to give anything to me even if I ask her for fifty rupees when I am in need." "What are you going to eat if you do not work, Chemi? It's not as if you have a husband or son who can take care of you. Go and have a wash. Bang your head at the feet of Maa Bhuasuni (a goddess). You will see Maa will look after you."

Chemi went to the backyard without saying anything. Sukibou was lost in the past looking at her. Chemi had come to this house in an inauspicious moment. She had been filled with grief ever since she had set foot in this house. Her mother-in-law had been ill since a long time. She survived for a few days with Chemi's nursing. But she finally went her way. But poor Chemi turned into a corpse the day her rascal husband Parsu ran away with his sister-in-law. The scoundrel did not even come to the village for the *shraadh* ceremony of his mother. Poor Chemi fed the Brahmins and gave a feast to the people of the village by begging money from other people. The ill-fated girl's looks had turned into her enemy. Nakhi entered the house at this time calling out to *Khudi*. She said, "You are here! I just returned from your doorstep. Your daughter-in-law curled her lips and said, 'She must be talking against me sitting in someone's house.'" Sukibou was not able to see Nakhi's face clearly in the semi-darkness. But she knew that she empathised with her.

"What can I say? I have been leading a despicable life ever since getting my daughter Suki married. My daughter-in-law has been giving me a piece of her mind every now and then. She says, 'You gave everything we had to your daughter. Your son mortgaged all your landed property and blew it on booze. Where do I find the money to feed you? I will give you two bowls of watered rice in the morning and evening.' I cannot blame her. She is telling the truth. My son is always in a drunken stupor. There are more liquor shops than grocery shops in the village."

Chemi lit a lamp near the deities. She took out a piece

of cloth from the thatch and wiped the glass of the lantern. She looked around for a matchbox. But she found only an empty box. Sukibou said, "What do we need two lanterns for? One is already lit. This will see us through the night." Nakhi asked, "Aren't you going to cook this evening, *Nuabou* (sister-in-law)?" "No, I will drink some *torani* (fermented watery portion of watered rice). Do you know something? Some fragmented rice was lying in the house for some time. I brought some molasses today and made a few ghee *pitha* today." "When did you do all this? Is any guest coming home today? Has Parsu Bhai sent you word that he would be coming today?" Chemi's eyes became heavy like Sukibou's dirty lantern. She was finding it difficult to breathe. Nakhi was not able to see the darkness in Chemi's eyes. She was looking for life in the fragrance of ghee *pitha*. Chemi gave two ghee *pithas* to each of them.

Sukibou *Khudi* caressed the emaciated face of Chemi and said, "Chemi dear! I have not eaten such delicious ghee *pithas* in any marriage or elsewhere." A smile appeared briefly on Chemi's face and disappeared in a moment.

The night was playing multi-coloured hide and seek with the sky. The clouds were floating away somewhere in rows. The moon was smiling at her at times and hiding behind the clouds again. Chemi lay on the bed made of wooden planks in the courtyard and stared at the sky. Sukibou *Khudi* slept beside her on a mat on the floor. She turned on her side. Her indigent state was reflected on her face like a tree shorn of its branches and leaves. Tears did not come to Chemi's eyes. The blood from her chest flowed out as water. What a miserable life she led!

She was constantly bashed up by her stepmother when she was in her father's house. There was life in her. But she was thin like a stick. Her father looked like a ghost because of the hard work he had to do every day. His eyes had turned to stone. There was neither any water nor sunshine in them. A distantly related brother of Shukibou *Khudi* had given the proposal to Chemi's stepmother to get her married to Parsu. He said, "There is an ailing old woman and an alcoholic son at home. They have given their land for sharecropping and manage from what they get." But still the stepmother was not willing. Chemi did all the household work apart from giving her a massage every evening. How could she manage without her? But the mediator was not prepared to let go of things. He thought over the matter and said, "You take two thousand rupees from me. Give away your daughter with just the clothes that she is wearing and nothing else. People will sing paeans to you."

She had already begged her husband to get her a pair of earrings. The old man simply ignored her entreaties. The stepmother decided that it was better that Chemi should go. She could ask the goldsmith to make a nose ring along with the earrings if she could have two thousand rupees. She sent the mediator away with her consent. Fifteen days later Sukibou *Khudi*, Nakhi *Apa* and some other women of the street had welcomed her inside Parsu's house with some dried grass and *arua* rice. Parsu had spoken to her affectionately hardly for a day or two. Her ailing mother-in-law had hardly got an opportunity to look properly at her face. Chemi could understand very little of what her mother-in-law said to her as she had coughing fits all the time. She could have confided her sorrows to Parsu if only he could get away from the bottle of booze that was his constant companion. Still she thought that the faraway moon was in her hands when she lay beside Parsu in the open courtyard. Parsu's poverty-stricken family was dearer to her than her stepmother's constant nagging and reproaches. What would she do with love and affection? She was not fortunate enough to have a roof over her head, clothes for her back and some food for the stomach. It was the case even now.

Chemi was lost in thoughts. Did she find any happiness in life? What was the colour of happiness? How big was it? Was there a kingdom called happiness? She had not been able to cross the river of sorrow. How could she have seen the kingdom of happiness? Her fate had dragged her to her present state. God took pity on her miserable life. The ailing old woman was not only delivered from the living hell she was experiencing. Chemi too found some rest for herself. Chemi's stepmother had sent her daughter Raji to help her in observing the funeral rites of her mother-in-law. Not even ten days had passed after the old woman's death when her alcoholic husband eloped with his sister-in-law. Three years had passed in the meantime. But there was no news of either of them. Chemi stared at the veranda. Oil was getting exhausted from Sukibou *Khudi's* lantern. The glass had turned completely black. She moved to the lantern and shook it. No! There was enough oil in it for another night. Chemi was no longer scared of darkness. The stars were no longer visible in the sky. It must be past midnight. There were only nights in her life. She hummed under her breath and cleaned the glass of the lantern with a piece of cloth that had been stuck in the thatch. The glass that was completely black a while ago shone like a new glass. But her hand had turned black. Anyway, the glass was cleaned. The dim light of the lantern seemed to have turned into electric light. Someone seemed to have lighted a new lantern in Chemi's mind.

She had not studied much. But she had completed class

seven from the village school in spite of all her stepmother's restrictions. Chemi made *ukhudas* (fried paddy seasoned with molasses) at the time of Saraswati Puja and Ganesh Puja. She fried *murhi* in a pot and made *muans* (balls of parched rice baked with molasses). She sang songs at the time of Khudurukuni Puja. She drew figures on the village street at the time of Laxmi Puja. She had learnt knitting from the new bride of the Choudhury family. She had thought about knitting a sweater for Parsu. What was the meaning of such thoughts for an ill-fated woman like her? Chemi had fallen asleep leaning against the wall of the veranda as she thought about the past. Sukibou *Khudi* sprinkled some water on her face and said, "Chemi, why are you sitting like a zombie here?" Chemi was startled. It was already morning. Sukibou extinguished her lantern and was about to leave for her house. She said, "Chemi dear, I want to talk to you about something. I will tell you about it when I come next." Chemi said, "Why don't you tell it to me now?" "No … it's about this ghee *pithas* of yours." The inside of Chemi's mind was shining like the clean glass of the lantern. She was fighting a battle for survival like a thin wick.

The bird that had been tied in her mind flew away flapping its wings after *Khudi* left. She finished her morning chores as quickly as possible. She plucked some flowers from the backyard and strung a garland for the tutelary goddess of the village.

She was going to live. She didn't want to lead a life paved with roses. All that she needed was a little bit of self-respect. She was now surviving only to eat two meals a day. Was it really necessary to live like this? She didn't have a matchbox to light the hearth. She didn't have eight annas with her to get a matchbox. She slogged from morning till night to earn only fifty rupees a month. She did the same kind of work in her mistress's house. Now she was going to do it for herself. She was constantly reminded about Sukibou *Khudi's* words that she had not eaten such ghee *pithas* anywhere. Was nobody going to buy them if she made such ghee *pithas* and sold them? She was startled for a while. How her imagination ran away with her! She was a woman who had been deserted by her husband. Where were the nights for her to see so many dreams? A desire lay curled up somewhere in her mind. A desire to live! A green leaf was sprouting on the dry branch.

Chemi offered a ghee *pitha* that she had kept aside as *bhog* before the framed photograph. She sprinkled some water with *tulsi* leaves and flowers. She closed the front door behind her and went outside. Why, Sukibou *Khudi* was nowhere to be seen. Chemi's mind was not able to rest after she had heard *Khudi*. She came inside the house and rummaged through her mother-in-law's trunk. She might have left some money inside it. Two ten-rupee notes fell on Chemi's feet as she shook a sari. She held the currency notes in her hand and explored further. She found a tin pot with loose changes inside it. Someone seemed to have blown a conch near her ears. Sukibou's voice calling out to her floated in at this time. She thought that it was the voice of the gods.

Sukibou *Khudi* was reminded of the face of the tutelary goddess of the village on looking at Chemi's smiling face. Chemi said, "*Khudi*, take this. This is the ghee *pitha* that I offered as the *bhog*. Give it to your grandson." *Khudi* laughed. Colours seemed to be dripping from her teeth stained with *paan*. Chemi wondered if she was a lone woman in this world or there were other people to help her out. Chemi made tea without milk for the three of them. She said, "I have some *murhi* at home. I could make a few *muans* if I could get some molasses. Why don't you send for your grandson? He could get me some." *Khudi's* grandson got her some molasses and she made a few *muans*. Chemi had stared at Nakhi's sad face that looked like a dry wick.

The three of them had one sorrow. They were extremely needy people. Sukibou *Khudi's* grandson Haria said while munching a *muan*, "*Bhauja*! Won't you give me two *muans*? Nakula Sir is going to bash me up at school today. I have been telling *Bou* to buy the mathematics book for me. She does not listen." Chemi laughed and said, "What would you do if you do not study? Buy the book somehow first." She gave him four *muans* in a paper bag. Sukibou shouted at her, "Why are you giving it to him for nothing?"

Haria ran to the school in a flash before Sukibou was finished. Nakhi was thinking looking at the smiling face of Chemi. She too was a girl of this village. She had hardly spent a couple of years with her husband after which she was living at her father's place for the past three years. Her mother-in-law and sister-in-law nagged her constantly and made her life miserable. But what really broke her spirits was the way she was beaten black and blue by her husband. Dowry was at the root of everything. Was her father capable of giving a dowry? There were three more girls and a lame boy after her in the family. The father had turned into a hunchback in the process of carrying his son on his back. He thinks that his son would take over the burden of the girls someday. Her mother had become prematurely old because of working from morning till night every day. Nakhi's husband had a *paan* shop in the village. He wanted a Luna moped and six thousand rupees as dowry. Her father gave him everything he wanted. But her husband was back to square one after two years. He started beating

Nakhi mercilessly demanding more money from her. "Go and get the money from your father. Otherwise, sleep on the veranda." She would have committed suicide since long if she were not in the carrying stage.

"Nakhi *Apa*! What are you thinking about? Are you aware where you are?" Nakhi was startled for a moment. How long could she sit idly in her father's house doing nothing? Her brother was young now. That was why he didn't say anything. But could she continue to live in their one-roomed house for all time to come? Chemi looked at Sukibou and Nakhi and said, "I could stand on my feet if both of you would help me out." Sukibou *Khudi* said, "What are you implying?" They found that Sukibou's grandson was running towards them and waited for him. He said, "Grandma! Sir asked me to get *muan* worth ten rupees. He has some guests in the house." "Ten rupees!" All three of them shouted in unison. Haria said, "Sir asked me to get the *muans* immediately."

Haria vanished in a flash with the *muans*. Chemi's face looked brighter than the glass of a lantern holding the ten-rupee note in her hand. She said, "*Khudi*! I could find a way for us to live if you and Nakhi *Apa* give me a helping hand. I have twenty rupees with me. If we could get some more money as capital .... Our life is a jumbled ball of thread. The more we try to put it in order, the more haywire it would go. We do not know when death is going to overtake us. Why shouldn't we make an effort to lead an honourable life?"

A wick of hope was burning in Nakhi's eyes. Chemi became somewhat scared on looking at the disapproving face of Sukibou. With tears in her eyes, she said, "*Khudi*! I had made a few *muans* at home just for the fun of it. I now have ten rupees in my hand for it. I could make a variety of sweetmeats if both of you sit beside me. Nakhi *Apa* could deliver them to shops. We could share in the profit." Sukibou curled her lips and said, "You are a newly married woman. How can you open a confectioner's shop in the village?" Nakhi said, "You have no shame, *Khudi*. Your daughter-in-law is sleeping at home after eating a bowl of watered rice. You cook for them at your old age. *Nuabou!* Don't worry in the least. I have a pair of earrings with me. My father had given them to me. I can hock it and get one hundred rupees. Make a bigger hearth at this place. The one who has provided us ground beneath our feet will also provide us with a roof above our head. Don't worry about a thing!"

The clay beneath Chemi's feet was turning into solid rock with those few words of Nakhi. She was looking skyward in despair. A shower seemed to pour down in the hot afternoon.

There were so many wants. Still there was a desire to live. She had been dependent on handouts till now. But she wished she too could give something to someone. She wished she could count fifty or a hundred rupees at a time and keep the money in her trunk. She wished she could buy a new sari and bangles that she fancied. Parsu had deserted her. But the girls of the village addressed her as *Khudi* or *Nuabou* because she was the daughter-in-law of the village. Where would she have been otherwise? Parsu had thrown her into a bottomless river. She was able to see the bank now. She was certain that God was going to help her. It was getting late in the day. She would cook rice. She would dress some spinach. She had boiled vegetables almost every day. It was seasoned on rare occasions. She was about to close the front door.

Someone called her at this time, "*Nuabou!* I am Raghu,

Mohan *Mastre's* (teacher) son." "What's the matter?" asked Chemi. "My sister Mituna will go to her in-laws' house for the first time tomorrow. Gifts have to be sent with her. She liked the *muans* made by you a great deal. Nakhi *Apa* was saying that you made scrumptious ghee *pithas*. Father has asked you to send one tin of ghee *pithas* and two tins of *muans*." Chemi's chest started thumping. How could she tell the boy that she didn't have the money with her to execute the order? When Chemi kept quiet, Raghu took out two hundred-rupee notes from his pocket and gave them to Chemi. He said, "You will get the rest of the money at the time of the delivery." Should she take the money or not? She had no idea how much she had to spend for three tins of sweetmeats. "*Nuabou,* here is the money," said Raghu and ran away. Chemi found herself in an unknown kingdom holding the two hundred-rupee notes in her hand. Sacks of rice stood against the wall there. There were rows of saris inside the cupboard. She was wondering which sari she was going to wear. She came back to her senses when she heard Nakhi calling out to her. She opened the door. Nakhi was smiling looking at her.

She had come with her father. Nakhi *Apa* could not hide her joy on hearing everything from Chemi. Nakhi's father said, "*Bohu* (daughter-in-law), start making the sweetmeats. Nakhi will help you out in everything. I will deliver the sweetmeats in different shops." Sukibou arrived with a bucketful of clay. "What is this, *Khudi*?" "The hearth has to be made. Have you forgotten what we were discussing a while ago?" Chemi smiled. The three of them forgot about their lunch that day. The hearth was made and dried in the sun. The three of them were searching for their lives inside their thoughts in the fragrance of ghee *pithas* and *muans.* Chemi's hands seemed to have turned into machine after the sweetmeats were sent to the house of *Maastre's* daughter. Orders started pouring in from different households in the village. It became gradually difficult for Chemi to execute the orders. Sukibou and Nakhi were constantly by her side. But that was not enough. The grown-up girls of the entire village joined hands with Chemi.   Gradually, the doorstep of Chemi turned into a small scale industry of food items cooked by hand. Chemi paid everyone according to the work they did. The items made by Chemi became famous in all the surrounding villages. The grown-up girls and women who remained idle earlier found employment at Chemi's place. Chemi found the place to be insufficient for her needs. She took a loan from the cooperative society and built a two-roomed building. She also opened a centre that imparted training in sewing. Sukibou was no longer taken to task by her daughter-in-law. She too wore clean saris with *chappals* on her feet. Her daughter-in-law did not mind taking care of her.

Money was no longer a constraint to buy books for Sukibou's grandson Haria. Life had become smooth for everyone. Poverty was getting eradicated slowly but steadily. Chemi could see a long road ahead of her. But she was not able to proceed further on that road. Lack of education proved a deterrent for her. A new moon rose again in her mind. She opened a school in her house. Nakhi was the first woman to enrol in the school. Nakhi persuaded all the elderly and old women to come to the school. Chemi explained to everyone that everyone did not take up a job after studying. There was no limit on the age at which a person should get educated. They should be able to write their names. They should learn how to keep accounts of the money they were spending. Everyone in the village had joined Chemi's programme. Chemi tried to show them the world through her own eyes. Chemi had turned into the toast of the village people.

Chemi wondered about how old she was. She was around fifteen or sixteen when she had come to Parsu's house. She might be twenty-two or twenty-three now at the most. She spoke to Ranka *Maastre*. She was going to prepare this year and appear at the matriculation examination the following year. Chemi's eyes were filled with dreams. She grew wings gradually and started flying around in her dreams. She lost her sleep. She got busy in studying day and night. The young daughter-in-law of the village who had been deserted by her husband. The girls and women of the village kept staring at her when she walked on the village street. They kept staring at Chemi when she got up on the veranda of the village school with a veil over her head. They eulogised her.

****

The Unparalleled

I ran into Sunita the other day at Connaught Place. She was wearing a pair of jeans, a t-shirt and a small Titan watch on the left wrist. Her right hand was bare. I was scared a great deal. The reason was that Sunita's marriage had been held twenty-two days after my marriage. It was not appreciated that the new daughter-in-law would go to attend her friend's marriage soon after stepping inside the house of her husband and that too by herself. My husband had not been invited to the marriage. Therefore, my in-laws had not permitted me to attend the marriage. I had heard later from other people that she had a very handsome and lively husband, just the opposite of Sunita. Sunita rarely smiled. When she found us rolling with laughter in our college days, it was obvious to see that she was not very pleased with us although she didn't say anything openly.

I had seen Sunita for the last time about twenty years ago in the marriage of Prannay Nayar who was doing post-graduation with us at Ravenshaw College. He had fallen in love with Mary Wright and married her. Mary was also one of our classmates. Prannay had to perhaps change his religion for the purpose. Sunita and I had married by that time. The marriage was held in a church during daytime. Mary looked really beautiful. She wore a white maxi with white stone settings and a gorgeously embroidered dress. Mary looked like a queen. As such she was quite glamorous. Prannay Nayar was just her opposite. He was most often dressed in a blue pant and white striped shirt. His smooth hair was always liberally oiled. There were several partings in his hair that ran zigzag like village roads. He had a thin moustache with very white teeth that looked very good on him. Both of them were doing their post-graduation in Psychology. Prannay was preparing for competitive examinations. We thought Sunita too liked Prannay as the latter too did not laugh unless it was absolutely necessary. It was difficult to know who wanted whom at what time.

But Prannay Nayar looked like a Greek king that day. He was wearing a white suit and red tie. His hairstyle had changed. He looked so handsome that I said in jest, "Mary, are you marrying Prannay's brother?" Everyone had laughed. Sunita's husband also arrived at this time. He was shaking hands with everyone with a smile on his face. Sunita was wearing a sari with matching bangles and *bindi.* She looked like the heroine of a novel although she was not very fair-complexioned. Our batch mates had a group photograph with their spouses. Sunita stood beside Prannay. I had stood beside Mary. My husband stood by my side. Sunita's husband was not present there. Prannay had sent me a copy of the photograph later. A drop of tear was visible in a corner of Sunita's eye as if she had found or lost something.

Twenty years had passed after that. I had gone away to New York with my husband. We had been able to get the green card there. I have been staying at Delhi now with my daughter since she has been studying at Delhi School of Economics. Time hangs heavy these days. I thought about my childhood days. I was reminded about the *golgappa* and *chat* vendors on the way. My friends in the college and the times that I had spent with them moved around me. I often stumbled against the moments that I had left behind when I recalled my childhood days. I had become mad with happiness on seeing Sunita after all these years. But she seemed to be indifferent. There was no change in her expression even though she was seeing me after such a long time. For a moment I wondered if she was someone else whose features looked like those of Sunita. But I had been stunned. The man who had accompanied her took the shopping bags from her hand and kept them on the back seat of the car. He got behind the steering wheel and held the other door of the car open for Sunita to get in. I had seen her from a distance. She was not looking at me. She had held a polythene shopping bag in her hand as she turned her back on me. I wondered if her world had completely changed in the past twenty years. Suddenly, I found myself calling out to her. She turned around to look at me. But she had not come to me. I had stared at the zigzag path that had stretched from the past to the present before her car vanished out of sight.

I decided to collect the telephone numbers of my old friends in Odisha that day on my return from the shopping centre. Then I went inside the kitchen to prepare dinner for my daughter. My mind was filled with the thoughts of the past.

My daughter said, "Mama, you have a letter. Daddy has redirected it from the U.S.A." Before the smell of boiled chicken poisoned my senses from inside the microwave oven, I asked her, "Who has sent the letter?" Holding the tray of food in my left hand, I tore open the letter with my teeth and the right hand. My daughter said, "What's the matter with you today, Mama? You look so upset!"

My daughter had stared at me in amazement as she took the tray from my hand and kept it on the dining table. I was reading the letter with my back to her. I was delighted on reading the letter. I had to go to Odisha within a day or two. Mary and Prannay, my classmates from the days when I was doing my M.A., were celebrating their twentieth marriage anniversary in Odisha. I had to go.

I had become quite emotional with the hope of meeting my old friends after such a long gap. My daughter had finished eating and left the dining table since long. I stood holding the railings of the window and was trying to see the game of hide and seek between light and darkness as far as I could see. I had been able to understand to some extent now why Sunita had pretended not to recognise me in order to hide herself. The past was flying before me page by page. Sunita, Mary, Prannay, Mugdha, Anuradha and Srimanta were studying in different departments. But Sunita's best friend Aniruddha was studying with me. He was somewhat abnormal. He followed me for hours together. He kept staring at me like a deranged man. But he had not been able to talk to me till we left the college.

I felt thrilled even after all these years when I thought about him. A narrow river seemed to be flowing silently beside a hill inside his silent stares. Was he in love with me in that case? My heart missed a beat. I turned around and saw that my daughter had switched off her computer and the light and stretched out on the bed after wishing me good night. She was a final year student at Delhi School of Economics. But I had never seen her emotions getting the better of her. How practical and materialistic she was! She had understood what was important in life in what measure. She had also tried to explain things to me at times. She would say, "Mama, you have studied so much. But you do not have a source of earning. You are a dependent wife. But I do not want a life like that."

I often wondered if it was really necessary for me to get married at the age of twenty-one. With the passage of time, I had lost the passion to have a separate identity for myself. It had perhaps been lost twenty years ago under the heap of ashes of family life. I could not recall my pin number when I used an A.T.M. to withdraw money. I felt embarrassed to remind my husband to deposit money in my account when the matter escaped his mind. Almost all my friends were working women. Sunita and I had not been able to do our M. Phil. because of our early marriage. I had no idea what she did later. All of us were in touch with each other for a few days. But we flew away like dry leaves with the passage of time. I became somewhat lazy when I settled down in the U.S.A. I could not know the distance between the past and the present with the world in my pocket. By the time I had slowed down, the grass forest of the past seemed like a soft and green lawn to me. The older I grew, the more I recalled my years when I had grown wings. I went to sleep that day. I booked my flight ticket the following day and came to Odisha after dropping my daughter with her friend in the hostel.

My city and the attraction of my land had turned me into a young woman once again. I removed my dress and wore a sari on reaching my younger brother's house. I was ecstatic in searching for Miss Barnali Mohanty of twenty years ago inside the mirror. Mary's anniversary party was scheduled for the following evening. I ran into Mary in the parlour. I did not know at the time that my classmate Mary was the owner of the famous Rosemary Parlour. She was still slim and beautiful like a young girl. Her lips quivered like a spring. But she seemed to have been carved out of a piece of rock. She had taken me to her room. She was completely formal about everything. I had come such a great distance on getting her invitation. But I did not think there was any sincerity in her demeanour. She was sitting on a chair. However, I was picking up sea shells from the beach without bothering about the tide rising inside her. I asked her, "What are you going to wear tomorrow, Mary? A dress or a sari? You seem not to have grown any older after marrying Prannay. You are looking so young." I got up and planted a light kiss on the dimple in her cheek. She stood up as if she had just woken up from sleep. Her beautiful, black eyes suddenly became solemn. She gave me a smile and said, "You too look the same as before. Perhaps you have put on a bit of weight. But you haven't grown much older too." Both of us laughed. But there was not much mirth in her laughter. It seemed to be cool like darkness. I took leave of Mary and went to the market to buy a gift for her. A huge tide rose inside me and breached the banks of my mind after I bought a good gift for Mary. I was certain that Sunita must have been invited to this celebration of the twentieth anniversary of Mary and Prannay. Mary's eyes made it clear that something had got stuck somewhere. Was it possible for a human being to change so much? Times kept on changing. Lectures may be given to others reassuring them about everything. But one had to look for a word of solace for herself.

My younger brother left me at the hotel before it was evening. Someone shouted from behind me, "Hello Barnali!" I turned around and looked. A handsome man wearing a white suit and white tie was wishing me. I said hello to him and was moving away when I retraced my steps. This man was wearing a full pant and a half pant of the same colour for months on end. The oil that he used on his hair saw him through for a week. I recalled the face of that boy. I opened the door again and looked behind me. Was that fellow Aniruddha? There was no one behind me. As I entered the hall, I thought I was in the conference hall or canteen of Ravenshaw College. A woman ran towards me at this time. I could not imagine that she could have been Sucharita. "Have you become so fat Suchi Aunty?" "Damn you! I have a thyroid problem. It's because of that. You look fine. Hasn't your husband come?" "No, he is in the U.S.A." Mugdha introduced me to her son. She had married late. Her son was quite young.

I was looking for Sunita. There were many familiar and unfamiliar faces. But everyone seemed like my own. Mugdha had introduced me to her husband. I had been startled on looking at the face of the man wearing a white suit. I blurted out, "Aniruddha, is that you?" Aniruddha had given a sweet and cool smile like the last touch of the spring. "Do you still remember me, Barnali?" Mugdha said, "You know, Barnali? I met him at New Delhi railway station one day eight years after joining D.M. College. After travelling together on the Rajdhani Express for two days, we decided to have one destination for both of us. The interesting part of it is that he proposed first to marry me. Before I could respond to him, he asked, 'Where is your friend Barnali, Mugdha?'"

The three of us laughed so loudly that Prannay, Mary and a few others ran to us. But Sunita had not come although she was standing about two metres away from us. Mary stood close to Prannay as on her wedding day. I had not looked at Prannay properly. Mary and Prannay stood close together. But I had a feeling that they looked in opposite directions. Everyone had a glass in his hand. We were taking soft drinks. A huge cake had been ordered.

Mary and Prannay had cut the cake. They fed a piece to each other. I cut the rest of the cake into small pieces and distributed it among our friends. Singing and dancing were in progress. But it seemed as if something was breaking into pieces somewhere nearby.

Mugdha whispered in my ears, "Do you know something? Prannay and Mary are no longer living together. They are here together today on Mary's request." "What do you mean?" I blurted out. Mugdha went on, "Mary's daughter is nineteen now. Prannay had agreed to marry in a church twenty years ago for Mary's sake. None of Prannay's relations had attended the marriage. At a later time, Mary had converted into Hinduism to make her parents-in-law happy and married Prannay according to the Vedic rites. You had left for America by that time. Mary had turned her life into a deserted beach in order to make Prannay her own. I met Mary once again two years later on the occasion of her daughter Rosy's birthday. Mary seemed to have turned into Meera. Her face was filled with happiness. But I learnt that day that her parents had severed all relations with her and had gone back to Kerala. Prannay is the only person who matters to her at the present time. But a huge rock now stands in between their conjugal life. She was unaware of it. She had not been able to free herself from the dreams that she saw about Prannay. She felt reassured after losing her identity inside Prannay. Mary had not been able to hear the sound of her family being destroyed as she was drawing the picture of a triangular, colourful life with Prannay and Rosy. Do you know, Barnali? Prannay and Sunita are now staying together at Delhi after a court marriage."

I recalled that I had met Sunita two days ago in Connaught Place. I had not been able to understand why she acted as if she didn't know me. But everything was falling into place now. I had not been able to say anything to Mugdha. Both of us felt shattered. At this time we turned around when someone's long sighs brushed against our napes. I was startled on seeing Mary so near us.

Mary looked at me with equanimity and said, "Barnali, age and experience made me into a wife from being a beloved and then a mother. I was Prannay's beloved one day. But he had not forced me to become his wife. Everyone has to pay a price for a particular time. He had treated my love with respect and given me the prestige of a wife. But I remained as his beloved. A beloved remains as a lamp for all time to come. Only the beloved has the right to burn for the man she cherishes. I had to flow like a river by the side of Prannay's mind." However, looking at a hint of revolt in Mugdha's eyes, Mary had lowered her eyes and looked at the ground beneath her feet. She continued, "I have a nineteen-year-old daughter. Therefore, I have been standing on the grave of this relationship and staring at the sky. I have not wanted that my daughter's future should float away in my tears. I have had to cover my superficial relationship with Prannay for years with coloured paper. The colour of the sunset had splashed across my world before I knew what this life was. I acted before Prannay as if I knew nothing although I knew everything. The bird of my happiness had flown away to another branch. But the nest still swayed in the breeze. I have been guarding over it all these years hoping that the bird might forget its way someday and return again."

I thought I was listening to a story on hearing Mary. Were there women today who could go on living carrying so much of grief in their chest? Mary seemed to have frozen into ice because of her unbearable grief. I found the huge injustice of Prannay to be unbearable. Mary placed her chilled hands on my inflamed hand and seemed to be consoling me, "Barnali, I still have faith that Prannay will someday return to my lonely life. How long can time keep him tied up? He will become exhausted as age catches up with him. He will recall the sweet memories of our love for each other and return to me. My daughter will again look at the sky resting her head on her Papa's chest after she completes her studies from London and returns. Is there another house that is bigger than the house of the mind?" Mary broke into a sob as she said this. I had held her in a tight embrace. Rainwater was dripping on my shoulders. I was getting drenched with Mary's grief. I said, "Really, Mary! You are not only a beloved. You are also not just a wife. You are unparalleled. You are unique." Prannay saw Mugdha who had moved away from me some time ago and asked her, "Mugdha, have you seen Mary?" Hearing Prannay's affectionate voice, Mary held me in an even tighter embrace as if the bird had sat down on that branch of her dream.

****

The Two Banks

Deepa came awake all of a sudden. She had no idea what time of the night it was. The calling bell of the adjacent flat was ringing constantly. She switched the bed lamp on and looked at the clock. Who was ringing the bell in this manner at two in the morning? Wasn't there anyone at Mohanty Babu's house? She stood up. She was able to hear the continuous sound of the calling bell as she bent down to retrieve her *chappals* from under the bed. She was forced to wake Rajesh up, "Do you hear me? The calling bell of Mohanty Babu has been ringing for the past fifteen minutes. No one is opening it." Rajesh woke up from deep slumber. The fear and excessive anxiety in Deepa's eyes forced him to sit up on bed. But he said in an irritated voice, "What's the matter? Their bell is ringing. Won't they get up? Why do you have to worry about everything? You won't sleep yourself and you don't allow me to sleep either. Times are bad. There could be a thief or dacoit at the door. It is wise not to open it. Mohanty Babu is perhaps not opening the door deliberately." Deepa continued to look worried. But she persisted, "Can't you imagine how anxious the caller seems to be. He has been ringing the bell nonstop." "Deepa, listen to me. Do not invite trouble." Deepa said, "Do something. Give a ring to Mohanty Babu." Rajesh checked the number from the telephone book and dialled the phone. The irritated voice of Mrs. Mohanty could be heard after a while, "Hello!" "Madam, someone has been ringing your bell for a long time." "All right," said Mrs. Mohanty and disconnected the line. Rajesh switched off the bed lamp and literally forced Deepa to go back to sleep. Deepa said, "Oh! What a selfish man you are, Rajesh. Listen to me. Don't fall asleep." Deepa was trying to shake Rajesh. Rajesh said, "Go back to sleep, Deepa. They will telephone us if there is any trouble." Rajesh turned on his side and went back to sleep. Deepa didn't realise in her absentmindedness that Rajesh was virtually forcing her to go back to sleep. She lay on the bed for some time with her eyes open and ears pricked.

She was not aware when she had fallen asleep. It was morning by the time she got up. The sun god had eradicated darkness and stared at Mother Earth just like a chick stared out from inside a nest. Deepa got up. Half of her work was over once she prepared her son for school. She finished her daily chores and *puja* before waking Rajesh up. The two of them had tea together. Deepa stood against the railings of the balcony with the sun at her back. Rajesh sat on a chair in front of her facing the sky. He read her the interesting news of the day from the newspaper. His eyes were riveted on a familiar face in the newspaper as he sipped his tea. He brought the newspaper closer to his face. He read the news item from one end to the other and glanced at Deepa's face carefully. Deepa seemed to be dreaming and lost in thought at the same time. She was always like that. She prided herself on her capacity to solve every problem under the sun. Rajesh knew that Deepa will come at him with all guns blazing for his imprudence after going through this news item. He knew that Deepa read the newspaper every day from one end to the other after he left for the office. He understood the gravity of the situation and asked her in a rather placating voice, "Deepa, what am I going to eat today?" Deepa was surprised. But she broke into a smile and said, "Why, I have already made rice, *dal* and vegetable curry. Only the fish needs to be fried." Rajesh folded that portion of the newspaper carefully and moved closer to Deepa. Going against his nature, he arranged her hair that was flying around and pulled her to him. "Have you gone out of your mind? This is the balcony of the flat, not the bedroom," said Deepa in mock anger and ran inside the house. Rajesh wanted some time to himself. He threw the folded portion of the newspaper to the ground and felt relieved. All kinds of thoughts were entering his mind. He decided to skip office that day and find the truth behind the matter. He wondered if he should ask Mrs. Mohanty about the last night. But his day would be certainly spoiled if he saw her rude face early in the morning. Oh! What a harridan! He felt pity for Mr. Mohanty. He had no idea how he spent his days with her. Deepa came running at this time and said, "Do you hear me? Our maid says that a guest has come to Mr. Mohanty's house last night." "How does it matter to you?" Rajesh felt irritated. "Serve food for me. It's time for the office." Deepa said, "I am not bothered about it. But Mrs. Mohanty just came and told me to ask the maid not to go to her house today. I was about to ask her about last night. But she hurried away as if she had not heard me." "Why do you poke your nose into their affairs?" said Rajesh. Deepa broke into a sob, "Don't they mean anything to us? My sister has married Mrs. Mohanty's brother. How can we ignore them?" Rajesh put on his thinking cap once again. He realised that he should leave home as quickly as possible. He said, "I am going for my bath. Get my clothes out of the cupboard." He entered the bathroom.

A small album fell on the floor when Deepa took out Rajesh's pant and shirt from the cupboard. She opened the album in an absentminded way. She had herself approved of this step of Rupa although it was very difficult to face the realities of life. Rupa was her younger sister. Her mother's world revolved around Deepa, Rupa, their younger brother and grandmother. Father had deserted them since a long time. She did not think about him any longer. She could only see her mother's sad eyes. She loved her mother a great deal. She had kept her mother's photograph in her bedroom in spite of Rajesh's opposition. He had never protested. But he said at times that the wall would have looked much better with their family photograph hanging on it. Deepa had hung three single photographs of Rajesh, their son and hers on the wall. Rajesh had become quiet after that as if he had appropriated his emotions. He believed that no husband ever deserted his wife without a valid reason. But she could never explain to him why her father had deserted her mother. She had always requested him not to raise the matter ever again.

Rajesh had fallen in love with Deepa and married her. It was Rajesh who had proposed to Deepa. He was a computer instructor where Deepa was taking coaching in computers before he completed M.B.A. and joined a company. He had liked Deepa at first sight. She was conservatively dressed and spoke little. They became acquainted with each other which later led to intimacy. But Deepa had refused the offer of marriage in the beginning. Two years passed after that. Rajesh was still in touch with Deepa. He found a good job after completing M.B.A. He thought Deepa should agree with his proposal now. But Rupa had certain conditions for marriage just as there were limits in their friendship. Rajesh was willing to agree to all the conditions in order to marry Deepa. But Rajesh could not compromise with the fact that her father had deserted her mother. He tried to explain it to Deepa clearly that women are deprived of their husband's love and affection because of their ego and arrogance. But all his efforts in this regard had failed and Deepa had her own views in the matter. They were married now for ten years. Therefore, Rajesh had accepted the fact that surrendering to one's wife was the best way to lead a happily married life. He had been content to hand over the reins of his family in the hands of a cultured woman like Deepa. She was soft-spoken, thrifty and conservative in nature. She didn't indulge in idle talk with her neighbours or friends. In a way, theirs was a happy family. Deepa never broke down under any circumstance. But she had been devastated when Rupa didn't return from college one day till late in the evening. She requested Rajesh to allow Rupa to live with them till she finished college.

Rupa had not returned till now and Rajesh too had gone out of town on a tour. Who could she ask about her? Should she telephone her mother? She had never stayed away for such a long time earlier. There was one other room apart from her bedroom. There were two beds in that room. Rupa and Deepa's son Gudul slept there. Toys and books lay here and there in the room. Where would she look for the reason of Rupa's absence from this devastated area? She rummaged through Rupa's books, bed, clothes, everything. Evening had passed and it was night in the meantime. She had been forced to telephone her mother who lived in the same town. She said, "Maa, send Rupa back to my house quickly. Rajesh is not at home. I feel lonely." Her mother was crying loudly. She could very well hear the sound made by her broken heart. But she could not understand why the door that had been closed for years in her mother's mind had opened all of a sudden. Her mother had told her softly, "Deepa, Rupa has run away with the brother of Mrs. Mohanty, your next door neighbour." She had come to know about it only a while ago. Deepa could not believe it. How could Rupa choose a loafer and alcoholic like Saugat who had such a loose character? Had she gone of her own accord or had Saugat kidnapped her? Deepa had been sitting like a zombie throughout the night. Why didn't the morning come sooner? She had dozed off towards the morning when the telephone rang. Rupa was on the line, "Forgive me, *Apa* (elder sister). I love Saugat. You will see I will make him mend his ways. I need your blessings." Deepa asked her where she was. She said, "When did you become close to Saugat? Rupa, there is still time. Come back home. Time never runs out during the course of a night. But the dream will be over before the night comes to an end. Come back! Listen to your *Apa*. You have no idea, Rupa. This is a cruel world. You will be exhausted in the process of stepping on thorns. No one will sympathise with you when you would be repenting. There would only be darkness everywhere." Deepa did not know when Rupa had disconnected the telephone. She had kept no relation with Mrs. Mohanty for a few days after that. She didn't even wish her when they ran into each other. Rajesh too did not lose this opportunity to take a dig at her, "Your mother was innocent then and your father was responsible for everything. Rupa is not to be blamed here too. Saugat would have taken her away after giving her a chocolate." The *Sravan* sky was overcast. Tears were dripping on the unforgettable memories of the album. The two sisters Deepa and Rupa were sitting with their hands on their mother's shoulders. Younger brother

Dwipankar was kneeling at mother's feet. There was a smile on Maa's lips. But the eyes looked sad like a dry cloud had hung in the sky.

She did not know when Rajesh had left for the office. She did not even know whether he had eaten or not. Rupa's shining face looked tenderly from the memories of the past that had been covered with layers of dust. Perhaps she was looking forward to receive some affection from her elder sister. Her mind was in a churn today. It was two years since Rupa had left home. She used to telephone once in a while in the beginning. But she had gradually stopped keeping in touch. Deepa too was gradually forgetting about Rupa's folly. But she never felt like asking Mrs. Mohanty about Saugat. She might give her a piece of her mind to her. Therefore, she never raised the matter before her. But she could not also sever her relationship with her as her darling sister had married Mrs. Mohanty's brother. She was constantly thinking about Rupa that day. She could hear her calling out to her. The fragrance of her body still lingered in their house. Her maid finished her work and asked Deepa to close the door behind her. Why did Mrs. Mohanty ask the maid not to come to their house today? Should she go to Mrs. Mohanty and ask her about the person ringing her bell at the dead of night? Deepa stood up. Her calling bell was ringing. She ran to the door. Rajesh had perhaps not eaten while leaving for the office. Had he come back home? The maid stood on the other side of the door. She held a newspaper in her hand that had been folded. She said, "Maa, This lay just below your balcony. Sir was reading the paper in the morning sitting there. I thought it must have fallen down. Therefore, I brought it here." Deepa smiled and said, "Just press their calling bell."

Mrs. Mohanty opened the door slightly on hearing

the bell and asked who was there. She was startled all of a sudden on seeing Deepa. As she was about to close the door, Deepa smiled at her and asked, "Who had come to your house at the dead of night yesterday?" Mrs. Mohanty looked at the paper in her hand and then at her face. She slammed the door shut without saying a word. She never acted that way earlier. Deepa felt humiliated. She closed her front door and came inside the house. Irritated, she took out bread and butter from the freeze and ate a slice. She spread the newspaper before her to read it. She was suddenly startled as if she had seen a ghost. Whose photograph was this? The girl was very thin and emaciated. The bones on her body could be counted. But the eyes shone exactly like those of Rupa. But no! She was just a beggar woman. She wore a tattered sari. The blouse was torn at several places. She was exposed. Why should this be Rupa? She read the news under the photograph breathlessly. It was an advertisement given by the lady manager of a short stay home. "This girl is around twenty to twenty-two. Her height is five feet four inches. She looks like a married woman. There are numerous wound marks all over her body. She has almost lost her speech. She has taken shelter at this place for the past ten days. If any of her relations want to take her with them, they should provide suitable proof to the authorities and take her."

Deepa's eyes were filled with tears. This was certainly Rupa. The dreams of the entire world seemed to be still visible in her eyes. "Oh no! Rupa!" cried Deepa. Her eyes were raining fire. She got up and banged loudly on Mrs. Mohanty's door. She opened the door. She shouted at Deepa, "Do you disturb gentlemen in such an uncivilised manner?" "Who is a gentleman here? You or that depraved brother of yours? Who is a gentleman? That eunuch of a husband of yours who has been providing a cover for your brother's sins?" Deepa opened the newspaper before her face. She roared, "Whose photograph is this?" The ghost-like picture of Rupa stared back from the newspaper.

Mrs. Mohanty glanced at the newspaper and acted as if she had completely lost her temper. She said, "Have you gone out of your mind? Whose photograph is that? And to whom are you showing it?" Mr. Mohanty came outside on hearing the noise. Someone else appeared after him for a moment like a thief and disappeared. Deepa realised immediately that he was none other than Saugat. She returned to her own house. She threatened Mrs. Mohanty before leaving, "The police will ask you for an explanation. You have to tell them whose photograph this is and who is responsible for her state." The fan was whirring at a great speed over her head. But she was drenched in sweat. The sad face of Rupa danced before her eyes. How could people stoop so low? The uncovered body of Rupa was clearly visible from under her tattered sari. Everyone must have seen it. People would have turned over the pages of her body to read the news. Her so-called lover and husband Saugat had chopped her into mincemeat. Two years had passed in the meantime. She had kept no relation with Rupa because of her anguish. God only knew since when she had been suffering this. She never uttered Saugat's name out of loathing for him. She looked once again at Rupa's photograph in the newspaper. She had been staring ahead with uncomprehending eyes. She seemed to be looking for a way out, a way to live. She caressed Rupa's body in the photograph. What would she do? Should she wait for Rajesh? Or should she herself go to that short stay home? One of the members of the Mahila Commission was studying with her in college. Should she approach her or should she lodge an F.I.R. against Saugat? Deepa could not come to a decision.

There was a hurdle like the insurmountable Himalayas before her. Rajesh loved her a great deal. But she was not certain how much support she would get from him for the step she was planning to take. She felt somewhat small before Rajesh on account of her mother. What was she going to do now? She looked at Rupa once again. Her beautiful face had been somewhat twisted in the crumpled newspaper. The old days were floating before her like pictures. She thought about Maa's helplessness when her younger sister went to the college after caressing her. She could hear her cry of distress from under the huge burden she carried. Rupa resembled their mother a great deal. That was perhaps the reason why both of them suffered the same fate in life. She could not watch her sister going into pieces before her eyes. She would bring her to her place. She would make her whole once again. She would fill her with confidence to face the world. Rupa was her younger sister. There was no meaning of relationships in this mechanical world if she did not stand beside her in her misfortune. She wondered if she should telephone Maa. Wouldn't she have gone through today's newspaper till now? Or had she not been able to realise that the picture in the photograph belonged to her daughter? Was there any relationship that was holier than the relationship with mother, daughter, sister, husband and wife? Rupa and she slept on the same bed before she got married to Rajesh. Rupa had all kinds of complaints against Deepa throughout the day. She didn't permit her to touch anything that belonged to her. But she slept beside *Apa* in the night. Their younger brother slept beside Maa. Rupa was as fickle as she was level-headed.

Deepa was often scared to look at her body that was filling up and her eyes that resembled blue lilies.

There was only the difference of the season of *Sravan* between the eyes of Maa and Rupa. Maa's eyes were always filled with tears while Rupa carried a world of dreams in her eyes. Therefore, she had kept Rupa beside her after her marriage. Deepa had thought that she would never allow Rupa to move away from before her eyes. But she had not been able to know when she had separated from her life. How could she even think that a beautiful girl like Rupa would fall in love with an uneducated, ugly-looking hooligan like Saugat? She was now able to recall the headaches that Mrs. Mohanty used to have in the afternoons and how she asked Rupa to visit her at odd hours. When father started distancing himself physically from Maa, she had perhaps not been able to understand the reality of that strange truth. Maa's younger sister (Deepa's aunt) used to live in their house like Rupa and studied under Maa's supervision. Their father had left behind his three growing children, his seventy-year-old mother and his young wife in order to set up home with her. Father had not allowed Maa to think or do anything in the matter. Two people had removed the light from the sky of their mother's life. One of them was her blood relation and the other was the father of her children. Could she have taken either of them to task? She was wounded all over and had bled profusely. But she had ensured the survival of the ten-year-old Deepa, the six-year-old Rupa and the young son who was still not able to talk properly. Grandma had lent support to Maa. She had pressed Maa to her chest and cried a great deal. They did not have a roof over their head or ground under their feet. Maa would be around thirty-two or thirty-three at the time. No relation of father or Maa had visited their house since that day. Maa gave private tuition to young children. She took up sewing as a profession. But she had taught her children to live with honour. She herself had lived likewise. She had not trusted any friend or relation after that. She knew that father was never coming back again. She kept on burning even after banishing all her hopes. The children had grown up before Maa was completely burned out. But there was perhaps a gap somewhere between her self-confidence and firm determination. Therefore, Maa would be once again shattered on hearing this sad news about Rupa.

Only God knew how the afternoon had passed. She was getting angry with Rajesh. He had never tried to understand her. He had only asserted his rights over her mind and body. Deepa had stared outside gripping the railings of the window in her hands. The sad face and the devastated body of Rupa floated before her eyes. She had perhaps neglected Rupa as she was constantly busy with Gudul. What was the difference between a grown-up girl and a river in spate? Saugat entered their life finding a gap between her affection and duty. What would Rajesh think when he comes to know everything? He was going to laugh at her. There were tears of helplessness in her eyes.

The wall clock struck three. She got up and changed. She looked at herself in the mirror. Her self-confidence was her only resource. She took out some money from the cupboard and kept it in her purse. She might need it. No! She decided that she would go by herself. She could not waste any more time waiting for Rajesh. She locked the house and got down. She would have given the keys to Mrs. Mohanty on another day as Rajesh was likely to come back anytime. But she decided to leave the keys at the gate. Mrs. Mohanty's brother Saugat was getting up the stairs. The kidnapper of her Rupa! A beautiful girl hung on his arms. She was perhaps as old as Rupa. A cigarette hung from Saugat's lips. And his face was creased in a smile as if he did not have a care in the world. That smile was unbearable for Deepa. She flew into a rage. But she pulled herself together and didn't say anything to Saugat. She looked at the girl hanging from his arms in disgust and shouted, "Don't you have eyes? Don't you have any tastes either? The lepers begging in front of Chandi Temple are better than this scoundrel. They do not have fingers and feet. But they have a heart. They will pray to Maa Chandi for you after taking a coin from you." The girl held on to Saugat even more tightly. Mrs. Mohanty came outside on hearing the noise. She asked her brother affectionately, "What's the matter?" Deepa turned towards Mrs. Mohanty and said, "Which short stay home have you arranged for this girl, madam? Before how many people are you going to fold your hands for your brother? It is better for you to open a short stay home yourself. Your daughter is already eighteen. She must also have found a broker like Saugat by this time. Listen to me! Rupa has a sister like me who can join the broken pieces of her body and mind and build a new image. But even God has to leave the heaven and descend down to serve you if someone has a sister like you."

Rajesh was getting up the stairs. There was a plain land before Deepa's eyes where she could see green grass, a blue river and a fragrant garden. Rajesh was her husband whom she loved more than her life. But she did not trust him. All her complaints against him seemed to be going up towards the sky as blue clouds. Her tears were likely to turn into the Ganges. Mrs. Mohanty pulled that girl towards her. But Rajesh had not allowed Saugat to walk up the staircase. He held him by his hair and turned him around. Saugat had perhaps not expected anything like it to happen. Rajesh had brought Rupa before him before he could react in any manner. He said, "Can you recognise her? Who is responsible for her situation?" Rupa was not able to stand properly. She had to seek the support of Rajesh in order to raise her head upwards. There were deep wounds below her eyes. Her swollen lips and her wounded feet described how she had suffered. As Saugat tried to flee, Deepa could hear the clanging sound of a handcuff in the hands of a police inspector. Deepa had been transported to a world of dreams on hearing that sound. She could not believe her eyes. Saugat had been arrested on the basis of the complaint lodged by Rupa. The other girl looked sadly at Rupa for a while before taking off her sandal and hitting Saugat on his cheeks with it. She vanished from the scene soon afterwards. Mrs. Mohanty's face was burning like fire with anger and humiliation.

Rajesh contacted a prominent doctor for Rupa's treatment. Rupa was sleeping on her bed as before. Deepa stood beside her lustreless body. She caressed her on the head and said, "You will be fine in a few days. Do not have any fears. Go to sleep. The results are likely to be terrible when girls of your age jump into fire to achieve their dreams and do not bother about the society or the family. You must have understood it by this time." Standing before Rupa, Rajesh said to Deepa, "You too are to be blamed in this matter. You did not allow me to talk to Rupa because your father had an illegitimate relationship with your mother's younger sister. I had tried to reason with you several times. But you could not free yourself from the prison of your mind. Therefore, I had become indifferent towards your family. You had seen the world with your father's eyes. Therefore, you could not trust me although you loved me. And the results are before you. Saugat will certainly be punished. But will it bring an end to the sins committed by men like Saugat? Girls like Rupa invite such trouble on themselves because they are weak-willed. Deepa! You are a writer. You write for the society. Show a lamp to such imprudent girls who are ignorant although they are educated, those who are ever ready to succumb to the unrestrained ways of the youth without being aware of their consequences. Your Rajesh will remain yours forever." Deepa smiled silently. Tears were no longer streaming down from her eyes. Instead, there was trust and love in those eyes. She had been looking at both the banks. Towards the eyes of her mother that resembled an overflowing river and towards the huge heart of Rajesh that resembled a still and motionless river.

****

When Life Speaks

The bride and the groom were receiving gifts standing on the impeccably decorated stage lit by bright lights. The bride was smiling at the groom while their photographs were being taken with the guests. They were very close to me. The mother of the groom studied in my lower batch and the girl was my student. I was known to both the sides. The people of the family had gathered around me on seeing me. I was gradually forgetting the untoward incident that had taken place a while ago.

There was light grass on the lawn. The open space was quite pleasant as a cool breeze was blowing. I didn't feel like eating in the least. On the contrary, I had a great desire to meet my old friends after a long time. But the aunt of the groom who was my erstwhile colleague embraced me on seeing me and pushed me into a chair. She said, "Madhumita, sit here. Let me get some starters. We will eat together." The vegetable and non-vegetable starters had been kept on one side. The stalls of the main courses had been arranged at a different place. The names of the items had been placed before each stall. A girl placed two plates of *paneer pakoras* and a vegetable soup before me. Extending a paper napkin towards me, she said, "Madam will be here shortly. You can go ahead." I thanked the girl and wanted to know her identity. But I could hear a noise at some distance at this time. My eyes moved to a place where a nauseating experience was waiting for me. I had just taken one sip of the hot soup. I could hear someone shouting from among the crowd, "Who are you? Who has invited you? These rascals are barging in as if they own the place. Hand him over to the police." The blue shirt that a man wore seemed to be beckoning to me. I stopped sipping the soup and walked to the crowded place. The crowd was just in front of the chicken counter. I could not see that man. But he was saying, "I have come here with two ladies." But who were the ladies? They should have some name!

Someone had snatched the plate from out of his hand. Someone else was trying to push him from behind. But the man had stared at the chicken pieces on his plate. Before reaching the man, I shouted, "What's going on here?" The gentleman tried to calm down on seeing me. He said, "Madam, the food costs us four to five hundred rupees a plate. Many outsiders are picking up plates masquerading as guests." "So what? You should have written on the invitation card that plates will be handed over to you only if you hang the invitation card around your necks. How unfortunate!" I was looking at the man. He had retrieved his plate and was pushing the chicken pieces to the centre of the plate for fear that they would fall down. He was also trying to hide his shame as if he did not know anything about the incident that had taken place a while ago. The so-called gentlemen apologised to me and moved away with a smile. But I was feeling dejected. That man too was worried. But he tried to act normally and turned his back on me. Looking at him, I prayed to God, "O God! Why do you make human beings so helpless? You have already given what you had to give everyone. But do not make man so helpless as this helplessness is the reason of all weaknesses." The man was pretending not to have seen me when I moved in front of him. I felt my heart choking when I laid my eyes on him. I did not know if it was out of anger or grief.

I extended my hand to take the plate from his hand. He said, "Madam, so many people are eating here. They are wasting more food than they are eating. The dustbins are full of leftover food. But you want to take the plate from my hand ...." He had not been able to say anything more. My eyes had become so hazy that I could only guess his presence from his voice. I felt bad to take off my glasses and polish them. I didn't know what to tell him. I told him, "Get anything you want to eat from the stalls. If anyone objects, tell them that you have come with me." He looked at me like the last devotee in a temple before the doors are closed. He was trying to wipe away the helplessness dripping from his eyes with his dirty handkerchief.

Man has an unassailable desire to live. If a choice had to be made between living and dying, man won't balk at doing anything to go on living. Did that mean that man was alive only to eat? The man had not moved his gaze from the plate to look at me once even after such humiliation. On the contrary, he was trying to save the chicken pieces on his plate the moment the situation was becoming somewhat normal. He didn't bother about the way he had been ill-treated. He looked more confident of himself now. But still he could not muster enough courage to collect the food from the stalls. He looked over his shoulders as he went towards the stalls. He was taking much more from each item than he could reasonably eat. I felt irritated. Was he a human being or an animal?

I came back and sat on a chair. A stand fan was moving near me. I relaxed for a while and looked around for my son. The lawn was getting full with people. That man came out of the crowd and put his plate on the table in front of me. When I stood up with my mobile and purse, he said again, "Madam, how can I carry all this home?" I was even more startled. Give these people an inch and they would like to take a yard. I said in irritation, "Is this my house that I will arrange a packet of food for your home? Considering the circumstances, you should have left immediately after eating." I had said so in a controlled voice. He said hurriedly, "Madam, my two children have been pestering me since a long time to get some food from a grand feast. I have planning since long to come to a feast like this one."

I slumped back into my chair. I thought I had read somewhere that truth was the only shape of truth. Truth had no meaning or alternative. The biggest truth of life was to live. Man never hesitates to stoop as low as possible in order to keep someone alive. And if that man is a father! Oh! Could living be as painful as this?

My son had parked the car on the extreme left hand side of the road. Therefore, I had difficulty in getting down on the left side. My son stepped out of the car on the right side. As I tried to follow him and come out of the car on the right side, an auto rickshaw came and braked hard near my feet. My feet would have been under its wheel if I had not removed them in a hurry. My son tried to stop that auto driver. But he was in a hurry to reach the marriage venue along with the passengers who had accompanied him. I had come out of the car with a great deal of difficulty. A few people had stared at me in amazement. But I had looked at the blue shirt of the auto driver who was running inside.

I said as if I had recalled it just then, "You are the auto rickshaw driver, aren't you?" He was quiet for a moment before he said, "No, madam. I am a rickshaw puller." I said that I had seen him while parking his auto rickshaw. I felt disgusted once again. He could realise on looking at my face that I was not going to trust him any longer. She dropped the 'madam' and addressed me as 'Maa'. He said, "Maa, I am acquainted with a few auto rickshaw drivers while keeping my rickshaw in the stand. I have learnt driving an auto rickshaw from them. Could I have come to a feast like this driving a rickshaw? I have been planning to come to one such feast for a long time. The two women who had accompanied me are also poor people. They work as maidservants. They told me that I could get ironed clothes on hire from a laundry. I thought that my problem would be solved if I could only get an auto rickshaw on hire. Those women came with me in the auto rickshaw. They would have finished eating and left this place long since. But my misfortune has been following me. These people already know that I am neither an invitee nor someone's driver. I am able to know today that living with honour is much more important than going through the motions of living. I am prepared to face any kind of hardship for my children. You saved me from acute embarrassment at this place today. But it might happen again someday in the future. Mothers like you are not going to materialise everywhere to save me. Let us go, Maa. I need nothing. I will follow you and leave this place. This place is worse than hell. The fragrance of humanity has been lost in the aroma of chicken and mutton here." I had become silent. People had to live in this manner too.

I asked him to wait for me and went to my erstwhile colleague, the aunt of the bridegroom. I told her without any reservations, "I don't feel like eating anything right now. Can you pack a little bit from each item and give it to me? I would like to have the dinner at home." She looked at me happily and assured me that she would take care of the matter. She sent about fifteen to twenty packets to my car and came till the gate to see me off. The man wearing the blue shirt was walking behind me. I didn't know his name. Nor did I have any inclination to know it. My son looked at me and that man in turn and was about to say something. I indicated to him to keep quiet. Our host and his family members were somewhat embarrassed when they found the man wearing the blue shirt following me. But the man had stared behind him at the overloaded plate he had left behind and the dogs that were happily eating everything with their heads inside the dustbins. His eyes betrayed the suffering he experienced.

My son started the car. I could see that he was in an irritated mood. He pushed the accelerator the moment I sat on my seat absentmindedly. I turned around a few moments later to keep my purse on the back seat. I was startled when I did so. I shouted at my son, "Please stop the car. For Heaven's sake!" My son brought the car to a stop and asked me if I had left something behind. I said, "Turn the car around. I lost my face. But his family would go hungry. I asked for those food packets for him. But ...." There was a vacuum inside my chest. On my return, I found that the auto rickshaw was no longer there. I was feeling helpless. The crowd had thinned by this time. A few drivers were chatting among themselves near their cars. But there was no auto rickshaw and no one wore a blue shirt there. My son went looking for him and returned to say that no one had seen him. My son could see my heart breaking into pieces. He stood beside me leaning against the car. He was searching for words to console me. I thought about the man. How miserable was his fatherhood! He had stooped so low for his children. But still he stood there mustering enough courage. He would certainly have carried away some food home on the sly. But I would not have got another chance to show my magnanimity. I had become still. What would his children have said to him on seeing him empty-handed? His wife would have turned her head away in disgust. He himself had not eaten a piece of chicken in spite of all his humiliation. He had put up with everything with the certain knowledge that he was going to carry good food home.

Tears started flowing down from my eyes. My son took a last look around him and started the car. But I was feeling his existence somewhere near me inside the darkness and light. I was earnestly praying to God to come to my aid. That moment changed the path of my life. The long wall of my education, ideals and commitments was about to crumble. I could see his blue shirt before me like a tattered sari left behind by someone on a cyclone-ravaged house. I closed the car door with a broken heart. Someone seemed to be chasing me and saying, "Maa! Where are you going away carrying the food for my children?" I was trying one last time to control my grief. I began praying, "God! Are you really there? Can't you see my helplessness?"

He had stared vacantly leaning against the electric pole on the first turn. The huge rock of regret that lay on my mind felt as light as a leaf on seeing his blue shirt so near me.

He was moving away from before my eyes. His blue shirt looked like the moon and the food packets hanging from his hands seemed like stars to me.

****

The Last Bouquet

The number of onlookers was gradually on the increase at the marketplace. A long row of human heads had stretched ahead by the side of a number of cars, rickshaws, bicycle riders, etc. The last mantra of life *Ram naam satya hai* was being lost in the noise made by the vehicles like the murmurings of rain inside the noise of thunder. It was still not quite dark in the evening. But someone had passed away.

The flower shop of Sapana, the *mali*, was at the turn of the street. Flower garlands of different colours hung all around his shop like fragrant garlands hanging around the bed on a wedding night. He sat inside the shop on a mat. There was a flat basket for flowers, a large needle and some old newspapers near him. A bundle of thread rolled around him like his wheel of fate. His shop was open from six in the morning till nine in the evening. He loved his flowers and his cabin. He also loved the sixty watt bulb burning dimly in his shop when it was dark. He kept on humming under his breath as he strung the flowers. He made bouquets. He kept the loose flowers in a way that showed that he had an aesthetic sense. He sprinkled water on the flowers at intervals. He had his food in the shop. He took a nap there in the hot afternoon when customers were not there. He wound up his business at nine in the evening and went home. He had only an old grandmother at home. She kept waiting for him till his return. He was often late in returning home in the marriage season. At times, the entire night passed in decorating a car. He often extended credit to his regular customers. He had no objection to that. *Rajanigandha* garlands were in demand on auspicious occasions. People took wild flowers and marigolds for inauspicious occasions. His flowers were in great demand at the time of Ganesh Puja and Saraswati Puja. He gave a rebate to the children. They were going to study. The gods will make them learned only if they offered them flowers. He had no resources when he was a child. His father was dead long since. Mother too passed away last year. Only his grandmother had been left behind.

He kept moving from one shop to another for about ten to fifteen years before that gentleman arranged a cabin for him at this place. But it was at the turn on the street. The gentleman bought flowers from him almost twenty days in a month. He purchased garlands or bouquets from him. Sapana did not dare ask him about the job he did. How could he spend so much money on flowers? He had often seen the gentleman's photograph in the old newspapers he purchased for his shop. He was among the people who garlanded an image on certain occasions. He laid wreaths at the feet of dead men. He held garlands made in his shop in his hand on such occasions. Sapana felt overjoyed. He called the boys working in nearby shops and showed them the photographs. "Look, this garland is from my shop," he boasted. He did not know who the gentleman was. But he was his biggest customer. The important thing about him was that he paid cash for everything. He never asked for credit. Therefore, Sapana always gave him a discount. He looked different to Sapana clad in a dhoti, a *panjabi* and a jacket. A flicker of a smile could always be seen on his face.

There was a rush in front of his shop one morning. The gentleman got down from a rickshaw. Sapana pushed aside everyone else and wished him with folded hands. He asked humbly, "You are quite early today."

"Sapana, my boy! My daughter's marriage has been fixed. You have half the responsibilities. You will decorate the car and the altar. You have to go to the bridegroom's house too. I have not seen another honest man like you in my sixty years on earth." Sapana felt elated. The gentleman likes a non-entity like him so much. He trusts him so much. But he didn't even know the name of the gentleman. He used to steal flowers from some people's houses a few years ago and sold them on the sly. He used the few rupees he got to buy some biscuits or a *chat* for him. He had carried away a great deal of jasmines one day. He strung them into a garland and stood at the street crossing to sell it. No one bought it from him although he kept shouting at the top of his lungs. He had lost his patience when he had to reduce the price from five rupees to fifty paise. Sapana felt terrible when he recalled that day. It was almost ten in the evening. He wondered if he should go back home. A gentleman got down beside him from a rickshaw. He bought two packets of incense sticks from the nearby shop. He carried a matchbox from another shop and got up on the rickshaw. Sapana ran to the rickshaw in despair. "Sir, Sir! Take this garland of jasmine. It is worth five rupees. You can have it for two rupees. I have been standing here for the past three hours." He could hear people chanting *Ram nam satya hai, Hari nam satya hai* from a distance. The procession came closer. Sapana could see the dead body. He had held on to the rickshaw like a dying patient grabbing the hands of the doctor.

The gentleman got down from the rickshaw suddenly. He took the wilting garland from his hand and placed it on the dead body of the unknown woman. Sapana's hands folded automatically. Was it meant for the dead woman or for the gentleman who had provided him with the food for the night? The procession had moved away from them. The gentleman gave him a five-rupee note. He asked, "What is your name? Are you a *mali* by caste? Why don't you open a flower shop in that case?" He had already sat on the rickshaw by that time. He kept the things he had purchased on the rickshaw carefully and said, "Wait for me at this place at nine in the morning tomorrow. We will work out something for you." He went away after that. But he planted the saplings of flower plants in Sapana's mind. He has been stringing garlands of jasmines, marigolds and roses for the past five years since that day. He supplied flowers when people married and when they died. He was earning enough money for his family. His grandmother was very happy with him. She also blessed the old gentleman. Sapana was hesitant in the beginning. But he took the plunge one day and asked him, "Sir, you are a very decent human being. I have been thinking of asking you something since long. But I have been afraid that you might take offense at my words. I understand it very well that one does not take liberties with his regular customers. Sir, how many sons have you got?"

There were no customers at the shop. Fragments of flowers had been strewn around the mat in the shop. Sapana cleaned the space and requested the gentleman to be seated. The gentleman took out a *paan* from his shining *paan* box and put it inside the mouth before sitting down. He looked very sad. Sapana was cursing himself. The gentleman had felt anguished by the question. He could have saved the question for another day. With his face enveloped in sadness, he said, "Do you know why God created human beings?" Sapana kept looking at him with a question mark on his face. He addressed him as 'Sir' looking at the way he was attired. He didn't know his name. He had also never bothered about it. A dog slept under the cabin and was whining. The gentleman lifted his legs up carefully. He said, "Sapana, look at this dog lying under the cabin. My leg was hanging over its head. It would have certainly bitten me if my leg would have touched its head. Do you know why? It's an animal. Does it have a conscience? Still God has created many animals, birds, insects, etc. Do you know what is the greatest in God's Creation? Human beings ….He has given hands, legs, nose and eyes to every living being. There is a difference among human beings because of their conscience. There are good people and bad people." A beggar came and stood in front of his shop. He hadn't sold any flowers that day. But that did not deter him. He took out a four anna piece and gave it to the beggar. But the beggar did not seem to be happy. The gentleman said, "Look Sapana. He does not have anything. But he is not happy with what you gave him. That is the reason they remain poor and unhappy for all time to come. A man receives God's blessings and becomes happy in life when he has the quality of converting his beastly qualities into godlike qualities." Sapana was thinking. The gentleman possessed all the good qualities. Why did he look so sad all the time in that case? Was he physically ill? A customer arrived at the shop. As he made a bouquet for him, Sapana asked again, "Sir, how many children do you have?"

A thorn seemed to have pierced his chest in some

corner. He was bleeding inside him. He stood up as his eyes turned moist. He said, "My legs have become useless today in the process of walking up all the steps of my years hurriedly in order to make something out of one child. I am unwanted myself. Life on this earth would have been a blessing if you would have been my son in place of Dr. Raviranjan, the famous doctor of the capital city. I have no share in the money that he earns. But I am certain that you will pour all the flowers of your shop on my body the day I die. That would make me immortal. Even the onlookers would place a bouquet on my body when they see so much flowers being laid on it. I would become an important person rather than a non-entity that day for a short while. You are in fact my godson. I will come again tomorrow. There is a meeting. Flowers will be needed. I have given your address to the organisers."

Tears of joy flowed down from Sapana's eyes after the gentleman left. He said to himself that the gentleman had made him great by calling him his godson. He was indeed his godfather. The people organising the meeting collected flowers from him the following day. But the gentleman had not come to his shop for a number of days. He arrived one day to discuss his daughter's wedding. Sapana had sent garlands, bouquets and loose flowers as ordered by him. The gentleman had sent someone to his shop to take him to his house. The altar was to be decorated according to Sapana's specifications. Sapana stood rooted to the ground for a while after reaching the house. The palatial building belonged to the gentleman's ancestors. There were people everywhere. He did not feel very comfortable there. But the gentleman introduced him to his family members. His son was just his opposite in nature. The gentleman was calling his daughter-in-law. But she was busy otherwise. Her sister-in-law was getting married. He looked around for the gentleman's wife. He thought she might be sitting beside her daughter. The daughter was sitting all decked up. A bed of flowers was behind her. Flowers from his shop. He decorated the altar with flowers. Sapana could see that the gentleman was pleased with his work. He finished all his work. He had his food in their house before leaving. But something seemed to be out of place. The gentleman knew so many people in town. The house was crowded. But an inexplicable sadness seemed to have seeped into his mind passing through his white *panjabi*. His face looked very sad to Sapana. Perhaps he felt that way as he was sending his daughter away. Many people were wishing the gentleman with folded hands. Many others touched his feet. Sapana thought that he was indeed fortunate to be at the place.

Such an important person treated him as his son. He must have been related to him in a previous birth. He was perhaps his servant. He was able to know everything within a few hours of his arrival in his house. The gentleman's wife had passed away. His only son was a doctor in the capital city. He had adopted this girl. He had given her his surname. In a moment, he had changed the fortune of the girl who was a scavenger earlier. In fact, he was telling the truth. There would be no sorrows in this world if everyone could be like him.

He would find food to eat when he sold flowers. How did his thoughts matter? There was no dearth of leaders in the country to think. He wished the gentleman every day with folded hands. But he felt like bowing down at his feet that day. He was waiting to leave. The gentleman handed over two packets to him. He presented him with a shirt apart from the money for the flowers. He gave him a sari for his grandmother. Sapana cried in happiness. The gentleman rose a great deal in esteem before him. These days the father thinks that the son is a burden. People do not bother about their mother and sister. But the gentleman had treated a mere flower seller as a close relation. He didn't make distinction among people. What was God after all? He must be like this gentleman. He must be giving *darshan* to poor people in this manner. He came with him till the front gate to see him off. He introduced him to all the people present there. He made everyone promise that they would be buying their flowers from him. He wrote down the address of his shop on pieces of paper and gave them to people. His sales were likely to increase manifold now. He too would build a house somewhere. He would get married and start a family. The gentleman was going to give him a variety of gifts at the time. Sapana had returned home lost in thought.

He did not go to the shop anymore that day. He went straightaway to home. He slept with his head in his grandmother's lap.

Days passed. His business started growing exponentially. He had to open one more shop to handle the rush. It was difficult for him to procure such a great deal of flowers. He engaged two boys to help him out. The gentleman came rarely to his shop these days. He too was gradually forgetting him, his help and humanity. His grandmother passed away. His wife Renu and son Binay had filled up the vacant space in his life. The gentleman had come to his son's birthday. He had named him Binay.

He had built a two-roomed house with asbestos roofing. He had a bank balance. He supplied flowers to different places these days. People thronged his shops from morning till evening. He received orders over the phone these days. He had a small office behind the cabin. A boy had been engaged to attend to the telephone. The boy informed him one day that someone had called him twice that day. One Binay Babu was frantically looking for him. Sapana could not understand anything. Who was Binay Babu? How did he come to know him? A few days had passed while he remained busy. He was having all kinds of misgivings one morning. His eyes were getting moist. His son Binay was also not well.

He slept throughout the day. He took his son to a doctor. He came to the shop in the evening. The boy in the shop said, "Sir, all the flowers have been sold today. An important person died today." He could hear people chanting *Ram nam satya hai* from afar. Who was the fortunate man that had died on a day like this? It was the last day of the current marriage season. There were no flowers in any shop. The bier was getting near his shop. The dead body had been hid among heaps of flowers. Sapana told the boy, "Close the shop. Let me go home. I too don't feel well." As he pulled the mat, a bunch of roses fell down. Sapana picked them up. He reprimanded the boy, "We would have got at least fifty rupees if we had sold it. You wasted them. All right! Let it go."

A few pages fluttered inside his memory. He recalled the gentleman. He still didn't know his name. He had paid him five rupees one day for a garland and placed it on an unknown dead body. The bier was very close to him. Sapana ran to the bier. He wanted to display his magnanimity. But what was he seeing? Whose face was this? That dry smile still stuck to the withered face. The gentleman lay there. He had stopped the bier as he broke into tears. He had covered his body with the petals from the last bouquet of his shop. He could hear him explaining the difference between a good man and bad man. A man lost his way when he forgot the objective of his life. He went away from humanity when he ignored the man who had provided him with shelter.

He too had done the same thing. Had he given the gift of humanity to the man who had picked him up from the street corner and taught him how to live? The gentleman had passed away that day. Tears were streaming down from his eyes. He had told him one day, "Sapana dear! I will leave this world being buried under the flowers from your shop." He kept his word all right. But he taught him to recognise the value of humanity being buried under the flowers sold by his shop.

The bier was moving away. Sapana was reminded about the words of the gentleman, ""My legs have become useless today in the process of walking up all the steps of my years hurriedly in order to make something out of one child. I am unwanted myself. Life on this earth would have been a blessing if you would have been my son in place of Dr. Raviranjan, the famous doctor of the capital city. I have no share in the money that he earns. But I am certain that you will pour all the flowers of your shop on my body the day I die. That would make me immortal. Even the onlookers would place a bouquet on my body when they see so much flowers being laid on it. I would become an important person rather than a non-entity that day for a short while. You are in fact my godson."

Sapana shouted, "Father! Father!" He broke into tears.

***

Black Eagle Books

www.blackeaglebooks.org
info@blackeaglebooks.org

Black Eagle Books, an independent publisher, was founded as a nonprofit organization in April, 2019. It is our mission to connect and engage the Indian diaspora and the world at large with the best of works of world literature published on a collaborative platform, with special emphasis on foregrounding Contemporary Classics and New Writing.